A Grave in
the Woods

A Grave in
the Woods

A BRUNO, CHIEF OF POLICE NOVEL

Martin Walker

Alfred A. Knopf   New York 2024

THIS IS A BORZOI BOOK
PUBLISHED BY ALFRED A. KNOPF

www.aaknopf.com

Knopf, Borzoi Books, and the colophon are registered trademarks of
Penguin Random House LLC.

Library of Congress Cataloging-in-Publication Data
Names: Walker, Martin, [date] author.
Title: A grave in the woods / Martin Walker.
Description: First edition. | New York : Alfred A. Knopf, 2024. |
Series: A Bruno, Chief of Police Novel
Identifiers: LCCN 2024013797 (print) | LCCN 2024013798 (ebook) |
ISBN 9780593536629 (hardcover) | ISBN 9780593536636 (ebook)
Subjects: LCGFT: Detective and mystery fiction. | Novels.
Classification: LCC PR6073.A413 G73 2024 (print) |
LCC PR6073.A413 (ebook) | DDC 823/.914—dc23/eng/20240329
LC record available at https://lccn.loc.gov/2024013797
LC ebook record available at https://lccn.loc.gov/2024013798

Jacket photograph by Chris Archinet / Getty Images
Jacket design by Stephanie Ross

Manufactured in the United States of America
First American Edition

In memory of my dear friend, Pierre Simonet, an orphan who became a soldier and then a fine cook, and a village policeman whose wise and generous personality inspired me to write the Bruno novels. Like my fictional Bruno, Pierre knew everybody, danced at all the weddings and taught the children to play rugby and tennis. He died this year after a short illness, not long after his retirement. The real Pierre was also a husband and father, who had a strong and enduring marriage with Francine, and they raised a fine son, Adrien.

So this book is dedicated to all three Simonets.

A Grave in
the Woods

Chapter 1

Bruno Courrèges, chief of police of the Vézère Valley in the Périgord region of France, eased himself a little stiffly from his venerable Land Rover and gazed up affectionately at the Hôtel de Ville of the small town of St. Denis. Behind the flags of France and Europe on the balcony was the office that had been his for over a decade but which he had not seen for more than two months. After being shot in the shoulder, he had spent several weeks in the hospital followed by six weeks at a convalescent center reserved for French police injured in the line of duty. On the less fashionable part of the Mediterranean coast, it had offered good food, congenial company, excellent nursing and physiotherapy, and Bruno felt restored if not yet fully recovered.

His faithful basset hound, Balzac, who had given Bruno a lavish welcome on his return to St. Denis, scrambled down from the vehicle and stood beside him. Balzac's welcome the previous evening, and that of Bruno's horse, Hector, and of his closest companions who had gathered at the familiar dining table of the riding school to celebrate his return, had touched Bruno's heart. (Each of his friends had visited him in the hospital, first in Périgueux and then in Bordeaux, where his shattered collarbone had been rebuilt.) At the end of the meal, when all the others had discreetly left, Pamela had invited him upstairs to her room. A former lover who was now a very dear friend, she sometimes, when the mood was on her, claimed amorous privileges. This time was just to ensure, she had said playfully, that everything was in working order. And, gloriously, it was.

The flags drooped and the roofs around the square glistened from the heavy rains overnight. Glancing down over the balustrade, Bruno noted that the River Vézère was running very high, lapping over the quayside below. He was reminded that the weather always turned in late October, in time to make his winter hobbies of rugby and hunting into muddy affairs. But the rain was good for the Brussels sprouts and broccoli he'd planted back in August, he assured himself. There were few customers in the weekly market, and some were carrying umbrellas; others, like Bruno, were wearing woolen caps against the chill wind. Perhaps that was why, even with Balzac at his heels, nobody in the market seemed to recognize him as he walked to the familiar entrance.

Bruno mounted the stone stairs of the *mairie,* each one bow shaped by centuries of footsteps, up to the first floor where his office was located. Word of his return had spread, and a crowd was there to greet him: the mayor and his deputy, Xavier; Claire, the flirtatious secretary; Roberte, from the social security office; Michel, from public works; Marie, from the housing office; and even Laurent, the handyman, and his wife, Clémentine, the cleaner. His police colleagues, Juliette, the municipal policewoman from Les Eyzies, and Yveline, the local commander of gendarmes, were the first to greet him with a hug. They were followed by everyone else, save the mayor, who had been at the welcoming dinner the previous evening.

Genuine as the *mairie* welcome was, Bruno was aware of a certain stiffness among his colleagues, a disturbance in the atmosphere, as though something in the building had gone sour. He could not define it, but the place had changed. He was accustomed to being on a happy ship, where people worked well and amiably with one another, convinced that they were all doing something worthwhile. One or two of them glanced nervously at the closed door of Bruno's office.

"I still have two more weeks of convalescent leave to go, and then the *toubib* has to sign off that I'm fit for duty," he said, referring to the doctor. "I just came in to take a look in my office to be sure you haven't borrowed all my pens and broken my printer."

There was a slightly nervous laugh as the ranks parted and people shuffled aside, an expectancy in their eyes. Had they banded together to buy him a gift or filled his office with flowers? Bruno hoped not. Salaries in the *mairie* were notoriously low, and most of his colleagues had families to raise. "Good to be back, even briefly," he said as he opened the door.

For a moment Bruno thought he had entered the wrong office. The desk was now under the window and the rest of the furniture had been changed. His battered old metal filing cabinet had disappeared, along with the elderly printer which he'd kept on top. In its place stood a humidifier, and he could smell incense burning, a vanilla scent. He could not see if his own swivel chair with its signature squeak had gone as well, since it was now behind the desk and occupied by a woman, her face silhouetted by the light spilling in from the window behind.

"Didn't anybody ever teach you to knock?" came a sharp voice, her tone suggesting that his intrusion was yet another of many burdens to be borne.

"Not when entering my own office," he replied, trying to conceal his surprise. "Who are you and why are you sitting in my chair?"

"My name is Cantagnac, and I'm the new executive administrator to the chief of police. And who are you?"

"I'm the chief of police. What was wrong with the office that had been prepared for you?"

"It didn't meet the required norms. It was too small, with too little natural light. The workspace specifications for civilian officials supporting the police are very clear. I was told you were not due back to work until after your doctor's approval at the end of next week. And if that's your dog, it's against regulations to have animals in the workplace."

"He's a great deal more than an *animal,*" Bruno said, putting into his voice a calm that he did not feel. "He is a highly skilled hound dog who has saved two lost children and an elderly citizen suffering from Alzheimer's disease who was close to dying of hypothermia. He also helped us save a civilian hostage. His predecessor was shot dead saving me from an armed terrorist. I only hope, mademoiselle, that you might prove to be half as useful as Balzac, who was presented to me by the Ministry of the Interior to replace the dog that died. And now I'd like my chair and my privacy, please."

He held open the door for her, but she did not move.

"If this used to be your office," she snapped, "you should be ashamed of yourself. Files in disarray, worksheets not completed, proper records not kept, your annual health and fitness reports never filled out, letters unanswered, and you have yet to file a single report on the work of your subordinate officers in Les Eyzies and Montignac."

"Mademoiselle Cantagnac, I have a conference with the mayor which will last for about an hour. When I get back, I want this office vacated, the desk and chair returned to where they used to be and a report from you on what you claim to have achieved so far."

He pondered adding that if she did not comply, she faced arrest for obstructing a senior officer in pursuit of his duties, but he would save the big guns for later. And there would most certainly be a later.

"You're still on convalescent leave," she replied. "You have no status here until you're formally declared fit for duty. *Au'voir, Monsieur le Chef de Police.*"

Telling himself that this was but a temporary retreat and summoning what little dignity he could manage, Bruno walked out, leaving the door open. He wondered what on earth the woman had done in her previous job to have been assigned here. He would have to find out.

Then, as Bruno began to walk away, he heard a familiar but most unusual sound, that of a dog purring almost like a cat. It was a contented rumbling deep in the basset's throat, which Balzac only did when he was happy. Bruno turned and saw his trusted hound fraternizing with the enemy. Balzac was standing on his hind legs, his paws in her lap, while Mademoiselle Cantagnac tickled his favorite spot just behind the ear.

Well, he thought, she can't be all bad if Balzac likes her. Bruno had limitless faith in his dog's instincts.

"You survived your first encounter with our new battle-ax, I see," said the mayor when Bruno took his usual seat across the vast desk that was said to be even older than the *mairie* itself. "Watch your step with her, Bruno. She's an impressive woman, committed to public service and terrifyingly efficient. She even got a law degree in her spare time."

"I survived, but barely," Bruno replied. "She began by telling me that no dogs were allowed in the workplace and finished by charming Balzac into that special purr of his. She not only seems to have commandeered my office and changed the furniture but she reprimanded me for inadequate paperwork."

"You know that she's the queen bee of Interco?" the mayor asked, referring to the civil service labor union to which almost all *mairie* employees belonged. He put up his hands, palm first, as if to signal his helplessness in the matter. This was unusual. A former senator, he had learned his politics while working for Jacques Chirac, first when Chirac was mayor of Paris and then when he became prime minister. The mayor had then gone on to hone his bureaucratic skills in Brussels. One of the three or four most powerful officials in the *département,* and probably the most experienced, he very seldom waved the white flag.

"What was her last job?" Bruno asked.

"Running the Nouvelle-Aquitaine task force on diversity, rooting out sexism, racism and any other ism you can think of," the mayor said. "Her last report was received with great public acclaim and private relief; her task force was wound up with the thanks of a grateful bureaucracy, and she no longer had a position. She has been assigned to you as executive administrator, to make sure this experiment in modernizing municipal policing is properly managed and committed to the latest principles of enlightened public service. Blame your friend Amélie at the justice ministry in Paris. She dreamed up this pilot program and put you in charge of it."

"I'm surprised that with her skills Mademoiselle Cantagnac hasn't taken over your office rather than mine," Bruno said.

"My plan is to move her into the big new gendarmerie we're building near the station when it's ready. It's twice the size of the old one, so there'll be lots of room. My argument will be that such a move will improve coordination between the various arms of the police, which may be sufficient to convince the head of the gendarmes to accept the arrangement. With luck, you'll have your office back in six months."

"And in the meantime?"

"You're hardly ever in your office anyway," the mayor said. "You're patrolling the market, or should I say taking Balzac for a stroll. You're out meeting people, teaching the kids to play tennis and rugby, visiting the communes up and down the valley, having a drink in all the hunting clubs, making connections and building trust. As you always say, Bruno, preventing crime is much better than having to solve it."

"So now that I've been banned from my office, why don't I move in here with you?" Bruno asked, leaning back and gesturing at the big, high-ceilinged room with its walls of bookshelves and its views up and down the river. "If I don't, Mademoiselle Cantagnac will probably have you evicted and move in."

"Nice try, Bruno. Just leave this with me, and I'll have something sorted out by the time you come back on duty, which the battle-ax tells me is not for another two weeks, and you have to be judged physically fit first. Now, changing the subject, what do you know about abandoned graves?"

"Not much. Is this our business? Or is it a church problem?"

"You know the old disused hotel, the Domaine de la Barde, on the road to Périgueux just outside town? It's a lovely eighteenth-century building, classic Palladian design, but now pretty run down. It went bankrupt before you arrived here, about fifteen years ago or more, leaving lots of creditors. Since we are the main ones, for unpaid property taxes, I had thought vaguely of taking it over and turning it into an arts complex or maybe some new center for computer training. But we now have a potential buyer, except that this abandoned grave on the property may be a problem. Are you fit enough for a stroll? It's not far."

"A stroll will do me good, and Balzac. Who's the buyer?"

"An Englishman, a Monsieur Birch, somewhere in his late thirties, with a wife and young child. He has an interesting idea, turning the outbuildings into *gîtes,* with bed-and-breakfast rooms in the château and a cooking school in the offseason. Apparently, he used to be a chef. He already took over another old building outside Sarlat, restored it, got it running as a business and sold it at a handsome profit. And there's another interesting aspect that I'll explain as we walk."

Chapter 2

They set off across the road and up the steps to the higher square and avoided the market stalls that filled the long Rue de Paris and took the narrower rue Gambetta to the old parade ground by the gendarmerie. As they walked, the mayor explained that there was a British TV company involved. They were the makers of *Do-It-Yourself Château,* a program popular on daytime TV and now sold to other broadcasters around the world. They would follow the trials and tribulations of five or six British families who were each restoring a different French château, usually with a happy ending as old ruins became hotels or grand family homes. Apparently, transforming such ruins into wedding venues was very popular, the mayor said, since such episodes ended with some attractive couple tying the knot.

"It seems weddings make wonderful television, usually having at least one crisis and being very telegenic," the mayor continued, adding that he could show Bruno the TV recording Monsieur Birch had made of his previous restoration.

A couple of hundred meters beyond the old gendarmerie they came to a belt of shrubland with trees on the left. The mayor stopped.

"Look down here," he said. "You see that big square of dirt?

That's the old tennis court. He cleared off a couple of patches to see if it was still sound beneath, and it seems to be fine, easily restored."

After another fifty meters they came to a pair of rusted iron gates that still bore patches of faded blue paint. The gates opened with a screech of metal, and they entered, walking along a narrow driveway shaded by trees. On their left was a solid but dilapidated building, perhaps the old stables, since it had a tall double door for coaches and what looked like a hayloft above. That space would be turned into four self-contained *gîtes,* the mayor explained. Beyond it to the right was the château, a handsome structure despite the missing shutters, the overgrowth of ivy and missing roof tiles. It had an imposing central door, two stories—each boasting six double windows—and more rooms and smaller windows in the roof, all topped with a tall chimney stack.

"There's a lot of work to be done," said Bruno, as Balzac trotted off to explore the overgrown garden, pausing to lift his leg on an apple tree that had been left unpruned for many years. "How much land goes with it?"

"A bit more than four hectares, stretching beyond the tennis court and across the stream. It reaches most of the way up to the Resistance memorial on the road leading to St. Avit." Looking around, Bruno focused on the remains of what had once been a formal garden, with rows of trees, unkempt paths and a long-dry fountain of crumbling stone.

"Down there is what used to be the restaurant and then farther on, behind that low building, is the swimming pool. That will need restoring," the mayor said. "Behind those trees is an old forge, which Monsieur Birch says could be made into another fine *gîte.* I asked Michel to take a good look at the various buildings, and he said the main structures and roof timbers were all sound. There'll be a lot of work, new plumbing, electric circuits, repairing the roof and bringing the insulation up to code, but very little that's structural. And since Monsieur Birch has already done a fine job on the other old château, he should be able to handle this, and it would be a handsome addition to our town."

"So, what's this about a grave? Where is it?"

"I don't know. But there was a reference to it in the property deed, a small separate plot, three meters by two, and part of the overall estate. I'd hate for that to block what could be a fine project."

"If it's in the deed there should be coordinates for the exact location. What does the *notaire* say?" Bruno asked. "Was it our own Brosseil who drew up the deed?"

"No, Brosseil's grandfather added the grave to the deed some sixty or so years ago. The date is not entirely clear. Michel tried to find the exact spot, but the whole area is overgrown woodland. It would need clearing to know if the grave is there, and if it's occupied, if that's the right word."

"Anything in the town records about a burial? I presume you've asked Father Sentout about the church records. I seem to recall that family members could traditionally be buried on private property."

"Theoretically that's still the case, but so hedged in with conditions and inspections of water tables by hydrological and other experts that I thought I'd leave all that to you, Bruno. Father Sentout says he has no record of such a grave. But he told me that if a grave has been abandoned for more than thirty years, it can be emptied and the remains properly interred elsewhere or cremated with a proper record of the location of the ashes. A formal legal notice would have to be published so that lawyers and *notaires* could have a chance to contact any descendants who might file objections."

"Well, I can go see Brosseil and learn what I can. Do you have an address for this Monsieur Birch?"

"Yes, he's rented a place in Audrix so he could register his boy for school here. He seems like a decent enough fellow and he speaks reasonable French. He told me he'd learned it when working in the Alps during the skiing season. He was the chef at various luxury chalets."

"Hence the cooking school idea," Bruno said.

"Indeed. Birch has his head screwed on right. He said it wouldn't make sense to run the château as a hotel, since it would only be filled for four months of the year. So he plans to live in it with his family in one wing and rent out the other five or six rooms as bed-and-breakfast places so he wouldn't have to employ staff all year-round. And he'd have four *gîtes* to rent out, five when he restores the old forge. I think you'll like him; he cooks and he used to play rugby. What's more, he seems keen to get the tennis court back in order."

"What about the bankruptcy and the creditors?" Bruno asked.

"I had a quiet word with the judge. Our unpaid property taxes have priority among the creditors, and if we suspend that claim, Birch has offered to pay enough money to the court to give the other creditors about a third of what they are owed. Since they wrote off those bad debts more than ten years ago they'll be happily surprised by their windfall. The judge is prepared to approve that, and then we would start getting about six thousand a year in property taxes, plus a couple of year-round jobs and three or four more part-time jobs in season. And there'll be work for our craftsmen and decorators for a year or so. St. Denis will have a paying asset rather than a crumbling liability."

"You said suspend the town's claim on the unpaid taxes, rather than waive them," Bruno said.

"That's right. And when Birch eventually sells the place, we'd want our unpaid taxes, which he agrees would come out of his profit. He obviously believes he'd make more than enough on the deal and most of it would have been swallowed by inflation. Everybody would win, Bruno, so long as you can sort out the problem of the grave, which may well be empty for all I know. And now I understand that you're going to meet some friends for lunch at Ivan's, where we'll part company."

Chapter 3

The friends in question—Horst and Clothilde—were waiting for him at the restaurant. Both were prominent archaeologists at the museum of prehistory in Les Eyzies. A stranger was with them, a woman who looked to be in her thirties, dressed in jeans and a fleece jacket over a military-style khaki shirt. She had dark hair tied into a neat bun at the back of her neck. Her expression was serious, almost solemn, and she wore not a scrap of makeup that Bruno could discern. Her eyes were a clear blue and she had a pleasant, slightly guarded smile, as if she were nervous, or perhaps naturally shy.

Before any introductions, Clothilde, a small, redheaded powerhouse of a woman, rushed up to give Bruno a hug and a kiss on each cheek.

"We were so worried about you, but the mayor always said you'd make a full recovery. And nobody believes that story about Russian criminals shooting you at a traffic stop when half the French army just happened to be on hand for your rescue. Speculation has been running wild, as you can imagine."

"It always does," said Bruno. "But I'm almost as good as new." He broke off to shake the hand of Horst, a cheerful German professor with a white beard who had finally married Clothilde in the St. Denis *mairie* after years of on-again, off-again romance. They had pursued each other from rock paintings in Australia to tombs in Egypt; from prehistoric burials in southern Africa to Scythian sites in Ukraine. Bruno had been a witness at their wedding. Clothilde joked that she'd agreed to marry Horst only because of the bathroom he had installed in his house. It boasted a shower with different nozzles firing jets of hot water from every direction, with a sauna and hot tub attached. Bruno had long been promised an invitation to try it.

"This is our friend Abigail Howard," said Clothilde, "known to all her friends as Abby. She's a former pupil of mine from the U.S. who's staying with us. She'd like to stay longer, so she's currently house hunting. She wants to pick your brains about starting a business here as a specialist guide for American visitors."

When he shook Abby's hand Bruno felt calluses, which made him suspect she might be a serious tennis player. She went down on one knee to make friends with Balzac, murmuring something in excellent French about having grown up with basset hounds. Balzac seemed to take to her at once. Ivan now came out of the kitchen, arms outstretched to embrace Bruno, but then held back, asking if Bruno's shoulder was yet healed.

"Almost," said Bruno, using his good arm to embrace the chef who was also the owner of the restaurant. "And who is your new friend in the kitchen whose cooking all my friends have been recommending?"

"Marta, from Kraków," said Ivan. "She makes wonderful pierogi, and you'll love her *zurek,* a white borscht made with sour rye, celery root and hard-boiled egg. And she makes the most delicious apple-and-sour-cream cake with rum. You can have that for dessert."

"Where did you meet her?" Bruno asked with a grin, knowing Ivan's habit of coming back from each annual vacation with a woman of a different nationality who would bring her local cuisine to titillate the taste buds of the residents of St. Denis.

"I haven't had a vacation yet this year, but now that she's here I don't need one," Ivan said, casting a fond look toward the kitchen. "No, she came to me. She heard from someone in Bergerac that I was looking for a deputy chef. She was working as a waitress in a place where the owner kept trying to entice her into the pantry, and the owner's wife suggested she try here. I'm glad she did, and you will be, too."

As they took their places at the table, Bruno asked Abby if she played tennis, and Horst answered quickly, "She'll wipe the floor with you, Bruno. She was on a team that won the U.S. college championships."

"Really?" asked Bruno, suitably impressed. "I help to run a kind of tennis school for our youngsters at the local club. Maybe you could come along one day and do some coaching."

Her reaction startled him. Abby was looking over his shoulder, her mouth open and her eyes wide. He turned to see what she was staring at and saw a Valkyrie.

Bruno was no midget at one meter eighty-five, but the woman who appeared through the kitchen door was at least fifteen centimeters taller, with shoulders to match. A burst of tightly curled blonde hair was piled up above a thick white headband. She greeted them all and put a beefy arm around Ivan, who barely came up to her chin and gazed up at her adoringly.

"You are all welcome," she said in an unusual accent that seemed both guttural and liquid at the same time. "I am Marta and I am cooking today. The soup is *zurek*, the main course is to choose between a chicken schnitzel or fresh trout with caraway seeds, and my special cake for dessert. Which one of you is the policeman?"

"I am," Bruno said, putting out his hand to be shaken, but she took it to pull him toward her and kissed him on both cheeks.

"Ivan told me you stepped in to cook for him when he was ill, and Father Sentout says you have a good soul, for a pagan."

"And he's a real expert on rugby, for a priest," Bruno replied. "Have you ever played? We have a good women's team here." He was thinking that with Marta playing number 8, adding her weight and strength to the back row of the forwards and her height in jumping for the ball when it had to be thrown back in after going off the field, she'd be a formidable asset.

"I have never played, but I need some exercise," Marta replied. "Maybe I could come to watch your women practice and do some running?"

"Tomorrow afternoon at five," said Bruno. "If Ivan can spare you."

"Good. I know where your club is. I pass it when I go jogging. I should be back here soon after six to help Ivan cook. Now I have to return to the kitchen."

"Believe me, her cooking matches her personality, so we're in for a feast," said Clothilde, as they took their seats. "Now, as I said, Abby wants to know about the regulations for guides and whether she would need a *brevet*, since in France we seem to need formal qualifications for most jobs. She wants to put together a special tour of American connections to the region."

To be a licensed guide authorized by the tourist board, with the right to escort visitors into museums and national monuments, evidence of special skills and training was usually required, Bruno explained. A two-year training course would be followed by an exam to earn the *brevet*. But to be a private guide, particularly in a specialist field like American links to the Périgord, there'd be more leeway, especially with a recommendation from someone like Clothilde, a curator of a national museum.

"Abby is an archaeologist with a doctorate from the University of Virginia," said Clothilde. "Horst and I would be glad to write a letter of recommendation to the prefect and to the tourist board, stressing her excellent qualifications to be a guide for our regional archaeology sites. If it would help, we could make her a visiting curator at the museum; she would give a course of lectures in English as well as French."

Bruno thought that Clothilde was going to unusual lengths to help this friend. There would be more to this than met the eye. But Clothilde and Horst were old friends. Naturally, he'd help if he could.

"Making her an official *adjointe* of the museum should more than suffice," said Bruno, and then turned to Abby. "If you plan to make a living from this, you might want to establish yourself as an *auto-entrepreneur,* paying a modest fee for social insurance. But you'd need a *carte de séjour,* proof of legal residence."

"That's not a problem," she told him briskly. "I had an Irish grandmother, so I qualified for an Irish passport, which makes me a European citizen with the right to live and work anywhere in Europe."

"Lucky you," said Bruno. "Does this mean you'll be living in France permanently?"

"I only have a year's sabbatical from my teaching job in the States, which should be time enough to see if this can work or not. I'm staying with Clothilde and Horst for the moment, but I'm looking for a small place to rent," she said. "I think somewhere around St. Denis would make sense."

"We may be able to help with that," Bruno said. "I have two friends who rent out *gîtes* on their property, and I think they may have one available. It's a small house but comfortable, with a private garden and access to their pool and grass tennis court. I think Fabiola—she's the owner—asks about five hundred a month, which includes electricity, and there's a big woodburning stove in the living room."

"It sounds perfect," said Abby. "I'm grateful, and I'm also curious that you've just tried to recruit me as a tennis coach and get

Marta to join your rugby team. You sound more like the local sports director than a policeman."

"That's just my hobby," Bruno said, and swiftly changed the subject. "I'm curious about something, too. What special American connections do you intend to feature?"

"Well, I'd start with Thomas Jefferson and his admiration for Archbishop Fénelon as a leading intellectual father of the Enlightenment, and take them to visit the château where Fénelon was born, and to Rouffillac where he stayed. I'd also take them to the château at La Bachellerie near Terrasson, whose plans we think Jefferson copied as the design for the White House. Then there is Ezra Pound and his friend T. S. Eliot, who began writing *The Waste Land* while the two poets were on a walking tour in the Périgord. Many people, including me, think it's the greatest poem of the twentieth century," she said, almost vehemently, warming to her theme.

"And of course," she went on, "Pound virtually adopted the troubadours of the Périgord, translated the songs of Bertran de Born and even wrote poems in their Occitan language. Since Eliot also wrote the verse play *Murder in the Cathedral,* about the killing of Thomas Becket, I'd take visitors to the Chapel of St. Martin, near Limeuil. It was one of three churches the pope ordered Henry II to build as a penance for Becket's murder, two in England and one in France."

She paused, and gave a gentle smile that Bruno thought made her look much more attractive. "I love the medieval frescoes in that Chapel of St. Martin, not just the big ones behind the altar but the little ones, too. They're fading but still so beautiful."

Bruno smiled in return and nodded approval. "You can tell your clients that the experts say they represent two Old Testament prophets, but we locals all think that the fresco of the two men with the bottle in the side chapel represents Becket and King

Henry in happier times, when they were bosom buddies and drinking companions."

"I'll make a point of it," she said, for the first time smiling at him warmly. Bruno felt a little like a schoolboy being praised by a teacher.

"I'd also want to talk about the American paratroopers who were dropped near Cadouin in August 1944 to help the Resistance. There weren't many Germans left here by then, but the Americans were able to join the liberation parade in Périgueux. Then there are the Lindberghs, the family of the first pilot to fly across the Atlantic. His son married Monique Watteau, a local writer who had earlier been the mistress of the actor Yul Brynner. Then I'd take them to Josephine Baker's Château des Milandes. She wasn't just a superstar of the Jazz Age; Martin Luther King Jr.'s widow asked her to take over the leadership of the civil rights movement after her husband was assassinated."

"She declined," Bruno interjected, "saying she felt obliged to continue raising her rainbow family, children she had adopted from almost every race on earth."

Horst then broke in to say, "We took Abby to that American-owned vineyard you recommended to us, Bruno, the Château de Fayolle near Saussignac, with that lovely red Sang du Sanglier wine you raved about. So Abby's also thinking of a day touring the vineyards."

"*Sang du sanglier.* Blood of the wild boar," Bruno murmured, smiling. "And then you could cross the river to the Montravel region and take them to Montaigne's tower, where you could read out his essay on the American Indians he met."

"Great idea! I'd been wondering how to bring in Montaigne," Abby said, giving him that warm smile again. "That would make an excellent bridge. And just a little farther is the Château de Montréal, one of whose sons explored the St. Lawrence River in the seventeenth century and gave the name of his family home to the place that became Montreal."

"Congratulations," Bruno said, looking at her with respect as Ivan came in with the soup tureen. He was impressed by her research and the look of keen intelligence on her face, though there was a tension about her, as if she were a woman under pressure. And maybe there was one link between the Périgord and her homeland that she might not know. He'd only come across it by accident.

"You've certainly done your homework on our region, so I hesitate to bring up something that you may already know, but have you heard of the duc de Lauzun?" he asked.

Abby shook her head. "No, is Lauzun in the Périgord?"

"Not quite," Bruno replied as Clothilde served the soup. "It's just over the border in Lot-et-Garonne. But the duke was also the Marquis of Biron, a splendid medieval fortress in the south of the Dordogne, close to the bastide of Monpazier. And this Marquis of Biron deserves to be better known as one of the founders of your country."

"As an explorer?" she asked. "I've never heard of him."

"No, not as an explorer but as a soldier. He was an aristocrat, but he was also a professional soldier, and he commanded a legion of volunteers who fought alongside the Marquis of Lafayette in the liberation of the United States. Above all, he fought with George Washington and Lafayette at the siege of Yorktown in 1781. That was the battle which forced the surrender of the British army under General Cornwallis and secured American independence. The duke did well enough to be chosen by Washington and Lafayette for the honor of taking the news of the great victory back to the king in Paris."

"That's a wonderful addition to my list," said Abby. "How on earth did you come across that special piece of history?"

"Through my dog," Bruno said. "Balzac is descended from the

old royal hunting pack of King Louis XIV at Cheverny, but you may have heard that basset hounds were introduced to America by the Marquis of Lafayette. He took a breeding pair as a gift to George Washington, who imported several more, and that led to what is known as the Stonewall Jackson breed of bassets. Balzac has some of that ancestry, a fact that prompted me to do some research into Lafayette and his adventures in your War of Independence. That's how I came across the memoirs of the Marquis of Biron."

"That's a lovely story," said Clothilde. "I've always known, Bruno, that your dog was a natural aristocrat. This soup is very good. Do you think Balzac might enjoy a little bowl of it? Might Ivan object?"

"I think Ivan would be delighted," said Bruno, grinning. "Balzac always gets something to eat whenever I'm here. And I think that like me he'd enjoy that tangy taste from the sour rye. I think it would make for a fine *chabrol.*"

Having said that, he poured half a glass of Ivan's house red wine that came from the town vineyard into the last couple of mouthfuls of soup, stirred the mixture with his spoon, then picked up the bowl with both hands, raised it to his lips and drank.

"*Chabrol,* which drives away the doctors and leaves no need for pharmacists," he said as Horst and Clothilde followed suit. "It's a local tradition."

Gingerly, Abby poured some wine into the remains of her soup, glanced at the eagerly expectant faces of her companions and tried it.

"That certainly works with this excellent soup," she said. "I was brought up on an American diet of bland white bread, breakfast cereals and processed cheese in slices, so I'm a pushover for anything tasty." She gave Bruno a swift grin, then turned to Clothilde and asked, "Should I tell him now about our secret weapon?"

Clothilde nodded. "Bruno knows enough about archaeology to understand the significance."

"I first met Clothilde at an archaeological dig in Virginia, near my home, when I was a schoolgirl, at a place called Cactus Hill," Abby said, smiling across the table at her friend. "I had a teacher who was fascinated by archaeology and she took our class to the site where she volunteered on weekends. They had begun excavating, and the first indications were so startling for American history that extraordinary efforts were made over the next several years to be sure of what the site really told us."

She glanced affectionately at Clothilde again. "I'll never forget meeting you then—erudite and intimidating and exotic all at once. I was twelve at the time, tall for my age, and you and I were the same height. But you were this little French dynamo of a woman with the really cute accent, telling us that the whole story of America's origins was being rewritten around us. I could hardly believe it, but I caught the archaeology bug and kept coming back with my teacher on weekends to help out, mostly making coffee and sandwiches. But there was an area that was left for us young volunteers to work on—under supervision—led by Clothilde."

Abby paused as Ivan cleared away the soup plates and served the main course, fish for all of them except Horst, who had chosen the chicken schnitzel. As they began to eat, Abby glanced at Bruno and asked what he knew of human settlement in the Americas. At that moment Bruno was thinking that the caraway seeds gave an interesting flavor to the trout. They had obviously been roasted first, and he was trying to decide whether they were more like fennel or anise. He pointed to his mouth, which was still chewing. Then he swallowed and took a sip of wine before answering.

"Only what I've read, that it happened during a great ice age about eleven or twelve thousand years ago when glaciers came down beyond the Loire here in France," he said. "There was so much ice locked up in glaciers that people were able to cross the Bering Strait from Siberia to what is now Alaska, maybe even on foot. Then over several thousand years they explored down deep into South America, killing off mammoths and other great beasts along the way."

"That's the conventional wisdom," said Abby. "Well, at Cactus Hill we found human artifacts, tools and so on that were dated to between eighteen and twenty thousand years ago. That was the first shock, almost doubling our idea of the length of human habitation in the Americas. Then came the second shock: some of those tools looked extraordinarily similar to those of the Solutrean culture in Europe at that time. This raised the fascinating possibility that people may have come from Europe across the Atlantic ice, or in boats skirting the pack ice, living off the sea as they came, like Inuit."

"So, the original Americans could have come from Europe?" Bruno said, amazed. "But I thought there was DNA evidence linking Native Americans to Siberian tribes."

"There is, and more than that," Abby replied, the enthusiasm mounting in her voice, "there's even DNA evidence suggesting that some of the earliest Americans may have come across the Pacific Ocean from Polynesia to Chile and Ecuador."

Bruno laughed aloud in delight. "The extraordinary human race—you can't keep us down. Show us a sea, and some fearless explorer will want to see what's on the far side. But how do you explain all this to visiting tourists? Do you take them to Clothilde's museum?"

"That's certainly one option, but I thought I'd also take them to some of the sites, perhaps starting with La Madeleine, the origins of the Magdalenian culture that followed the Solutrean. The place has so much more to excite visitors, that church built into the rock and the medieval village built into the cliff. And then there are these." Abby dipped into her shoulder bag to bring out replicas of some of the carved bones from the Les Eyzies museum. "You probably know this one of the bison licking its own neck from La Madeleine and the prowling hyena and these bone harpoons. And now look at these." She pulled out photographs of very similar carvings in bone, saying of each one in turn, "Lakota Sioux, early nineteenth century; Ojibwa wolverine carving, early twentieth century; and then these Inuit harpoons, bones carved into barbs, also nineteenth century."

"I see your point," said Bruno. "But might not different peoples at different times reinvent the barbed spear to catch fish? I recall one of Clothilde's lectures on the way different cultures reinvented the spear-thrower," he said.

"You're right," said Abby. "It's not proof, but the style suggests a cultural connection, enough to get people's imaginations working."

"It will certainly intrigue tourists," said Bruno. He turned to Horst and Clothilde. "What about you two? Do you think prehistoric people crossed the Atlantic in the glacial period?"

"I'd like to think so, but the evidence is still very thin," said Horst. "Archaeologists have spent twenty years looking for similar sites on the east coast of the Americas without definitive success."

At that point, Ivan brought out large servings of Marta's special cake. By the end of the meal Bruno found himself committed to introducing Abby to Fabiola and Gilles to view their *gîte* and to the mayor to help her obtain the various bureaucratic approvals required to be a guide. He had also promised to lend her his copy of the memoirs of the duc de Lauzun.

"If you ever get the chance to try Bruno's cooking, seize the opportunity at once," Clothilde said as they rose from the table.

"Since you're staying there, have you been invited yet to try Horst's special shower?" Bruno asked Abby.

"No, but the hot tub is great," she said, sounding a little distracted as she glanced anxiously at the door to the street, as if wary of whatever might lie beyond it.

Bruno had noticed that she had taken a seat with her back to the wall, and her eyes had been watchful, even when talking enthusiastically about her plans. She was evidently in good health, and yet there were dark rings beneath her eyes as though she was short of sleep. This was a troubled and nervous woman, he thought. But Balzac had evidently taken to her, settling comfortably at her feet beneath the table. So, on an impulse as Horst paid the bill and Clothilde rose to leave, Bruno turned to Abby.

"We can go and take a look at this house that's becoming available now, if you like," he said. "We can take my car and I'll drop you back at the museum or at Horst's house."

Chapter 4

As they approached Bruno's vintage Land Rover, still parked in the town square, Abby asked, "Why is that stone cross standing there, overlooking the river?"

"It's to mark the site of the old nunnery," Bruno explained. "It dates back to the tenth century, and it was the first convent to declare for the reformed religion when the Protestants emerged in the sixteenth century. Then Catholic troops came along, evicted the women and looted the place and installed Catholic nuns. Then Protestant troops evicted the Catholic nuns, probably very brutally, and so it went. The nunnery limped on until it was finally closed and the ruins demolished after the Revolution."

Bruno paused, as if remembering something. "Follow me," he said as he headed down a ramp that led from the square to the riverbank. Halfway down he paused in front of padlocked metal gates protecting a small, vaulted chamber built of stone. He pointed out the stone remnants of the old nunnery inside: a broken pillar, half a cherub, part of a window frame and an impressive marble font. It stood waist high and was finely carved with vines and flowers. At Bruno's feet, Balzac raised a paw and stared with canine longing at this font, but the iron bars were set too closely together for the dog to squeeze through. The basset hound turned aside and, with a natural courtesy, raised his leg to sprinkle the ramp downhill from the two humans.

"That's all that remains of the nunnery," Bruno said as they peered in. "But you should also see this." He led Abby down to the quayside and beneath the first arch of the bridge. Once there, he pointed out the marks, each of them dated, that showed the peak flood levels of the Vézère River, some within a hand's width of the highest point of the arch.

"Wow, that highest one, marked 1944, must have flooded the whole of the far bank," Abby said.

"We've never seen the river quite that high since they built the big dams upstream. The river's source is on the Millevaches plateau in the Massif Central, nearly a thousand meters above sea level, and it falls nearly eight hundred meters to this point. But we still get floods when the dams get full, and they have to open the sluices. Only last winter, parts of Les Eyzies were flooded, and the road to Bergerac was cut off near Le Buisson where the Dordogne overflowed its banks. A few years ago we had to evacuate the aquarium and the offices downstream in the old water mill, and we lost electricity in half the town. That was when we decided to get rid of the streetlamps along the quayside."

"So the river was flowing seven or eight meters higher than it is now?"

"Close to that," he said. "The far bank was all meadows, and before the dams were built they flooded regularly. It's why this region is so famous for ducks and geese. You can imagine all those flocks of birds, getting tired on their migration flights, looking down and seeing great expanses of water. It must have looked like a perfect spot, their own little St. Tropez. And then there's the energy factor: the dams on this river and on the Dordogne provide electricity for half a million people."

"And it's clean power," she said.

"Yes, of course, but more than that," Bruno said, "it's our

history. The rivers explain why people settled here—the Neanderthals more than two hundred thousand years ago, the Cro-Magnons who made the cave paintings and engravings came along a bit later. But the same iron ore that gave them colors to paint made this valley an industrial powerhouse. It produced weapons and armor in the Middle Ages, and then in the age of sail many of the cannons for French warships were made right here and floated downriver to Bordeaux. In the eighteenth century there were a dozen blacksmiths on this stretch of riverbank, all making big guns."

"Maybe you should be the guide here, rather than me," she said, grinning at him. "You know more about it."

"It's not that," said Bruno, surprised at her words and a little flattered. "I'm simply fascinated. What makes me mad is that we had so little of this when I was at school. We never even heard of Lascaux. It was all Julius Caesar and the Gauls, Charlemagne, the Crusades and Joan of Arc, the Sun King, the Revolution and Napoléon. The history of great men and one woman who happened to be French. But did they tell us that the word 'France' came from the Germanic Franks? No, they kept telling us that our ancestors were the Gauls."

"After all this time, does it matter that much? It's not as though it was a secret. You were able to find out for yourself, to visit the caves and read some history."

"I suppose you're right. But I just wish our teachers had been more open with us, or perhaps more imaginative."

"It's better these days, no?"

"Yes, a lot better. All the schoolkids in the region are taken to the caves and learn about Lascaux and that these ancestors of ours were not primitive but serious artists, hunters, inventors of bows and arrows and so on. They even invented smokeless lamps that allowed them to work inside the caves."

"You see, there's progress," Abby said, and grinned at him

again. Bruno had initially been wary of her guarded manner, but she seemed to have relaxed, and her warmth was coming through. "And talking of progress, are we going to see this house I might be renting?"

"What? Oh, yes, I'm sorry," Bruno said, taking out his phone to check that Gilles was home. Then he steered Abby to the Land Rover, Balzac trotting ahead to wait for the rear door to be opened.

"Fabiola is still at the medical center where she works, but Gilles is there. I met him in the Balkans when he was a reporter for *Libération* and more recently with *Paris Match*. He also writes books. His latest is about Ukraine. He's become a specialist, having learned the language. He visits often, knows the new president and government. He's sure a full-scale war is coming."

"The newspapers say Washington seems to agree with him," she said. "What do you think?"

Bruno shrugged. "Who knows? But Gilles is a good reporter and I take his views seriously. And Fabiola, his partner, is the best doctor we've ever had. You'll like their place. It's in a delightful setting, an old manor house in a handsome courtyard, with the old stables and carriage house to one side and a farm building on the other. That's the one I think is coming vacant."

Abby made the appropriate sounds of approval as Bruno turned off up the gravel road that led to the house, sheltered from the prevailing wind by a wooded ridge. A small herd of Blonde d'Aquitaine cattle with that year's calves were grazing on the pasture, and six poplar trees lined the last fifty meters of roadway to the house. Bruno explained that the fields were rented out to a local farmer.

"It's charming," said Abby and checked her watch. "And less than ten minutes from town. Presumably I could rent a horse from the riding school you mentioned if I wanted a canter?"

"Of course, and I'd be happy to introduce you," said Bruno, sounding the horn as he pulled into the courtyard and released the rear door to let Balzac jump out to greet Gilles, who had emerged. The two men embraced, Abby's hand was shaken, and coffee was offered but declined. Gilles led Abby into the vacant house and left her to look around.

"I'm no good at this rental business," Gilles said as they each took a seat at the courtyard table and Balzac curled up at Bruno's feet. "Can I offer you a drink?"

"No, but thanks. We just had lunch and I'm supposed to do a little work this afternoon, investigating an old and we hope disused grave," Bruno said, and went on to explain Abby's connection to Clothilde and her plan to be a guide.

"How long does she expect to be here?" Gilles asked. "I ask because we like to do short rentals so that we can rent the place out to tourists in the summer when the rents are higher."

"That's up to you," said Bruno. "I learned she has a doctorate in archaeology and visiting lecturer status at the museum in Les Eyzies. And she's an old friend of Clothilde, which is a recommendation in itself. You might want to bear in mind that she's a horsewoman, so you're probably going to run into her at the riding school. She also plays serious tennis, so you'll be seeing her at the club. And as she's a native English speaker, you can bet she'll become a regular member of the social circle with Pamela and Jack Crimson. So, be warned."

Gilles rolled his eyes. "Ten thousand *gîtes* in the Périgord and she has to walk into mine," he said as Bruno's phone vibrated with an incoming message, and he saw it was from Clothilde. "Sorry—I meant to warn you Abby's recovering from a grim divorce back in the U.S."

Bruno closed his phone, wondering how he was supposed to interpret that. Women seemed able to communicate whole layers of meaning in a casual phrase that left men baffled.

Abby came out, said the house looked great and that she liked the setting. She would need it for about six months, she said, perhaps longer.

"Five hundred a month, until the end of March, six hundred for April," said Gilles.

"Okay. Five hundred until the end of March," Abby said, and thrust out her hand. As Gilles shook it, she said, "If I move in this week, can I have the rest of this month free? It's only a few days."

Gilles shrugged and nodded, and Abby turned, beaming, to look at Bruno. "Well, thank you both, and could you give me a lift back, please, Bruno? You can tell me about this mysterious grave on the way back." Then she pulled a checkbook from her bag, wrote a check and handed it to Gilles. "Two months in advance, one thousand euros, and thank you again."

"That's only one month in advance," said Gilles, with barely a hint of apology in his voice as he wrote out a receipt. "The other five hundred is a security deposit that you'll get back at the end of the lease unless there are damages. I'll have a lease ready for you to sign when you arrive."

"How are you going to get around?" Bruno asked as he drove Abby back to town.

"I need something cheap. Clothilde said I should talk to the man at the garage, I think his name is Lespinasse? You must know him."

"He's a good man, loves getting old cars back into running order, though it's hard to make a living that way," Bruno said. "He gave up selling gas because he couldn't match the prices at the supermarket, so his son persuaded him to move into other areas like trail bikes, restoring classic cars or old wrecks like my Land Rover."

"It seems to run smoothly. How old is it?"

"It's a 1955 model, and Lespinasse loves it even more than I do. But he has ordinary cars to rent or buy."

"May I take up even more of your time and see what he has for leasing?"

Bruno drove through town, out on the Périgueux road, past the old château where he'd been with the mayor that morning and pulled into Lespinasse's garage. To one side was a field with rows of used cars. To the other was a new glass-fronted showroom displaying glossy motorcycles, electric scooters and trail bikes. Between them was a big shed, its sliding doors open to reveal three cars, each partly dismantled. Bruno climbed out and let Balzac down to sniff around.

Lespinasse, a short, rotund man, backed out from the innards of a Citroën Traction Avant from the 1940s, brushed cheeks with Bruno and then brandished his forearm at Abby to be shaken. His hand was covered in grease.

Bruno introduced Abby. "She needs a cheap rental car while she's here. Maybe one of those old Peugeot 106s that you're so fond of."

Abby shook the proffered forearm.

"Cash or lease?" he asked.

"What's the difference?" Abby asked.

"With cash you get a three-month guarantee, with a lease I'll give you another one if yours breaks down. You can buy one for nine hundred ninety euros and pay your own insurance or lease for two hundred down and ninety a month, insurance and servicing included. I'll need your license. Can you drive a stick shift?"

"I have an international license and my dad loved English sports cars."

"Which did he prefer—Jaguars or MGs?"

"I learned to drive on a Triumph Spitfire," she said proudly.

Lespinasse led the way into an untidy office and pointed with a greasy finger to one of several rows of car keys hanging from hooks. "It's the red Peugeot 106 diesel, and it has close to four hundred thousand kilometers on it, but she runs sweet. Take her out and try her. The tires and brakes are good, and I rebuilt the transmission. Turn on the ignition and watch for the light to show the coil has warmed up before you try to start her, maybe six, seven seconds."

Perhaps it was the presence of a policeman in the passenger seat, but Abby drove cautiously but with skill, downshifting as much as braking to control her speed when coming down the hill from Audrix. She observed speed limits, stopped at pedestrian crossings, slowed before blind corners and kept an eye on her mirrors. If Bruno had been conducting a driver's test, she would have passed with flying colors.

"I like it," she said as she pulled back into Lespinasse's garage. She gave Lespinasse a check for the deposit and three months in advance.

"We're close to the grave I mentioned," Bruno said as Lespinasse handed Abby the car keys, insurance papers and a form naming her as the leaseholder. "Since you're an archaeologist, you may know more about it than I do."

"Graves are us," she said cheerfully, evidently pleased with her car and her new lodgings. "And bodies, of course."

Chapter 5

Bruno could not recall whether Brosseil was the fifth or sixth generation of his family to have been *notaires* in St. Denis. That was the kind of detail the mayor always remembered. At least once a year, the latest Brosseil would be reminded, usually in some public context, how much easier the mayor's mission of writing the town's history had been thanks to the Brosseil dynasty which had, in the days of the Emperor Napoléon III, taken over the legal paperwork. Last wills and testaments, sales and leases of property, the fate of insurance settlements and rights of way—they had all been written down and witnessed by a Brosseil. The *notaire*'s office was the obvious place for Bruno to obtain a copy of the deed to the Domaine de la Barde, including a map of the grounds.

"If you ever get a chance to dance with him, I mean classic ballroom dancing, do it," Bruno told Abby as they strolled down the main street of St. Denis to the *notaire*'s office. "Brosseil wins prizes for it. You name it, waltzes, foxtrots, even the tango. Friends of mine who have never learned to dance come back from a spin around the floor with him with their eyes shining with delight. He may be short and plump and a little overdressed in his old-fashioned way, but the women all say he makes them feel like a prima ballerina."

Abby laughed and raised an eyebrow. "In that case, I hope to get an invitation to take a twirl around the floor with this maestro of the ballroom!"

"Brosseil makes a point of dancing with all his clients, his wife's friends, the local notables and the attractive newcomers," Bruno said, grinning, as they approached Brosseil's door. "So I'm pretty sure you qualify."

Brosseil, in his suit, high collar, foulard tie and with a dark red rose in his buttonhole, bowed to put his lips within a centimeter of Abby's hand and declared himself enchanted. He shook Bruno's hand, and, speaking as though he were sharing some secret of national significance, said quietly that the mayor had called to say Bruno would be coming.

"I've made a copy of the map, but I'm not sure I can vouch for its reliability," he murmured. "Let me know if I can be of any further assistance. I'd be delighted to see that grand old building restored and lived in again."

"Can you date the grave, or tell us who drew the map?" Bruno asked.

"The grave was already marked when my father handled the sale in the 1960s, just before I was born," Brosseil said. "It's not his handwriting on the map, perhaps my grandfather's, and it would certainly be after 1945 because of that war memorial on the road below Bara-Bahau. It was put up for some *résistant* from the region who was shot by German troops." He glanced up at Abby and explained courteously that Bara-Bahau was a local cave with some notable prehistoric engravings inside.

"Did you ever hear how the man was shot?" Bruno asked. "I've never heard of a skirmish this close to the town."

"My father said there was some ambush near there but not when the main action took place in June," Brosseil said. He explained to Abby that the main fighting in the region had been immediately after D-Day, on June 6. The Resistance had tried to delay an SS armored division based in the South of France which had been ordered to head north to attack the Allied beachhead in Normandy, some three hundred miles away.

Suddenly Abby intervened. "Yes, I know," she said briskly. "The Das Reich Division should have reached Normandy in a few days, but thanks to the Resistance slowing them down, it took three weeks. It was the most important contribution to the war effort made by any of the Resistance movements anywhere. So, if this ambush did not take place in June, it must have been in August, after the German front in Normandy collapsed and the Allies landed in southern France."

The two men stared at her in surprise, glanced at each other, then Bruno said, "That's right, French and American troops landed near St. Tropez on the fifteenth of August and began chasing the Germans up the Rhône Valley. I'm impressed that you know so much about this."

"I've been reading a lot about it. Of course, many of them weren't German," Abby went on. "There were all those who'd been captured from the Red Army on the eastern front—Kazakhs, Georgians and so on. They probably thought that a quiet life on garrison duty in France was better than spending years in a Nazi prisoner-of-war stockade, even if they did have to wear a Wehrmacht uniform. All in all, the Allies took more than a quarter of a million Wehrmacht prisoners in France alone. And don't forget that many of the Georgians had deserted and joined the Resistance."

Bruno and Brosseil were silent, glanced briefly at each other as if at a loss for words.

"Why look so startled?" Abby asked, then laughed. "Do you really think I'd try to set myself up as a guide on the American connections in France without researching our role here in World War Two? British and American special forces were parachuted in to help train the Resistance all over France. But let's focus on the local issue. If there were German forces retreating through St. Denis in August, they would probably have been units from the Bordeaux U-boat base, possibly with some of the Luftwaffe troops who manned the antiaircraft defenses. Altogether there were more than twenty thousand of them, led by General Elster, and they got as far as the Loire River, where they surrendered later in September. Like so many other German units, Elster's troops were desperate to surrender to a Brit or an American rather than the Resistance, who had a reputation for killing lots of prisoners."

"You know more about this than I do," said Bruno. "Maybe I should introduce you to some of our local historians."

"I'd like to meet Guy Penaud and Patrice Rolli, if you know them," Abby replied. "I've read both their books. And then there's someone who wrote an encyclopedia of the Resistance in the southwest."

"Jean-Jacques Gillot," said Bruno. "He, Patrice and Guy are all members of our local history and archaeological society. I'll take you to the next meeting and you can get to know them. Penaud is an ex-cop, so I know him pretty well. But if we're going to take a look at this grave we should get moving."

Brosseil asked to join them, so all three set off down the rue de Paris, Bruno with the map and Brosseil carrying a portable theodolite on a folding tripod to help find the precise location. Thus equipped, finding the grave should have been easy, but Brosseil turned away from the eyepiece of the theodolite once he'd erected it.

"This makes no sense," he said. "The coordinates on the deeds must be wrong, they're pointing me to a place over on the far side of that road, two hundred meters beyond the property limit. It seems to me the coordinates refer to that Resistance martyr's monument we talked about."

"We could set out on the same compass bearing and see what we find," suggested Abby.

"Yes, good idea," said Bruno, and began thinking aloud. "This is low ground, probably a meadow in the old days, regularly flooded in the springtime and autumn. The house itself is built on higher ground, and I imagine any grave would be the same. They wouldn't want it to be drowned. There's some higher ground on the far side of the stream on the right compass bearing. Let's look there."

There was an ancient wooden bridge in need of repair over the stream. After the rains the water was flowing high enough almost to touch the supporting timbers beneath their feet. They crossed one at a time, and then squelched damply through long, wet grass until they came to a modest ridge, half hidden in bushes of wild brambles. They skirted them and found a slope where the brambles thinned out. Bruno clambered up and almost at once felt something like stone beneath his feet. He kicked away the tendrils of bramble and grass and saw rough concrete. The others helped him clear away more of the undergrowth and found a slab that was more than a meter wide and at least two meters long. Bruno used his index finger to measure its thickness. He knew that from his knuckle to the end of his nail was twelve centimeters and the slab's depth was a fraction deeper.

"Looks like a grave to me," Bruno said. He knelt down to pull the vegetation away from one side, revealing a concrete wall emerging from the ground to support the slab. Crumbling mortar held the two together.

"You'll need crowbars to lift that slab, maybe some machinery," Brosseil said, pulling a penknife from his pocket and poking at the mortar.

Bruno was already phoning Michel to ask if the town's public works department was using the ditcher. Once Bruno had explained the problem, Michel said it was in the yard behind his office and promised to bring it right away.

"Don't come by the main road and past the château," Bruno

told him. "The bridge over the stream is too flimsy. Come by the road beneath Bara-Bahau and then across the field. I'll meet you there by the road."

He asked Abby and Brosseil to wait for him and then set off across the meadow to await Michel's arrival. On the way, he called the mayor, to tell him the grave had been found and he was about to open its concrete lid.

"I thought you might want to be there, and we can use my phone to take photos," Bruno said. "But I'd like to see how deep the sides are, so if you could bring that old saber that hangs on the wall of the council chamber, I could slide it down between the earth and the concrete side of the grave."

Fifteen minutes later, having made the introductions of Abby to Michel and the mayor, they stood back to watch Michel at the controls of the ditchdigger. First he moved the metal scoop to try and insert its forward edge beneath the lip of the concrete block that topped the grave, but there wasn't enough clearance between it and the ground for the jaw of the scoop to fit. Undismayed, Michel reversed, turned the machine so it was parallel with one side of the grave and then used the scoop to dig a small ditch along the graveside.

Bruno looked at the crumbling mortar in the joint and asked the mayor for the saber. As he poked it at the seam, much of the mortar crumbled, then came away as he pulled the saber back toward him.

"I don't think that mortar will give you much trouble," he said. "Try levering the lid off now."

This time the blade of the scoop fit easily under the rim of the grave lid. Michel extended the four metal legs of the machine to stabilize it, and only then did he start to apply pressure to lift the slab. As he did so, Bruno used the saber to push away more of the old mortar. Once he had cleared one corner where the mortar seemed to be holding, the whole grave lid lifted a few centimeters.

"Stand farther back," Michel shouted. "The lid might crack apart when I try to push it off."

Bruno stepped back, gave the saber to the mayor and pulled out his phone to record the opening of the grave. Michel increased the lifting power on the arm, and the lid quivered briefly, rose up to the vertical and stood there a moment, balancing on its edge, before it toppled away from the grave, crushing some bramble bushes as it fell. They all darted forward to stare into the grave, and their spirits fell as they saw what appeared to be the skeleton of a small dog.

Chapter 6

"That's a very shallow grave for all the concrete," said Abby, breaking the disappointed silence.

Its depth looked to be about the length of Bruno's forearm. He put away his phone, took back the saber from the mayor and slid it point first between the earth and the concrete side of the grave. They could all hear the screech of metal on stone as Bruno pushed until only the saber's handle could be seen. The concrete wall went much deeper than the dog's grave.

"Stand back," said Michel. "Let's see how deep it is." He maneuvered his machine so that it was parallel to the grave and began scooping up the earth alongside it. At two or three scoops a minute, it took barely ten minutes to establish that the concrete wall of the grave descended at least two meters.

"Looks as though the dog's grave is a decoy," said the mayor. "What's the base of it?" He took the saber from Bruno and jabbed at the floor beside the dog's skeleton.

"I wonder what breed it was," mused Abby. "Medium-small, I'd say, perhaps some kind of terrier. Is there anything around its neck?"

"No sign of any identification," said Michel as the mayor continued to poke down with the saber.

"Looks like tarpaulin over something harder," the mayor said, and tried using the point to pull back the cloth. It tore without moving.

"Hold my legs, please," Michel said. He crouched and then lay full length on the ground, his head and shoulders over the rim, and began pulling at the tear in the tarpaulin. "Looks like planks of wood, old and well seasoned."

The mayor used the saber to cut away some of the cloth around the dog's skeleton. Then, supporting himself with his arms on each side of the grave, he lowered his legs and gingerly tested the wood's resilience. It felt stable and secure, so he let it take his full weight.

"Let me do this," said Bruno, but the mayor waved him away. "You're still convalescing."

"It seems solid enough, looks like an old door." The mayor used his own knife to cut a length of the tarpaulin to wrap the dog's bones. He handed the parcel to Michel and clambered out of the grave.

Michel used the saber to try to lift the wood, but it didn't budge. He went back to his machine and brought out a sturdy crowbar, working it into the wood this way and that. Finally, with a scream of metal on concrete and much creaking of the wood, it began to lift. Again, Bruno used his phone to film the process. Brosseil, the mayor and Abby each grabbed the raised edge of the wood and tilted it back.

"*Mon Dieu,* there are bodies in here," the mayor exclaimed. "Skeletons, I think three of them. And some kind of box that looks like metal. Hold it like that so Bruno can get a photographic record."

The old door seemed to have rested on wooden supports, four poles, one for each corner. Bruno put his phone away as Michel and the others lifted the door. They all clustered to look down and were stunned into silence. Two skeletons lay close together with a third, partly clothed, body at their side.

Abby moved as close as she could and knelt on the ground to peer in.

"I'm pretty sure from the pelvic girdles that the two smaller ones are female, and there's no sign of clothing," she said, her voice almost booming from the echo. To Bruno's surprise she seemed not in the least awed by the sudden presence of death, and he was reminded of Clothilde's joke about her profession, that all archaeologists were "ghouls with credentials."

"The bigger one seems to be wearing some kind of uniform, and there's a peaked cap that suggests something military," Abby continued. "I'd really like to bring up that box and see what it contains. But maybe we should stop now and call in the police."

"Bruno is the police," said the mayor. "And I am the mayor of this town, which means I am the chief magistrate. So we have full powers to investigate before calling in anyone else. Bruno, are you able to get down there and bring up the box? I think there's just room for you to stand in the corner beyond those two skulls."

After a brief discussion of the best way to achieve this, Michel brought his digger close so that the scoop was poised above the center of the grave and lowered it by half a meter. After donning evidence gloves Bruno stepped onto the scoop. He held the metal arm as Michel lowered it farther until he could step off into the corner and retrieve the box. It was about the size of a tin of cookies. He put it under his arm, stepped back onto the scoop and told Michel to start lifting.

"I'd like to go down as well and get a closer look at those remains," said Abby as Bruno stepped back onto the ground. "I've spent much of my professional life looking at skeletons, and they can tell us a lot. Do you have another pair of gloves, Bruno?"

"No, but you can have mine as soon as we've had a look at

what's in this tin," he said, putting it onto the ground and taking photos from each side.

"Pale green paint and what could have been red lettering," said the mayor, his voice almost wistful. "I think I remember a box like that from my childhood, a Breton brand that contained *galettes*. My mother kept it on a high shelf in the kitchen, too high for me to reach."

Bruno tried and failed to open the lid, then took out his penknife to lever it open. Inside were some items of cloth and papers, or perhaps small booklets. For the first time since the grave had been opened, he caught a smell of rot coming from the sealed box. One of the bits of cloth was a blue triangle with a white stripe, perhaps a badge of rank that had been cut from a uniform. It had been pinned to another piece of cloth, two oblongs of faded red, looking like the opened pages of a book, with two birdlike shapes on each page. Beneath them were more scraps of cloth, similar but with two stripes on the triangle, and the oblongs were a faded yellow with three birdlike shapes. They were clearly badges of rank. The pin holding these together was shaped like a laurel wreath with an eagle and a swastika on top, and what looked like a piece of artillery.

Abby was focused on her phone, a model unfamiliar to Bruno, but it looked new and expensive. She looked up, a glint of triumph in her eye, reminding Bruno of a clever schoolgirl eagerly thrusting a hand into the air to be first to answer a teacher's question.

"They are Luftwaffe rank badges from World War Two," she said. "The single stripe is a *Gefreiter,* or an airman, and the second is an *Obergefreiter,* like a corporal or sergeant, and the badge is *Flak-Kampfabzeichen,* for distinguished service as an antiaircraft gunner," she announced. "They had antiaircraft units at Bordeaux, guarding the harbor and submarine pens."

Bruno was examining two small booklets with blue covers

and the words *Soldbuch* and *Luftwaffe* in Gothic print on the cover. They were reminiscent of the paybook he had carried in the French army.

"Anna-Liese Weber, born in Königsberg, June 2, 1925," he read out from the first paybook. "She joined the Luftwaffe in 1943 and she's the *Obergefreiter*. The other is Hannelore Franke, born in Münster in January 1926 and joined the Luftwaffe in January 1944."

"Two female skeletons in the grave," said the mayor. "That seems to fit. What about the third body?"

"There's an Italian naval paybook here for a *capitano di fregata*," Bruno replied, opening it carefully. "He was promoted in 1942 from *capitano di corvetta*, named Salvatore Todaro, born in Messina, September 16, 1908. He was made a knight of the Order of the Roman Eagle in 1942 when he was commanding a submarine called *Comandante Cappellini*."

Abby was working her phone again.

"That submarine sank five Allied ships while in the region. It was part of BETASOM, the Italian submarine flotilla based in Bordeaux until the Italian surrender in 1943. Todaro must have stayed on, still loyal to the cause. Or he preferred that to being imprisoned in a German detention camp. Hold on, I'll see if Wikipedia has anything on that sub."

The men all watched her as they waited.

"Ah, the submarine was confiscated when the Italians surrendered and was then used to carry strategic materials to Japan. When the Germans surrendered in May 1945, it was confiscated by the Japanese."

On his own phone, Bruno pulled up the photo he had taken of the insignia on what had looked like the remains of a uniform. He tapped at the screen to enlarge the faded image on the sleeve, one thick golden stripe and two narrow ones, topped by a circle. He showed it to Abby.

"That denotes a *capitano di fregata,*" she said. "That must be him."

"There's a metal badge in the box, looks like silver, a circle with a dolphin inside," he said.

"Submariner's badge," said Abby, her finger flicking over her phone. "That's him for sure."

"I'd better get in touch with our foreign ministry and the German and Italian Embassies," said the mayor, and then looked solemnly at Abby. "I don't want any word of this to leak before I have done that, so no mention of it beyond us here, and above all not a word to any media. That includes in particular our own Philippe Delaron of *Sud Ouest.*"

"Should we replace the cover on the grave, seal it again?" asked Bruno.

"I think that would be fitting, as well as a wise precaution," the mayor agreed.

"Before you do, please could I go down and take a closer look at the female skeletons, just to confirm their age?" asked Abby.

"How do you do that?" asked the mayor.

"The epiphyses, where the long bones join, don't fully lock in until age twenty or more. We can learn something from this grave. I might even be able to find a cause of death."

"Then please go ahead," the mayor said.

She climbed into the scoop and Michel lowered her down.

"Should I call my friend Julien at the Resistance research center in Bordeaux?" Bruno asked as they watched her descend. "He's discreet, and he may be able to discover which Resistance units were involved. They, or somebody, went to considerable effort not just to hide these bodies but to be sure that their identity papers were preserved. In the fighting against the German units fleeing this area in August not much care was taken with the bodies. Mass graves at best. This strikes me as unusual. What's more, I never heard about any gun battle so close to town, apart from that memorial to some dead Resistance fighter." He turned to the mayor and Brosseil. "Do either of you know about any skirmishes near here?"

"Only what my father told me about a small German convoy being shot up after it came through town, leaving a burned-out Wehrmacht truck and motorbike and some dead troops who were tossed into the river," said the mayor. "All our men were up north trying to force the Germans out of Périgueux, so it must have been some other Resistance group involved. We'd better leave this grave as it is for the moment, and I should talk to the diplomats. I must say I can't see even the roughest Resistance people shooting women, even if they were in uniform."

"No, captured women might well have been raped first," said Abby, her head just above ground level. "It's significant that the two women were buried naked and the Italian officer was fully clothed."

"Yes," said the mayor. "The political and international implications of that is one of the factors that worries me."

"I can confirm from the femurs that the two female bodies are teenagers. Their collarbones are not fully connected to the sternum," Abby's voice came from the grave. "Otherwise they appear undamaged. On the male body there's a diagonal pattern of holes in what's left of the uniform, which could have been caused by a burst of automatic fire."

In silence, the four men exchanged glances. Then Brosseil crossed himself and spoke.

"Maybe we should have let these sleeping bodies lie in peace," he said. "We could bury them and their documents again and agree to forget that this ever happened."

"One person can keep a secret, and we are five," the mayor said as Abby called for the scoop to lift her out. They watched her emerge. He glanced solemnly at Brosseil before continuing, "Don't think that the same idea hasn't crossed my mind. We could just close the grave and try to forget it. But this is going to come out somehow, if only when the next owner of this property investigates the known grave on his land. So I have decided it's best that we handle this by the book."

At that moment, a cheery voice with a pronounced English accent called out, "I see you're opening our mysterious grave, Monsieur le Maire. Did you find anything with that digger of yours?"

A solidly built man with short red hair and a neat ginger beard was crossing the flimsy bridge and heading toward them.

"Michel, get that lid back on top of the grave and we'll head him off," the mayor said quietly. "Bruno, come with me," he added as he marched briskly to intercept the Englishman who wanted to restore Domaine de la Barde.

"Monsieur Birch, I want to introduce you to our local policeman, Bruno Courrèges, chief of police for the Vézère Valley, still on convalescent leave but back on duty soon. I wanted his advice on what best to do about the grave, so we arranged for our public works team to open it."

Birch came forward to shake Bruno's hand as Balzac trotted up to make his acquaintance and sniff at his feet. "I've heard of you, Monsieur Courrèges, and it's a pleasure to meet you. Is this your dog? I've always liked bassets."

"Bonjour, monsieur," Bruno replied. "My dog's name is Balzac, and he's very friendly. The mayor was telling me about your plans for the place. It will be good to see the old building and its gardens brought back to life."

"Let's hope we can bring them to reality," Birch said. "And please call me Tim. What about the grave? Anything there?"

"The skeleton of a dog," the mayor said, taking Birch's arm and steering him back across the bridge toward the château. "I'm sure you can describe our plans for the place far better than I'm able to, and Bruno here is a pillar of our local tennis club. I wanted to put you two in touch because of your son. Bruno spends his spare time teaching our local youngsters to play rugby in winter and tennis in summer. Perhaps you could show us the way to your court."

Bruno shook his head slightly in admiration at the mayor's skill in social deflection and watched as he put an arm on Birch's shoulder and marched him past the château toward the undergrowth that almost hid the old tennis court. Bruno glanced back and saw the grave lid being replaced and Michel driving the digger back the way he'd come, with Brosseil and Abby strolling alongside.

Chapter 7

Bruno knocked once at the door of his own office and went straight in, to be greeted by the sound of some string quartet playing quietly, the scent of roses and the piercing eye of Mademoiselle Cantagnac over the raised lid of her laptop.

"Well?" she asked. "Are you proposing to throw me out of this office again?"

"Not yet," Bruno said, with a polite smile. "The mayor has asked me to brief you on our visit to the grave and what we found. He tells me you're a lawyer, in addition to your other role."

"Not quite. I have a law degree but don't practice. Nor have I been to magistrates' school. What's the news?"

Bruno explained what they had found at the grave site and she took notes. When he explained that the mayor was making calls, to the foreign ministry and the German and Italian Embassies, her pen paused.

"The property is under the authority of the bankruptcy judge," she said, leaning forward so that the light from the window fell on her face. She was handsome in a severe way, her features even and without enhancement by any obvious cosmetics. Her hair was pulled back into a disciplined bun, and she was wearing a dark blue blouse that buttoned up to her throat. He guessed her age at late forties, perhaps somewhat older.

"The judge should also be informed," she went on. "Since I have been dealing with him on this, I can inform him. As the leading creditor we have some rights. I doubt that the judge will object, since I will stress that the grave was opened to facilitate the sale of the property. That should allow the judge to close the file, which he's eager to do. Two young German women from an antiaircraft unit and an Italian submarine captain—that should make a stir. The mayor is right to start off with the diplomatic formalities."

She paused, and looked at him with that direct, almost intimidating gaze that he recalled from their first encounter. "Has the media been informed?"

"Not yet, but as I said, several people now know about this. It's unlikely to stay secret for long. I think the mayor is also concerned that it may prove to be an obstacle to the plans of Monsieur Birch to buy and restore the place."

"Not if Birch is as smart as I think he is," she said. "A dramatic history with a touch of the ghoulish should add to the place's attractions."

"I agree. Birch likes the place and the region. We spoke with him briefly, without revealing what we'd found. He seems very taken with the *domaine* and has some interesting plans for it."

"Let's hope he sticks to them. More to the point, any local Resistance people who were involved in the fate of the three bodies will almost certainly be dead by now, so we'll probably be spared any unpleasant trials, although there'll have to be some kind of formal inquest. Do you know of any locals who might know anything about this? I'd have thought there would've been rumors."

"None that the mayor has heard," Bruno replied. "My predecessor as the local municipal policeman, Joe, may be able to help. If there was anything known locally among the old *résistants,* he'd probably be aware of it. As a boy he acted as a courier, even got a Resistance medal after the war."

"I think you should find out what you can, discreetly, of course, while I call the judge, and then we can meet back here with the mayor when he's finished with the diplomats. I suppose we'll have to arrange for a formal visit."

"Tell him I'll be back after seeing Joe. He'll know who I mean," said Bruno, rising to go, pausing when he heard what sounded like the mewing of a cat.

"You're still officially on convalescent leave," she said. "You shouldn't be working."

"A stroll through town, watching Michel's digger open a grave, a visit to an old friend, I don't call that working. And I'm not even in uniform."

"How's that lovely dog of yours?"

"His name is Balzac and he's fine. He's outside in my van. Was that a cat I just heard?"

"Yes, she's on my lap. Her name is Minou. Oh, by the way, Philippe Delaron came looking for you. He wants to write something about our hero policeman coming back to work after being shot in the line of duty. I think he's really hoping to find out exactly what happened. There are some wild rumors flying around about how you got shot at that supposed traffic stop of yours."

"State secret," he said. "I can't talk about it."

"Understood, but I've come across your friend General Lannes before, and I know he came to see the mayor after you were shot. I think you should know that the mayor asked me to find out whether you should be put on the ministry's payroll when Lannes has you seconded to his staff. Of course, we'd reduce your local pay accordingly. It was interesting to learn how often you've been seconded to the staff of the interior ministry over the last three years."

Bruno raised an eyebrow. "I think all that is above my pay grade."

"Not at all. Your pay grade is the issue. When on secondment you are ranked as a *commissaire,* which is a much higher pay grade, and one of my duties is to ensure that my fellow employees are properly paid for their services."

"Good luck, but I suspect that General Lannes and the interior ministry might see it differently. He once threatened to call me back to military service at my old rank of *sergent-chef.*"

"The mayor said the same thing, but that's beyond the general's authority. You've been out of the army too long for you still to be in the reserves. I checked."

Bruno raised an eyebrow, recalling her secondary role as an official of the union for mayoral employees. "Good luck. I'll be curious to see what's in my paycheck."

"I think you'll be pleasantly surprised, Bruno. I enjoy this kind of bureaucratic combat."

Surprised at her use of his first name, Bruno said, "Since it appears that we're now on first-name terms, what should I call you?"

"Colette. And that means we can call each other *tu,* at least in private. In public, we should stick to *vous,* as you do with the mayor."

He grinned. "It will certainly be *vous* when I reclaim my office."

"Good," she said, with a warm smile that surprised him.

The mayor's door was closed when Bruno passed it. He descended the stairs to find Abby leaning against the door of his Land Rover. He opened the back to release Balzac, who went straight to Abby, glancing up at her appealingly. She bent down to stroke him.

"Thanks so much for taking me along to see the grave, although I guess we found more than we bargained for," she said. "But I really came to ask if I could take you to dinner to thank you for everything you've done—finding me a place to live and a car, and introducing me to the mayor and the town."

"I'd like that, but this evening looks busy. I have to see somebody about the grave and then have a meeting with the mayor, which may go on for some time."

"Another evening, then," she said, giving Balzac a final pat and rising. "What's your phone number?" Bruno gave it and took hers. "I suppose I should think about moving my stuff into the new house."

"You'll enjoy meeting Fabiola, the local doctor. She can introduce you to the riding school," he said. "I'd better go. Thanks for your professional help at the grave. That's put you into the mayor's good graces, which will be useful."

"By the way, and this could be important: the body of the Italian can't have been Captain Todaro, despite the identification papers," she said. "I looked up his name on the internet and Todaro was killed in the Mediterranean in December 1942. Apparently, he died on a boat in his sleep, strafed by a Spitfire. Seems like he was a decent guy. He towed the crews of two of the merchant ships his submarine sank to a safe spot ashore."

"Really?" Bruno replied, startled. "Thank you, Abby, that certainly sounds important. I'd better let the mayor know."

Chapter 8

Despite being in his eighties, Joe still worked in his *potager* every day. Bruno found him on his knees, taking advantage of the recent rain to plant onions and garlic in moist soil that would usually be hard and dry after the summer. Bruno stood back, knowing the old man would be offended if he tried to help him to his feet.

"Business or pleasure?" Joe asked, after shaking hands and greeting Balzac. He steered Bruno through the double wooden doors that led to his courtyard, where Bruno was given a seat at the rickety round table.

"Always a pleasure to see you, Joe, but some business. I want to pick your memory," Bruno said.

"Then we'll need a drink." Joe went to his kitchen and returned with two glasses and a bottle of his famous homemade eau-de-vie. From his pocket he took two sugar lumps and dropped one into each glass before filling them with the thick, clear liquid.

"*Santé,*" Joe said, and they clinked glasses. "So, what's this about?"

"It's something that dates back to the time after D-Day," Bruno began. "I don't mean the fighting in June, but later in August, when the Germans were fleeing from Bordeaux. You may remember the key dates: the Allies reaching the Loire on

August 13; the Allied landings in southern France on August 15. Then the Germans abandoning Périgueux on August 19, followed by the liberation parade on August 24, the day before the German surrender in Paris. Heady times."

"Yes, in general, I remember all that, though not the exact dates," Joe said.

"Same with me." Bruno held up his phone. "The wonders of modern technology. I checked the dates on the internet when I got here."

"The baron's grandmother was living here in the *chartreuse* and she had a radio that could get the BBC from London," Joe said. "I remember my father coming back to tell me about the *débarquement* on the sixth of June. He did the same for the big Soviet offensive that took Minsk in July, and the Allied landings in southern France in August. It was like having a birthday every month."

"Did you ever hear about the ambush of a small German convoy here, mid-to-late August, below the Bara-Bahau cave?" Bruno asked.

"I'm not sure," Joe said. "What's this about, Bruno?"

"I was just with the mayor and we found a grave. It was down in the meadow below Bara-Bahau, and it contained the remains of two young German women who'd been in the Luftwaffe and an Italian, a submarine officer still in uniform who must have come from Bordeaux."

"A grave?" Joe shook his head, not quite meeting Bruno's eye, which was unusual. "I never heard about any Italians—they'd surrendered in '43. Nor about any German women in uniform."

"Were you still here then, in August?"

"Yes, it was harvesttime, and my dad wouldn't let me go to Périgueux, where all the *résistants* had gone. We'd heard about some shooting near Bara-Bahau in August, a German motorcyclist and a couple of burned-out trucks and a staff car. Not really a convoy. The guys from the Lot had ambushed them and got some loot, cigarettes mainly. They traded them for a meal at the café by the bridge."

"Where were they from in the Lot?"

"No idea—no, wait. I remember hearing something about Castillonnès, but I might be wrong. They moved out fast, heading north to help liberate Périgueux. They'll all be dead now. It's seventy, nearly eighty years ago."

"What about the burned-out vehicles?"

"All of us kids went to see them the next morning, not that there was much to see, and we weren't allowed to get close. There was a German army motorbike and trucks, and a fancy Italian staff car, a Lancia, I think. We were all told to stay away from that place. Nobody said why, but there was a rumor that the house was being used to hide Jewish children. There was a fierce old lady who used to chase us kids away with a big stick. Well, not so old, maybe in her sixties. She knew my name because she was one of the 'postboxes.' There was a box for balls and towels under the umpire's chair at the tennis court where I could pick up and leave messages from the Resistance. I never went to the big house."

"Who was it who kept you away from the wrecked vehicles? Local people?"

"Not on the first day, when it was still the Francs-Tireurs et Partisans, the FTP guys from the Lot. But the day after they'd gone, it was being guarded by someone from the new team at our *mairie*. The old Vichy people had been forced out in June. But the real purge came in late August, when we watched women getting their heads shaved, like those who slept with Germans. We didn't have any Germans based around here, but they got the same treatment if they'd slept with those bastards from the Milice, the Vichy cops. A lot of private scores were settled in those days. Bad times."

"Some of those women had husbands in POW camps in Germany," said Bruno. "They had kids to feed, and some Milice guys would demand sexual favors in return for ration books, so they acquiesced."

"I can't say I blame them. That's what my *maman* always told my dad whenever it came up." Joe refilled their glasses. "As I said, they were bad times."

"What happened to the wrecked vehicles?"

"Railwaymen came from Le Buisson and towed them away. They said they were collecting metal to be melted down to repair railway tracks."

"What about the bodies?"

Joe shook his head. "I don't know. I never heard anything about a mass grave. They must have been pretty burned up. Maybe the railwaymen cleared the remains away with the scrap metal. Or maybe they were just shoved into the river. That's what usually happened."

Bruno raised an eyebrow but said nothing.

"Bruno. I don't know anything more about it. Most of the Resistance guys I knew were conscripted into the French army. A lot of them were killed that winter in Alsace, fighting around Strasbourg and Colmar."

"And some of them came back, friends of your dad, guys who'd known you as their young messenger boy," Bruno said. "You didn't get that medal for nothing, Joe. You were an honorary member of the group at the reunion dinners. You must have heard things, maybe just rumors. I'm sure you agree it was unusual, German women in uniform and an Italian, a year after Italy had broken with Hitler. We even had Italian troops fighting on our side by then. I can't imagine that didn't come up when the old warriors got together to talk about their fighting days."

"But remember, it wasn't our guys, it was the FTP guys from the Lot. But yes, there were rumors, gossip."

"Some of those guys from the Lot were conscripted into the army in late '44, along with our local men," Bruno said. "You remember, when de Gaulle was rounding up every man he could. The Brits were running out of men, the Yanks were more and more focused on Japan. This was de Gaulle's chance to show how useful he was, sending a whole French army to the front line in Alsace. Joe, I was in the military, I know how it must have been when guys from nearby regions were thrown together in the Alsace battles that winter. Old comrades always compare notes when they start remembering, so I can't believe that somebody from St. Denis didn't ask guys from the Lot what really happened at that ambush back in August. What were these rumors?"

Joe poured himself another drink, but this time Bruno shook his head and put his hand over his glass. It was still more than half full.

"What do you think happened?" Joe's voice was surly. He emptied his glass, then smacked his lips. "Young Kraut girls in uniform taken prisoner when our guys had hardly seen a woman in weeks, months. And we'd just spent four years being occupied, Bruno. Think of the shame of that and the resentment building up. For some of those men it could have been their first time with a woman, for others probably their last. *Merde,* Bruno, I don't have to spell it out."

"So, then what? The German girls have been passed around, maybe they tried to run away. Maybe one or both of them tried to fight back, perhaps even to grab a weapon. They are shot, maybe in self-defense. The German trucks are still burning, but it's time to clear out. Do the guys dig a quick grave and cover them up? Do some of them come back later with slabs of concrete and try to make a proper grave in the woods, out of the way? I've seen that grave, Joe, it's a solid piece of work."

"*Tu me casses les couilles,* Bruno. Don't bust my balls. How the hell would I know? I wasn't there. You know how old soldiers tell tales, make it up half the time."

"Joe, I know that. But that grave wasn't made overnight. Jesus,

Joe, you have daughters, granddaughters, you're not some young buck who can laugh about some awful moment when women are stripped and raped. They'd have been drunk on gun smoke and power and determined to show the German girls that they were the masters now."

Joe sat stubborn and silent, his lips drawn into a thin line and his shoulders tight, looking grimly at the ground beneath his feet.

"This isn't going to end here, Joe," Bruno said. "The mayor has spent the last hour on the phone to our diplomats at the quai d'Orsay. And he'll call the German and Italian Embassies to tell them we've found the wartime remains of some of their citizens. They're our allies now, our friends and partners in Europe, so we're honor bound to treat those bodies with respect, just as we'd expect them to treat our dead. There is going to be a formal inquiry into all this, and we can't keep you out of it. You're too well known for that, the last of our Resistance heroes. It was the mayor who told me to come and ask you what happened, and he's waiting for me to come back and tell him."

Joe leaned forward, resting his elbows on his knees and clasping his hands over his mouth as if forcing himself to remain silent.

"Joe, you were a kid," Bruno went on. "It must have been like playing cowboys and Indians, a bit of a game with the spice of real danger. You can't have been there when the bad stuff happened. But you heard something. And then you grew up and became a cop, our village cop, a good one, still respected. You taught me damn near everything I know. And that means I learned from you that even in wartime, even after four years of occupation, there are some things that should not be done, that must not be done. Because if we do them, then we sink to the same bestial level as the Milice or the Nazis."

Bruno rose, put his hand on Joe's shoulder and squeezed it briefly. Then he raised his glass in salute and finished the contents.

Balzac was sitting beneath the table. The dog rose and took a pace forward to rub his head against Joe's leg in a friendly farewell. Almost automatically, Joe dropped a hand to scratch the place behind Balzac's ears that made him give a gentle growl of pleasure at this gesture from an old friend.

"I know you'll want to think about it, Joe, and we both know you'll do the right thing when the mayor says you need to tell him what you know, and what you think happened."

Chapter 9

Bruno found the mayor in his office with Colette Cantagnac, drawing up plans for the official visit that would take place later in the week. The mayor had been informed that the delegation would consist of one German and one Italian diplomat from the embassies, a French diplomat to escort them and possibly someone from the war graves office of the defense ministry. They would take the early high-speed train from Paris to Libourne, where a car from the Périgueux *préfecture* would meet them and bring them to St. Denis. The mayor, along with Bruno, the prefect of the *département* and the official historian from the Jean Moulin Resistance museum in Bordeaux would meet them at the grave site. After the visit, they would all have lunch at the *mairie* before the diplomats returned to Paris to arrange for the repatriation of the women's remains to Germany.

The Italians were undecided what to do about their naval officer. He had apparently continued to work with the German navy even though the Italian government had joined the Allies in 1943. The question of inviting Italian and German media to the ceremony was under discussion, as the French foreign ministry began digesting the news that the supposed Italian officer could not have been Captain Todaro. So who was he?

"What worries me is that if the skeleton in Italian uniform is not Todaro, how can we be sure that the two females are the German women named in their paybooks?" Bruno said.

"We can't," said Colette. "But now that the diplomatic machinery has begun to turn, it will grind on, generating paper trails like any other bureaucracy. I suppose we could do a DNA test on the skeletons."

"But with whom or what should we compare them?" the mayor asked. "Do we suggest the German government get DNA from any remaining family members, and should we invite them, too? This is becoming a real headache."

"Whatever the diplomats decide to do about the mystery man in the Italian uniform, maybe we should invite Joe to join us at the lunch, as the last surviving *résistant* in the commune," Bruno suggested.

"What did he have to say?"

"That the railwaymen had bought a truck to take away the burned-out vehicles for scrap metal, and he hadn't been allowed anywhere near the spot. He said the ambush had been carried out by an FTP group from the Lot that was hoping to help liberate Périgueux and that there were rumors that the two women had been raped before they were shot." Bruno paused. "I think at this stage I should consult my contact at the Centre Jean Moulin to see if we can pin down which FTP group it was."

"Which FTP group?" the mayor said, clearly disturbed. "I don't want to get into a pissing match with half the mayors and the prefect from the Lot."

"Perhaps we should contact Commissaire Jalipeau. Since he's with the Police Nationale he could ask their forensic chief to examine the bodies and give us an expert assessment of the causes of death."

"Could we not do that informally with one of our own doctors?" suggested Mademoiselle Cantagnac. "I think we need to keep as much control over this process as we can."

"I'll try," said Bruno. "What did the bankruptcy judge say?"

"He didn't see all this causing a problem for the sale, but he had one suggestion that the mayor thinks makes sense," she replied as the mayor nodded. "He proposed that we should carve off a tongue of land from the existing monument on the Bara-Bahau road and make that property part of our commune. We could compensate Monsieur Birch with an equivalent patch of land elsewhere. The judge is prepared to do that quickly because of this new development. He says it should be done as a private arrangement before the transfer to Monsieur Birch is made formal."

"That makes a lot of sense," said Bruno. "But does our commune already own the land on which the memorial stands? And has anybody checked the name on it? I just remember that it said, *Tombé sous les balles allemandes*—fell under German bullets—but was he one of ours? Or from the Lot?"

"Good point," said the mayor. "We'll check to see if it's our land, and Bruno, maybe you should take a quick look at the memorial before consulting your friend at the Bordeaux archives."

"I'd better do that now," Bruno said. "If the name on the memorial is one of ours, we could have a problem. Joe told me that our local *résistants* had all gone up to help liberate Périgueux. Our guys were mainly Forces Françaises de l'Intérieur, under de Gaulle's authority. But there must have been some Communists in St. Denis who kept allegiance to the FTP."

"*Merde*," grunted the mayor. "Politics at this stage is the last thing we need. Go and find out, Bruno, and then call your man at the Moulin center."

Bruno left the *mairie* and drove to the memorial. His heart sank a little when he saw the inscription:

MORT POUR LA FRANCE
JEAN-MAURICE MARTY
1919–1944
UN RÉSISTANT
TOMBÉ SOUS LES BALLES ALLEMANDES

"Marty" was a common name around St. Denis, which suggested he might be local, although Bruno had never heard of a Jean-Maurice. He copied the words down in his notebook to check against the names on St. Denis's war memorial. Then he drove back into town.

The memorial was mostly filled with names from the 1914 to 1918 war, but there were two names from the Algerian War, one from Indochina and five from 1939 to 1945, none of which was Jean-Maurice Marty.

He called a friend from the hunting club, Alphonse Marty, a member of a sprawling family spread across the region.

"Bonjour, Alphonse, it's Bruno. That Resistance war memorial near Bara-Bahau with the name Jean-Maurice Marty. That's not a name I know. Was he part of your family?"

"*Salut,* Bruno. Glad to hear you're back. He was not one of ours, more a distant cousin of the branch down in the Lot around Cahors. He was from Castillonnès, wounded in 1940 and then joined the FTP during the occupation. He was a Communist, and they were the ones who put up the memorial. We still put flowers there every August 17, the anniversary of his death. Why do you ask?"

"I was just curious. I was passing the place, noticed the name and wondered if this was someone from the local family. You must still be in touch with that part of the family."

"No, he was the last of the Castillonnès branch, but there's still lots of them around Cahors. You remember, the hunting club dinner where we shared an excellent bottle or two of Cahors."

"How could I forget? I trust all is well with you and yours, Alphonse?"

"Everybody's fine. Young Raymond passed his *baccalauréat*, and Monique is having another baby in January. I hope you'll come and help us wet the baby's head. My third grandchild."

"I wouldn't miss it. But I'll see you at the hunting club before then."

"So, your shoulder's better after that bullet you took? I'm glad to hear you're out of the hospital and back at work. I trust that means you can still fire your shotgun and get some of those *bécasses* you like. Good eating, those birds are."

"I'll look forward to eating some with you, Alphonse. *Au'voir.*"

Bruno strolled back thoughtfully across the bridge, looked down at the river and then called his friend Julien at the Centre Jean Moulin in Bordeaux, named after a hero of the Resistance. Moulin had joined de Gaulle in London and had been parachuted into occupied France to persuade the various wings of the Resistance to come together under de Gaulle's leadership. He had largely succeeded with his mission when he'd been arrested, tortured and died on the train taking him to a concentration camp. After years of dedicated research and interviews with most of the aging veterans, the center was now the largest regional archive of the Resistance in France.

"Ah, Bruno, it's good to know that you're back in harness," Julien said. "I think I know why you're calling. We had a call from Paris about this newfound grave in your town; two German women and an Italian submariner, I hear."

"*Salut,* Julien. I have a date for you, and a name of one of the *résistants* who died there. August the seventeenth, Jean-Maurice Marty, from Castillonnès, one of a group of FTP guys from the Lot."

"Where did you get that?"

"The war memorial on the roadside, close to the found grave, and I checked with a member of a very widespread local family. The one buried here was from Castillonnès."

"That would have been one of the memorials that the FTP erected all over France. It was part of their campaign to show that the Communist Party mounted the real Resistance, fighting the Gestapo, while de Gaulle sat safely back in London."

"Does the name Marty ring any bells?" Bruno asked.

"Yes, I've found him here on the computer. He was a member of the FTP's group Kursk, about thirty men and named after the Soviet victory the previous year. Some of them were Spaniards, refugees and veterans of the Spanish Civil War who hated the Nazis and also hated the Italians who had fought on Franco's side. If I had to bet, I'd say that they were the ones who made sure the Italian officer was killed. After the Germans evacuated Périgueux, the Kursk group stayed on for the liberation parade, took part in some local reprisals against alleged collaborators, and were then sent off to the siege of La Rochelle."

"Did any of them leave memoirs?" Bruno asked.

"We have two oral memoirs, interviews taken in the 1980s. The first is by someone called Claude Nemours, who named himself their commissar, a railwayman and militant trade union man; the second by a Max Crossin, who was wounded in the advance into Germany and brought home. He later became a journalist, the Cahors correspondent for *L'Humanité,* the party newspaper. I'll get the tapes out from the archives. I can let you know more when I come to St. Denis with the diplomats."

Bruno scribbled down the information in his notebook, wondering what all that might mean. A trade union leader with the *cheminots* could probably have called up the local railway station and organized for the remains of the ambush to be collected as scrap metal. He might also have been able to arrange for the concrete slabs and the building of the grave and could have wielded the *piston,* the political influence to get it done fast and discreetly.

Bruno then informed his friend that the man dressed as an Italian submarine captain could not have been Captain Todaro, since he'd been killed twenty months earlier.

"So, who was it?" Julien asked.

"That's for you historians to establish," said Bruno. "I'll buy you lunch at La Tupina if you succeed." La Tupina was their favorite Bordeaux restaurant. "But it was somebody who was able to get hold of a paybook and identity papers in Todaro's name, presumably forged."

Bruno returned to the mayor's office and recounted what he'd learned.

"All right, that's more than enough for this unhappy and memorable day," said the mayor. "Time for a drink, Mademoiselle Cantagnac, Bruno?"

"I'd better say no," Bruno replied. "I have to exercise my horse. While I'm there, I'll ask Fabiola if she'll be able to take a look at our skeletons."

"Why might that be important?" asked Colette. The mayor poured her a glass of *vin de noix* and added a slug of eau-de-vie from the bottle he kept in his desk.

"Forewarned is forearmed," said Bruno. "The more we know before this becomes official, the better we can weigh the interests of St. Denis. And the sooner you can get that judge to arrange the transfer of the land to the town, the more authority we'll have."

"Ah, Bruno, what a worthy pupil of administrative affairs you've become," said the mayor, chortling, as Bruno rose to go.

Chapter 10

Balzac on the passenger seat was quivering with excitement as Bruno turned onto the road to the stables that he knew so well. Bruno was just as thrilled as his dog to be back in this familiar place, looking forward to seeing his friends again and climbing aboard Hector for the first time in weeks. He knew he'd have to take it slowly with his wound not fully healed, but Pamela would no doubt ensure that he did.

They were saddling up as he parked. While Balzac darted into the stables to greet his friend Hector, Bruno's own friends turned to welcome him. Yet concern showed on their faces. Isn't this too soon? asked Félix, the stable boy. Are you sure you'll be okay? chimed in Miranda. We'll take it gently, said Pamela, in the voice of authority she used when horses were involved. Hector is in great shape, said Félix, who'd been riding him while Bruno had been in the hospital and in the convalescent home.

Bruno relished it all, the feel of straw beneath his feet in the stable, the smell of the leather as he took the saddle to Hector's stall and above all the way Hector's ears cocked and his fine head lifted in recognition as Bruno approached. He handed his horse an apple from the bucket where Pamela kept her windfalls and pressed his head against the animal's great neck before checking his horse's legs and fetlocks, saddling him up and leading Hector out into the yard.

"Nothing beyond a canter, Bruno, or I'll ban you from the stables for a week," said Pamela. But she smiled back as he grinned at her. She led them out through the paddock at a stately walk, then rose to a gentle trot as they took the longer, shallow route up to the ridge. The trees seemed to stir in welcome and the light breeze was like a blessing on his face as he felt the familiar play of Hector's muscles beneath him. He fell automatically into the rising and falling rhythm of the trot until they reached the ridge and reined in, gazing down to the Vézère River curving below them until it straightened to flow beneath the town bridge. The red roofs of St. Denis clambered up the far hillside like a scattering of children's toys as they always had. This was home, he knew, as he took a deep breath to savor the familiar scents, of horses and saddle soap, the rain-soaked vegetation of trees and wild grasses all overlaid with the faintest hint of basset hound.

"*Mon Dieu,* I've missed this," he cried out, and heard the affection in the chuckles of his friends.

"We missed you, all of us—in the market, in the shops, the tennis club, the rugby games," said Pamela. "Even in church, Florence told us. Do you know, Father Sentout said prayers for you every week?"

"I didn't know, but I'm touched. I received so many cards in the hospital, including one enormous one from the nursery school. The nurses were very impressed."

"Enjoy it while it lasts, my dear," Pamela teased. "People will soon be back to normal, bickering over the placement of their market stalls and grumbling about parking fines and speeding tickets and writing their anonymous letters."

"I don't have anything to do with speeding tickets," Bruno protested.

"We all know that and it doesn't matter. You're still a cop, the embodiment of the law."

Bruno nodded, shrugged and then tapped his heels gently against Hector's sides and they rode on in affectionate silence, until Pamela said, "Come on, this is far too slow, let's canter back down the long slope or the horses will get grumpy. Just a touch of rein on Hector."

She led them into a trot that became a canter, and she kept the pace there, riding with Bruno almost knee to knee. And somehow, with that extraordinary chemistry of communication between a horse and his familiar rider, Hector seemed content with the moderate pace. He did not surge ahead to take the lead as he usually did, but stayed alongside Pamela's mare, Primrose, while Fabiola surged off ahead with Félix and Miranda. Balzac, however, seemed happy to be running along beside Hector rather than toiling far in his wake.

"I've never known Hector to settle for the sight of other horses' rumps ahead," Bruno said.

"Horses are much wiser than we think," Pamela said. "And more forgiving. More civilized than humans altogether, if you ask me. That's why they're so good for us. And is there any sound more soothing to the heart than their hooves at this modest pace?"

"The best medicine," said Bruno, relieved that there was not the slightest twinge in his shoulder, no sense of the alien metal that had been inserted into his collarbone.

"It's so good for us all to be together again," Pamela said. "We missed you very much." And they each turned in the saddle to smile at one another, exchanging the warm look of old lovers, content in the deep, unquestioning affection that they shared. All too soon they were close to the end of the ridge where the others were patiently waiting.

"Not bad for a beginner," Fabiola called out as Bruno and

Pamela approached. Bruno waved a general greeting and said, "I know it's Balzac that you were really missing, but he insisted on bringing me along, too."

As if responding to his name, Balzac let out a cheerful bark, and they all took their horses in single file down the bridle path through the woods that led to the hunters' cabin and the long way home.

"By the way, Florence called to say your phone was engaged for ages and asked me to tell you she was sorry not to be here with the twins to welcome you back," Pamela said as they reached the wider path by the cabin and they could walk their horses side by side. "It's half-term holidays at the *collège* so she's up visiting her parents in the north. Apparently, they're reconciled at last after they all stayed together at your place when you were in the hospital. She gets back at the weekend and we can all get together for dinner then. She said it was your idea to introduce them to Father Sentout and to put on the choir concert. Apparently, her very religious parents were greatly moved."

"I hope the mayor and headmaster told them that Florence had become a pillar of our community."

"Indeed, they did, everything save a brass band. And we had them to supper here with all the gang."

"On that note, we're going to our place tonight for dinner," said Fabiola. "We all want to hear about this new American tenant, and for you to explain the latest rumor that flashed around town. I heard you were seen disappearing into the earth on a digger by Bara-Bahau while the mayor and Brosseil and the American woman stood watching."

"Don't tell me," said Bruno. "One of your gossipy patients must have driven by as we were working. Now, who could it have been? Madame Pasquier with her bunions or Batailler with his lumbago?"

"Close but no cigar," Fabiola replied, laughing. "It was Pasquier's daughter coming for her regular pregnancy checkup."

"You can see for yourself what we found, if you like. The mayor wanted me to ask you a favor, if you would take a look at a couple of skeletons dating back to the war and see if you can tell us how they died."

"Are you serious?"

"Yes, very much so. We found a hidden grave containing the remains of two young women, Germans, and an Italian naval officer. They'd been ambushed by a Resistance group. The dead German troops, at least the males, were disposed of, probably in the river, but for some reason they buried these three. We have a bunch of diplomats coming later this week to see about repatriating the bodies."

"Why not call in the police forensic guys you usually work with?" Fabiola asked. "They're the experts."

"We could, but then everything becomes official and they may not tell us the results. We need to know just what we're dealing with. This American lodger of yours is an archaeologist, an old pupil and friend of Clothilde, and she's worked with a lot of graves and skeletons. But unlike you, she's no medical expert, and she may not have the town's interests at heart."

"That, my dear Bruno, is the least tempting proposition I've ever heard. These are bodies that have been buried for close to eighty years. What state are they in? Were they in coffins?"

"No coffins. The two women must have been naked, they're just skeletons. The Italian officer, we're not so sure. He's still in uniform, but there are what might have been bullet holes."

"What does that mean, the women were naked? Were they raped?" Fabiola looked at him fiercely.

"We don't know, but it's possible," he said. "We think that the ambush was mounted by Resistance fighters from the Lot. And as you said, it was eighty years ago. They're all dead so there can be no question of any kind of trial."

"I'm not a qualified forensic specialist, I don't have access to the right kind of equipment. I think you should bring in the police. This is their job. And I can't say that I share the mayor's concern to protect the precious image of St. Denis."

"The mayor is seriously worried about all this. If you won't do it, I'll ask Dr. Gelletreau."

"Don't be silly. He's a nice old man, but he hasn't learned anything since he left medical school, and he's forgotten half of that. Call the cops, that's what they're for."

"Okay," he said, and smiled. "I'm persuaded. I think you're right. As usual."

Fabiola smiled back at him. "My feminist instincts make me want to say something waspish about it being unusual and welcome for a man to admit he's wrong to a woman, but I'll restrain them just this once because it's lovely to have you riding with us again. And you're coming to dinner. Don't worry, it's not my usual fondue. Gilles is learning to cook. That's why he went back early."

"Ah," said Bruno, who recalled that back in Bosnia, Gilles had not even been able to warm up the cans of French military rations without somehow making them even less palatable. "What is he cooking?"

"I'm not sure, but he's bought a wok and a book titled *Asian Cooking Made Easy*," Fabiola replied, rolling her eyes.

Chapter 11

"The guinea pigs are here," announced Fabiola, steering Pamela and Bruno into the kitchen. The table was set for four with a first course already laid out, smoked trout with quarters of lemon. Gilles turned to welcome them while opening a bottle of white wine from the Domaine de Perreau, a vineyard in the Montravel, close to the château of the immortal Montaigne. The *domaine* was now run by Gaëlle, the daughter of the house, who had recently become the first woman to be made winemaker of the year in the Bergerac while raising a family of young children. Bruno had been on the jury.

"This is a welcome surprise to see you cooking, Gilles," said Bruno. "I thought you writers spent your days chained to your desk."

"Fabiola was kind enough to remark that I was the only member of the Monday night dinner group who never cooked," Gilles replied, smiling at Fabiola. "Even Jack Crimson cooks, she reminded me. And the baron cooks, although he's twice my age. So do Miranda and Florence despite the fact that they have young children to raise. Pamela runs the riding school but cooks, and Bruno is our guarantor of law and order, but he also cooks."

"And I, with the health of our community in my graceful

hands, also cook sometimes," said Fabiola. "So I thought that Gilles had spent long enough being one of the lilies of the field, who toil not, neither do they spin."

"I know I'm in trouble when Fabiola comes out with biblical quotations," said Gilles. "I wasn't going to try competing with Bruno or Pamela, and Jack has cornered the market on the all-purpose stew, cooked in one pot, which always tastes much the same no matter what the ingredients. Then I was reminded of the Chinese, Thai and Vietnamese restaurants in Paris. They also cook with just one pan, the wok, so how hard could it be? I wondered."

"Something certainly smells rather good, and indeed reminds me of an Asian restaurant," said Pamela.

Bruno was looking at the worktop behind Gilles, where some small white onions, several cloves of garlic and a couple of red chili peppers waited to be sliced. A large bottle of soy sauce and a small one of *nuoc mam*—fermented fish sauce—another of coconut milk and a large jar of peanut butter stood alongside the vegetables. There was also a bowl filled with neatly sliced chicken breasts, a big salad bowl and a basket of bread. A wok waited ready on the stove, and an open cookbook was propped against a storage jar, where Gilles could consult it.

"We'd thought of inviting Abby to join us," said Fabiola, "but she was invited out by a colleague at the museum. What do you know about her, Bruno? And does she ride?"

"Yes, she asked about riding schools. I know she's an archae-ologist and an old friend and pupil of Clothilde who has just gone through a divorce. She wants to start a business as a tour guide specializing in American connections to the Périgord. She's done a lot of research into American poets and politicians who've come here and possible archaeological links. I'm sure you'll meet her over dinner at my place or chez Clothilde. And have any of you met the English couple who hopes to take over that lovely old building on the way out of town, the Domaine de la Barde?"

"Yes, the wife, Krys," said Fabiola. "She came to the clinic to sign up the family. She was friendly, I liked her. I haven't met the husband, though."

Gilles checked the cookbook, then measured out portions of *nuoc mam* and soy sauce into a small saucepan and began to peel and chop the onions, red peppers and garlic. He poured a generous amount of vegetable oil into the saucepan and waited for it to heat up before adding the onion, pepper and garlic. Bruno watched him surreptitiously, while sipping his wine and half listening to Pamela talking about the horses. Gilles seemed to know what he was doing, waiting for the onions to soften before adding honey and three large tablespoons of peanut butter. He must be making satay sauce, Bruno thought. Gilles turned the gas down low and began stirring the mixture with a wooden spoon while adding small amounts of coconut milk.

"Time for the first course," Gilles announced, waving them to their seats before opening a second bottle of white wine. "Smoked trout—even I can't mess this up."

He didn't join them, though. Returning to the stove, he poured a measured amount of sunflower oil into the wok and turned on the gas, leaving it on high. Then he took his place at the table, keeping his eye on the stove and twice getting up to check the wok and stir the sauce. Bruno could sense his nervousness and felt almost relieved when Gilles finished his trout and went back to the stove, where he started loading the sliced chicken breasts into the now hot oil in the wok. He turned them steadily with a tool that Bruno had never seen before, like a flat spoon with raised lips that flared out from a wooden handle. With his other hand, Gilles stirred the sauce.

The conversation died as the guests watched Gilles juggling the contents of the wok and the saucepan while bending down to look at the cookbook. With the gas turned up high beneath the wok, this was no time to focus on a cookbook, Bruno thought.

He forced himself to sit still rather than obey his instinct to move in and take charge. He glanced at Pamela, then at Fabiola, and cast his eyes around the large kitchen, wondering if Fabiola and Gilles kept a fire blanket nearby, as he and Pamela and most of his friends did. He didn't see one. Finally, Pamela broke the tension.

"Maybe you could turn down the heat a little under the wok, Gilles," she said.

Then Fabiola stood up. "Let me watch the wok, *chéri,* while you take care of the sauce."

She turned down the heat under the wok, poured some of the excess oil into a metal bowl and drew the strips of chicken up the sides of the wok, away from the sizzling fat below. Meanwhile Gilles was valiantly stirring the saucepan, adding more coconut milk and using a separate spoon to taste the result.

"The chicken strips are about done," said Fabiola. "I'll put them on a serving dish, okay?"

Red in the face, not entirely from the heat, Gilles grunted, tasted the sauce again and said, "I think we're ready." He turned off the heat beneath the pan and put the salad bowl onto the table followed by his satay sauce, explaining that they should help themselves to the chicken and the sauce. There was no rice, nor any of the stir-fried vegetables and noodles that Bruno had seen accompanying this dish in the Asian restaurants where he'd dined. Still, the chicken was fine, perhaps a fraction overdone; the satay sauce was good, if a little thick; and the two went well together.

"This is excellent, Gilles," he said. "Well done, a real taste of exotic cuisine. Is it Vietnamese or Chinese or what?"

"I think it's pretty common across Southeast Asia," he replied. "I thought since you and Pamela have European cuisine sewn up between you, I should try something different."

"There's a similar peanut sauce in West Africa, made with red palm oil and carrots, lots of ginger and cumin seed," Bruno said. "I had it in the Ivory Coast when the army sent us there for a course on jungle warfare. They served it with chicken thighs. Not as good as this, though, Gilles."

"What's so special about jungle warfare?" Fabiola asked.

"You can never see anything because of the vegetation, and everything happens at very close range, so your hearing becomes as important as your vision. It's a bit like hunting in the woods with Balzac. This satay is really good, Gilles."

Pamela joined in the praise, saying it was just the kind of dish they needed now that the days were getting shorter and the evenings were getting cooler.

"Might I have a little more, please?" she asked, and Bruno and Fabiola loyally held out their plates for second helpings until there was neither chicken nor sauce left, but enough sauce remained on their plates to add a tang to the salad.

"I cheated on the dessert," Gilles said. "It's an apple pie from the bakery and vanilla ice cream."

"Perfect," said Pamela.

"I do the same often enough," Bruno said. "There's only so much time in the day. Are you close to finishing the Ukraine book, Gilles?"

"Almost. I'm calling it *How the War Came,*" Gilles said. "The idea is to publish it the week war breaks out. Putin won't go now when it's still *rasputitsa,* the mud season. He'll wait for the frost to firm up the ground and then attack. *Paris Match* is going to run an excerpt."

Bruno knew that Gilles had covered the story since November 2013, when the pro-Russian president Yanukovych had refused to sign the long-planned association agreement with the European Union, and Ukraine erupted in revolt. Gilles had been in Kyiv's great square, the Maidan, in 2014 when hundreds of protesters had been gunned down and the Ukraine parliament had voted to impeach and depose Yanukovych. As the death toll mounted in the square, there'd been a frightening day or two when Fabiola had not known whether Gilles was alive or dead until she had heard him being interviewed on the radio.

Gilles had stayed with the story, learned Ukrainian and befriended the new Ukraine president, whom he had first known as a popular TV actor. Gilles returned to Kyiv or Odessa three or four times a year. In articles for the popular press and for specialist military and strategy journals, he argued that NATO and Europe were ill equipped to deter Putin while Europe's economy relied heavily on Russian oil and gas.

Bruno felt that Gilles could well be right and that most of Western Europe, with the exception of France and Britain, had become close to a postmilitary society. Their political systems and governing elites were averse to any threat of war and suspicious of the strategic judgment of their American ally. They had a point. The outcomes of America's recent forays, in Afghanistan and Iraq and all the way back to Vietnam, hardly inspired confidence. Perhaps because he had spent more than ten years in the military, Bruno suspected that there was something inherently unsafe about the way most Europeans took the protection of the NATO alliance for granted, while mostly failing to invest in their defense.

"May we please talk about something else?" Fabiola asked, an edge to her voice. "I sometimes feel we have the River Don flowing through our kitchen."

"It's not the Don, it's the Dnieper," said Gilles, who immediately realized that he had made matters worse.

Fabiola closed her eyes and placed her hands in her lap, as if forcing herself to relax, as Pamela intervened, saying, "I really enjoyed that dish, Gilles, and wish I was more prepared to risk unfamiliar cuisines. It's amazing how much more cosmopolitan we have become in our eating habits over recent years."

Bruno picked up her cue. "Yes, even in Périgueux there are Chinese and Indian restaurants."

"And sushi in the supermarkets," Pamela replied, and the two of them kept up the soft conversation while Gilles stared at his plate and Fabiola kept a fixed smile on her face. Bruno knew only one certain way to lure her back into the conversation, so he asked, "Where are we, by the way, with replacing our missing doctor? Wasn't there some talk of an Indian coming to St. Denis?"

"He got a better offer from Issigeac," Fabiola replied flatly. "They promised him a house, a new car and a flight back to Bombay every year for him and his family. We couldn't match that. It's ridiculous that we're reduced to haggling among ourselves to hire new doctors when it's our taxes that paid for their education, at least the French ones."

"I thought there was a proposal to require new doctors to spend at least three years working in the countryside before they could move to the cities," said Pamela. They each knew of Fabiola's anger at the way 30 percent of France's population was now living in places officially described as medical deserts.

"I remember that piece you wrote in *Paris Match*, Gilles," said Bruno, "about those demonstrations by the Yellow Vests, most of whom were more angry about the lack of doctors than the cost of gasoline or the new speed limits. I forget the figures now, but I think there were nearly three times as many doctors per head on the Mediterranean coast than in the rural areas. The worst was in the Paris suburbs with the high-rise public housing and immigrants. It's outrageous, when those are the very districts that most need medical care."

"The real problem is the aging of the population, which means more ailments, while the education authorities restrict the number of places at medical schools," said Gilles. "And there's no control over the number of French-trained doctors and dentists who immigrate to Quebec and double their salaries."

"Who can blame them?" asked Fabiola. "I have to say there

are times when I get tempted. The fact is that we are increasingly and dangerously short of doctors in this region, and don't even get me started about the dearth of dentists."

"And it's going to get much worse very quickly," said Gilles. "One doctor in three in France is over the age of sixty, and when it comes to general practitioners, one in two is now over sixty. Just think where we'll be in ten years."

"Right now, I'm thinking more about that apple pie with ice cream that you mentioned," said Pamela.

Bruno began talking about the discovery at the grave, while Gilles took the ice cream from the freezer. Bruno rambled on about Abby's attempt to assess the age of the two female skeletons as Gilles cut the pie into four and added a generous scoop of ice cream to each helping.

It was always the same whenever Gilles was preparing a trip back to Ukraine, as he was now. Fabiola would declare that she'd never stand in the way of his profession, even when she knew he might be heading into danger, but her body language said the opposite. This evening she seemed even more tightly wired than usual, but when she spoke, she appeared to have moved on.

"The parents of those two German women can never have known what happened to their daughters," said Fabiola. "It must have haunted them for the rest of their lives."

"Yes," agreed Pamela. "Think of those awful notices that parents would have received in wartime. The worst must have been to get a letter saying that your son or daughter was missing, believed killed. And there must have been thousands of such messages, for men in aircraft that never returned, or ships that never made it back to port, or units that were destroyed by shellfire. They must have clung on to hope that maybe their children were prisoners somewhere or wounded in some foreign hospital."

"Well, at least there is one family we know that seems to have been reunited," said Bruno. "It's great that Florence has been reconciled with her parents, who at last are getting to know their two grandchildren. Daniel and Dora deserve to have that connection across the generations."

"The relationship you never had, you mean?" Pamela asked.

"I suppose so," Bruno replied. "I had an aunt and cousins, and I knew my mother was dead, but I never heard anything about a father or grandparents. Kids aren't automatically curious until they grow older. At least, I wasn't, nor was my cousin, Alain. It's something we've talked about, trying to work out why we never asked about it."

"That reminds me, have you seen him and Rosalie since you got back?" Gilles asked. "They're a nice couple. I've been wondering where they are."

"They're in an accelerated program for ex-military people becoming teachers," Bruno said. "It's a weeklong course in Bordeaux. They left me a note at the *mairie* to say they'd see me when they get back next weekend."

"It must have been a bit disappointing, getting back to St. Denis to find no Alain and Rosalie," said Gilles. "And no Florence, nor those twins of hers that you're so fond of."

"Well, you all more than made up for it," Bruno replied, smiling as he rose to his feet, thanking Gilles for the exotic dinner. Pamela rose as well, hugged their friends good night and they left the house together. Pamela kissed Bruno and told him she'd see him and Balzac again at the riding school in the morning to exercise the horses.

Chapter 12

The next morning Bruno slept late, not waking until just after eight, far too late to join his friends at the riding school. He put on his tracksuit and running shoes for a jog with Balzac and headed through the woods and along the ridge as the sun peeked above the eastern hills. He kept a moderate pace, partly because it meant Balzac could keep up, but also because after the time in the hospital and convalescing he wasn't as fit as he liked and the ground was slick beneath his feet from the rains. He had been warned against doing push-ups or weight lifting until his next—he hoped final—examination in December to check that his shoulder and collarbone were fully healed.

Back at home, he put on the kettle to make coffee. He showered, dressed and grilled yesterday's baguette, listening to the morning news on the radio. There was nothing about the grave at St. Denis. He drove into town for one of Fauquet's incomparable croissants and was enjoying his second cup of coffee when his phone rang. It was Fabiola.

"I've changed my mind," she said. "I can take a look at those bodies this morning if you want. It's my day off, but Gilles has been called to do an online interview this morning instead of playing tennis with me."

"Well, thank you. Let me arrange to reopen the grave, and I'll come pick you up as soon as it's ready. Anything I can prepare to help you?"

"A table, three body bags, plus a plank to raise the bodies and a tent to examine them. I can use my phone for still and video photos. We'd better put them back in the grave if you have a diplomatic circus coming to town, so I'll examine them in place. Pick me up at the clinic."

"I'll call you back on your mobile, and thanks again."

Bruno called the mayor to inform him and then Michel to ask if he could reopen the grave.

"No problem," said Michel. "I suppose you'll want the tent we use at the entry for the night market. You can stand up in it. Anything else?"

"A long table for the examination, a plank to put the bodies on when we raise them, a bowl and water for washing hands."

Fabiola had suggested her phone for a camera, but Bruno thought they should have a better record. He could ask Philippe Delaron, but he didn't want the story to appear in *Sud Ouest* too soon. He'd ask Brosseil, who, as well as a ballroom dancer, was a keen photographer, and he'd been involved at the opening of the grave.

Within the hour everything was in place, the tent erected and the table ready within, covered with a plastic sheet. Brosseil was there with his camera and the mayor with the video camera and its stand. The grave had been opened again, and Michel had brought a ladder. Bruno had borrowed three new body bags from the gendarmerie, and a basin and towels.

He picked up Fabiola from the clinic and drove to the grave, where she approved the arrangement and inspected the papers in the cookie tin. Then she donned a white plastic suit, asked Brosseil to take some stills and the mayor to start filming. Finally, she clambered down the ladder.

"I want the man in uniform brought up first," she said, when she emerged again. "That will give us more room to move the two skeletons. Not you, Bruno, I want your shoulder fully healed."

Brosseil and Michel put on plastic gloves and went down the ladder, and the mayor lowered the plastic-wrapped plank to them. Gingerly, they eased the body onto the plank and secured ropes around each end. Then they climbed out and used the ropes to lift the body from the grave then placed it on the table.

From her bag Fabiola took out a mobile phone, fiddled with the controls and inserted a thin cable with a small microphone at one end. She clipped this to her collar and checked that the recording system was working. She announced the time, date and location of the examination. Then, as she began cutting the rotted uniform it crumbled, the two sleeves of the jacket and shirt falling away of their own accord. Bruno could only detect a general mustiness.

"This is the body of an adult male of middle age, perhaps forty or so," Fabiola said, then took a metallic tape from her medical bag and began measuring. "The height of the skeleton is one meter seventy-eight centimeters, forty-six centimeters wide at the shoulder. The skull is intact with no sign of injury, three metallic fillings in the teeth, one molar is missing."

She stood up and took a step back before returning to the trunk, using a metal probe to explore the remains of the uniform covering the chest. Bruno had expected it to crumble at her touch, but instead it seemed to fold back.

"I think from the severed fibers that there are three bullet holes in the chest of the uniform, one close to the heart, another a little higher in the region of the right lung, the third in the right shoulder."

Gently she teased aside the uniform jacket to expose the shredded and stained remains of a white undershirt or shirt beneath, and the skeleton's torso was revealed.

"Close-up photos here, here and here, please," she said, pointing to a shattered shoulder bone, two splintered ribs and the sternum. "Three bullets, I'd say, one of them must have hit the heart. The holster on his belt is empty, so I assume he had a gun and had brought it out."

When she turned to the trousers, there was a tinkling of metal—coins beneath the body that had probably fallen through the rotted trouser pocket.

"There's a clean, unused silk handkerchief in the left trouser pocket which is very well preserved," she said. "The coins appear to be French, but there are some other metal items close to them, higher up than the coins, roughly at chest level."

She took some long tweezers from her medical bag, poked them delicately through the rib bones and pulled out first one, then a second lump. She dropped them into a metal dish with a clatter. Bruno saw small, distorted metal shapes.

"Two distorted metal objects, probably bullets, damaged by hitting bones. I presume these to be the bullets that killed him, but from the evidence of bone damage I'd expect a third. We may find it at the bottom of the grave," she said. "The breast pockets of what remains of the jacket are loose and seem to have been unbuttoned, so I presume that's where they got his identification booklet. There are no other signs of injury except the ends of two fingers are missing on the left hand and what looks like a very old break in the left forearm, well healed, probably a childhood injury. I'm surprised the uniform held its structure so long, a tribute to Italian tailoring. His boots are also well preserved, his socks made of what seems to have been silk."

Fabiola used a scalpel to search through the remnants of cloth from the dark trousers and the surprising white of what must have been underpants, partly discolored by the dark brown of dried blood. The men standing around were silent, riveted and impressed by her professionalism.

"There's no sign of animal activity, and I see no trace of insect life, so the seal on the grave must have been extremely effective," she went on. "Some construction expert evidently knew what he or she was doing. A good laboratory might be able to give you a rough date for the composition of the concrete. The date of the killing is estimated as August 1944, which means summer, high temperature, so from the level of decomposition I'd say this body was entombed very quickly after death, perhaps within a day, not much more. There is little evidence of blood beneath the body, so he must have bled out after being shot elsewhere. From the evidence of his placement in the grave, he was treated with some respect, the body laid out with the arms crossed over the chest."

Fabiola stood to her full height, stretched out her arms and called for the next body. Again, Brosseil and Michel descended to the grave but found it impossible to separate the two remaining bodies without damaging the skeletons. As they tried, one of the skulls lolled to one side at a bizarre angle. Michel and Brosseil exchanged worried glances, as if asking what they might have done wrong. The mayor wrapped the plank in some new plastic sheeting and lowered it down. Michel stood in the grave to ensure that the skeletons did not fall off as the mayor and Brosseil lifted out the plank and then carried it to the table.

"I'm afraid that when we tried to separate them the skull of one seemed to twist and roll to one side," said Brosseil. "I'm sorry."

"I'm sure you did your best," Fabiola replied. "The skeletons seemed entwined when I looked."

She waved the two abashed men away and turned to her work, speaking into her microphone.

"Two female skeletons, no trace of any clothing and well preserved, with no obvious sign of frontal injury to the bones, although each shows the skull turned at an unusual angle, possibly signaling a broken neck. There are traces of blonde hair on one, darker but not black hair on the other. The female with blonde hair is one meter sixty in height, thirty-eight centimeters wide at the shoulder. The female with dark hair is one meter sixty-four in height and forty centimeters at the shoulder. From the evidence of epiphysis on the long bones and collarbones they were not yet mature adults. I estimate each to have been between sixteen and twenty years of age. There is no evidence of parturition scarring, so neither one had given birth. There are no visibly broken bones but possible signs of unusual leverage on the arms and shoulders.

"Turning the bodies, cause of death becomes apparent. Each female shows signs of the neck being severely twisted, which suggests deliberate and violent action."

She paused, swallowed hard and closed her eyes for a moment before continuing. "My tentative initial conclusion is that each of these women died as a result of a broken neck, cause unknown."

She turned off the microphone and placed a hand on the skull that lolled to one side. Then she stood silently for a long moment before turning to face Bruno and the other men with cold fury in her eyes.

"I am not in the least religious, *messieurs,* but I think it would be fitting to ask Father Sentout to come and say a few words over the bodies of these two women who died so young. I don't know who they were or where they came from. And I cannot say for sure why and how they died. But the fact that they were naked and their necks deliberately broken provokes the inevitable assumption that they were raped and murdered, like so many women in so many wars in so much of our human history."

She pulled off her gloves and placed them gently over the holes in the twisted skulls where there had once been eyes.

"It was almost eighty years ago, so the men involved are almost certainly dead, but these girls died before they had even begun to live," she murmured, almost to herself. She pulled off her white plastic covering and placed it over the two skeletons.

"That's all I can do for you, *messieurs,* and all I can do for them. I think I would like to walk back to the clinic. Alone."

Chapter 13

The four men stood silently as she left, their eyes downcast, not glancing at one another and not following Fabiola as she walked toward the bridge. At some point, each one of them had been examined, treated, even healed by her. She had seen them ill, or in pain, or frightened of the diagnosis she might make, and had comforted them. From a doctor there were few secrets. And now they felt shamefaced, not so much guilty as having somehow let down a woman for whom they had affection and deep respect.

"Let's clear out," said the mayor tiredly. "Leave the tent, but let's put the bodies into coffins. Don't seal them but cover them up until the diplomats arrive. I'm sorry to have put you through this. Again."

Bruno went back to his Land Rover and drove home, unusually conscious of the steady, insistent ache in his wounded shoulder. He put on the old army tracksuit he used for gardening and began by feeding and giving water to his chickens and collecting the fresh eggs. Then he started weeding, pruning, watering and restoring some kind of order to the vegetable patch that had been neglected for too long. The familiar work did not exactly calm him, but the almost mindless chores helped to ease the guilt he felt for putting Fabiola through that ordeal. He'd never dreamed that after so many years as a doctor she would react in that way to bones of the long dead.

Then he thought that his reaction had been that of an old soldier who had seen too many corpses. Many men like him had dampened their response to the horror by grabbing a bottle and drinking until oblivion. And he'd seen what that did to them—a path to a different kind of personal ruin. He did not like these thoughts and told himself it was time for another run. He put on his running shoes and led Balzac at a moderate pace through the woods and across a shallow valley to the farther ridge that gave a view of the Vézère River flowing down to its junction with the much greater flow of the Dordogne at Limeuil.

The old river port and hilltop fortress was one of Bruno's favorite places, despite the unhappy memory of that American girl, Claudia, who had died in the ancient well inside the old castle walls. Julius Caesar's legions had stormed that Gallic hilltop fort two thousand years ago, he remembered. The Romans had built their own watchtower in its place, and then Charlemagne had erected a stockade against the Vikings. French and English soldiers had taken and lost and taken again the medieval fortress they had constructed there, hauling the great stones up that endless hill. Then Protestant Frenchmen had hauled up cannons to blast away their fellow countrymen who happened to be Catholics. Over the two millennia, how many hundreds or thousands of men had died fighting for that place? he wondered. But at the back of his mind was the memory of the two German girls whose bones he had touched and whose grim fate was so much closer.

Somehow these thoughts of the bodies in the grave no longer haunted him as they had after Fabiola had walked away. Perhaps Balzac's unquestioning love had restored him. Or maybe the unending cruelties and slaughters of history had given him some crude kind of perspective, that deceptively forgiving sense that we were no longer responsible for the crimes committed long before we were born. Or perhaps it was something quite different, a distraction, the memory that suddenly came into his mind of the great stone archway above the old quayside of Limeuil that led up the hill into the old town. That archway was close to five meters high, he recalled, and it stood a good three meters above the road along the riverbank, and that road was usually four or five meters above the river. But what stuck in his mind were the grooves that had been carved into the stone gate to mark the peak floods. The highest was the winter of 1944, almost at the top of the archway, which would put the height of the flood twelve or even fifteen meters above the normal level of the blending rivers.

Of course, he told himself, that was just before the big dams had been built upriver to convert into electricity the power of the water dropping more than a thousand meters from the high ground of the long dead volcanoes of the Massif Central. The floods could never be that high again, he told himself. It was at that moment that Bruno realized that he had, for a policeman, committed the dreadful sin of forgetting his phone.

He whistled for Balzac to join him and began to jog home along the ridge and stepped up his speed to a long sprint until he was breathless and could do no more and Balzac was far behind, almost lost to view. Then Bruno stretched himself out, panting, on the ground, and waited for Balzac's strenuous assault. The hound positively leaped the last meter to land on Bruno's chest, so that Bruno could feel the beating of his dog's heart as his tongue lapped at Bruno's face. He put both arms around his dog and hugged him as their breathing slowed and they both dozed a little until the cold in his legs, bereft of Balzac's warmth, forced Bruno to move.

Clumsily and with a surprising slowness, he stirred and tried to rise but found it strangely difficult. He turned so that he was facing the ground, put his hands on the earth on either side of his face and drew up one leg after the other until he was on his knees, but he still felt too weak to rise. He managed finally to struggle to his feet but without using his injured arm, which was aching so badly that he tucked it into his shirt for support. He stood for a long moment, trying not to sway although he felt dizzy. He began to walk or, rather, stagger back through the woods, wondering whether he had suffered some kind of heart attack. He picked up a fallen branch for support as he climbed a hill so gentle he could usually jog up the slope. But then it was downhill to the point where he could see the roof of his house and then the chicken run and the row of truffle oaks he had planted more than ten years before.

Still feeling more tired than he could ever remember, with the dog at his heels he plodded heavily home and into his kitchen for a long drink of water, then filled Balzac's bowl, since he'd probably be just as thirsty. In the sitting room he opened the glass door of his woodburning stove, added some kindling to the glowing embers and opened the airflow. Once the wood caught, he put two logs, one at a time, onto the flames before he sank back on the sofa and looked at his phone. It surprised him, showing it was not long after eleven. He'd thought it was much, much later. There were messages from his friend J-J, chief detective of the region, one from his old love Isabelle, in Paris; and one from Pamela.

He returned J-J's calls first, to hear that familiar, weary voice demanding to know why Bruno was not answering his calls, and why J-J was being bombarded with demands from the prefect to explain this discovery of a wartime grave in St. Denis full of European bodies.

"I'm still on convalescent leave," Bruno said feebly, feeling guilty. "And the mayor swore me to secrecy." It sounded lame, even to him.

"A secret that's all over the diplomatic corps in Paris," J-J replied. "And I have media calls coming in from *Sud Ouest, Figaro, Frankfurter Allgemeine* and *Corriere della Sera. Merde,* Bruno, you can't drop me into the crap like this. The gendarmes know nothing about it and the mayor won't return my calls."

Bruno stumbled through a brief description of Fabiola's findings. He repeated that he was not well and still on sick leave and J-J should contact the mayor. When he hung up he called Isabelle.

"Isabelle, you called. How are you?"

She was all business.

"Yes, Bruno. The Elysée wants to know what the hell is going on down there with these corpses," she began. "The Germans are asking if these women were raped, and the Italians, depending on their politics, want to know whether this submarine commander is a martyred Italian hero or a tool of the Nazis who met his just deserts."

Again, he gave a brief summary, pleaded convalescence and referred her to the mayor. He ended the call and dialed Pamela, who demanded, "What on earth have you done to Fabiola? She's here sobbing and says it's all your fault."

"I'm very sorry, but I'm not feeling well, so I won't make much sense. Call the mayor, who knows all about this. If he won't talk, try Brosseil."

He then turned off his phone, lay back on the sofa and slept. He dreamed of that moment in the hospital after he had been shot and he was finally allowed visitors and Florence had woken him with a kiss, one on the brow and another on his lips.

Somehow Bruno had known it was her, even though he had decided that he was not the right man for this thoroughly impressive woman. With his own confused feelings for Isabelle still like stubborn chunks of grit in his heart, he'd told himself that he could never give Florence the absolute devotion that she and her twins needed. He knew his friends in St. Denis were all convinced otherwise and that her young twins already saw him as the nearest to a father they'd ever had. And yet, here she was, her lips soft and enticing on his own.

He could feel her kiss now, the signals that it sent to his wounded body, the sense it conveyed of healing, the assurance of complete support, the commitment of love so reassuring that he sank once more into a deep and peaceful sleep.

It was almost four in the afternoon when he woke up, feeling much better. He washed his face, ran a comb through his hair and slathered eucalyptus ointment onto the bullet scars on his aching shoulder. It cured most aches after rugby games and its warm glow on his flesh seemed to do the trick. Dressing once more in his tracksuit and running shoes, he dropped off his dog at the stables with Hector and drove on to the rugby club, where he'd arranged to meet Lespinasse. The gate was already open, so Bruno wasn't the first arrival. He heard the sound of female voices from the visitors' changing rooms and found Lespinasse in the storeroom beneath the stands. He carried a large net filled with rugby balls in one hand and blue plastic cones to mark the running lanes under his other arm. With no hand free, Lespinasse presented his cheek for the *bise* between male friends and asked Bruno if he was feeling up to it.

"I'm fine, not to play, but okay for a practice," Bruno replied, picking up a ball.

He rang the handbell and the women trotted out, twenty-four in all, which included the seven-a-side team, the team of reserves and several women who came mainly for the exercise. They were mostly in running shoes rather than rugby boots, with their hair pulled back into ponytails and wearing an assortment of colorful T-shirts.

"Welcome back," they called out, and most of them came to kiss him and ask how his injury was healing. At the rear, he was pleased to see Marta, the Valkyrie from Ivan's restaurant. He was more surprised to see Abby trotting out beside her.

"It's good to be back," he said. "We'll start off with running today, mainly sprints and jogs with some sidesteps and dodging.

I'd like you to begin with a couple of laps around the pitch while I put out the cones for the sidesteps. You can jog on the long side but please sprint on the two short ends."

He and Lespinasse set out the cones in two lines across the pitch about five meters apart. Two girls set off, and the one with the ball had to run at the cones, sidestepping the first one to the right, the second to the left and so on. That was the easy part, but each girl also had to pass the ball to her partner while side-stepping, and then receive the ball as she was dodging the next cone.

At first he spared Marta and Abby the passing routines, but after they showed skill at sidestepping, he gave them the ball and asked them to run up and down the length of the pitch, passing the ball back and forth as they went. Abby tried to pass like an American football player, passing with one hand holding the ball above her head. But the rugby ball was bigger and it didn't work. He called her over and showed her the technique, the swivel of the hips, the flat buildup and follow-through, as Marta looked on. Then he left them under the posts, passing the ball back and forth until they learned how to impart some spin, and only then did they really get the hang of it.

Since he'd spotted Marta trotting out from the changing room, Bruno had been nurturing an idea. With her height, Marta could win every line-out. When the ball went out of play in rugby, it was thrown back to two long lines of opposing forwards who leaped to catch it. Height was a real advantage, though Bruno knew that planning could defeat height. He lined up the two rows of players, noticing the grin on Marta's face, sure that she'd catch the ball. Instead, one burly player in the other line crouched, waiting, as another player ran at her and jumped, being grasped around the legs by the crouching player at the same time. The woman who jumped was then boosted high into the air and stayed there to catch the ball, while Marta fell back to the ground.

"Now you try that, Marta," Bruno said. "And Abby, you try being the lifter."

The two women, each one a beginner, did it perfectly. Abby grasped Marta around the thighs and boosted her even higher than Marta could jump. She caught the ball with ease, and her face broke into a broad grin as the other women gathered around to clap her and Abby on the back.

"We have ourselves a secret weapon, team," Bruno said, laughing in delight. "All we have to do now is teach you two beginners the other tricks of the game."

They played on until just before six, when Marta said she had to go help Ivan in the bistro. The training sessions normally ended at six, so Bruno let them all go at the same time. As he and Lespinasse gathered up the balls and cones, he watched the women chatting and hugging as they headed to the changing room—French, American and Pole—and knew he was watching the birth of a team.

"I can't tell you how much I enjoyed that," said Abby, her eyes shining when she came out a few minutes later. "When's the next practice?"

"Friday at four-thirty," Bruno said. "We play the games on Sunday mornings, and the two men's teams play in the afternoons. But I can't see Marta playing. Sunday lunches are usually very busy at Ivan's bistro."

"That's a shame, she was really enjoying herself," said Abby. "And it was great to meet all those local women. One of them told me that there's a girl who used to play here who's now on the French national team."

"That's Paulette," said Bruno fondly. "My star pupil. Her parents run the flower shop in town. She was on the seven-a-side team that won the silver medal at the Tokyo Olympics. She's a professional now and is studying to be a phys ed teacher."

"You seem to need qualifications for everything in France."

"Including to be a village policeman," Bruno said, smiling, as he walked her to her car. "But not to be president of the country or a government minister or even elected to the National Assembly. How's the car?"

"Fine, I like it," she said, opening the hatchback. Bruno was startled to see a burglar alarm, four heavy bolts and several window locks. He spotted a bill beside them from Bricomarché, the local do-it-yourself and hardware store in town.

"Are you expecting a siege?" he asked, keeping his voice light but wondering what had prompted such security measures. He recalled the wariness he'd noticed in her, gazing at the door and keeping her back to the wall when they had met at lunch with Horst and Clothilde.

She gave a nervous and unconvincing laugh. "I'm a single woman, living alone," she said. "You understand."

"That should keep them out."

"I'd heard there was a gang of burglars looking for empty places owned by foreigners who only come here in the summers."

"There was, but I arrested them," said Bruno. "What's more, you're not leaving your place empty for months at a time, and you share the property with Fabiola and Gilles."

"Better safe than sorry," she said, putting her sports bag on top of her purchases and closing the hatchback. "My invitation to a thank-you dinner is still open."

"I look forward to it. And if it's at Ivan's bistro, I think we'll get special treatment from Marta after your teamwork today."

"You're probably right, but you and Clothilde and Horst have been so good to me I thought I'd take us somewhere memorable, that place with the Michelin star, the Vieux Logis. Clothilde says it's the best place in the region."

"She's right, but for the four of us it will cost you well over a month's rent," Bruno told her. "And that reminds me, the Vieux Logis is another place on your list of American connections. I heard the story from Bernard Giraudel himself, God rest his soul, the owner-chef who made an old local inn into the place it is today. You know he was one of the founders of the Relais et Châteaux group? As a boy, he answered the doorbell one day and saw a guy on the doorstep dressed only in khaki shorts and a sunhat. He said he was paddling a canoe down the river and wanted a bed for the night. It was Henry Miller, and he ended up staying for over a month while he wrote *The Colossus of Maroussi,* in which he said something like: 'France may one day exist no more, but the Dordogne will live on just as dreams live on and nourish the souls of men.' I can lend you my copy, if you like."

"That's a great addition to my list, and that settles it, the Vieux Logis it will be," she said, smiling. "Now, give me a date."

"Let's see if they can do tomorrow evening," he said.

She darted her head forward to give him a fleeting peck on the cheek. "It's a date. And thanks again for the rugby lesson."

She drove off, leaving Bruno to wonder at the financial instincts of a woman who could shell out more than six hundred euros for dinner for four but had tried to negotiate Gilles down on the rent. And he didn't swallow her unconvincing response to his surprise at the security precautions she was taking at her new home. Perhaps he would check discreetly with Clothilde if she knew of any reason why Abby should be so nervous.

Chapter 14

"Hey, Bruno," came a familiar voice from the stands. "You're so focused on your lady friends that you don't even notice an old friend sitting here."

Bruno laughed as the baron came into the parking lot through the members' gate. He embraced his old friend, still spry and active in his eighties and an honorary president of the town rugby club he'd played for as a youth.

"Who's that young woman who just kissed you?" the old man asked. "She looks like a born athlete. And that giantess, who's she? With her on the team we'd never lose a line-out even if the other side gets the throw-in."

Knowing that the baron, like most locals, wanted to know the antecedents of each new arrival in St. Denis, Bruno explained that Abby was an American friend of Clothilde. "And I'm surprised you haven't seen the tall one before. She's Polish, her name is Marta, and she's Ivan's latest partner in the kitchen."

"Really? I haven't eaten there lately. I just hope she'll be playing on our team. I've got to go because Jack Crimson is coming for dinner. Why not join us? I caught some fat trout this morning and there's more than enough for the three of us. And please bring

Balzac. I got used to having him around the house when you were in the hospital. I miss him."

Bruno said he'd join them once he'd taken Hector for his evening ride and then watched the baron stroll off, as always walking home rather than driving his cherished vintage Citroën DS. A retired industrialist and probably the wealthiest man in St. Denis, he was certainly the most successful fisherman and usually on the river soon after dawn. Bruno stopped at the town's wineshop to choose something to take to dinner. He selected a bottle from Château des Eyssards called Mano a Mano. It was a special wine made by Flavie, the daughter of his friend Pascal, a genial giant who played the tuba in the winemakers' band. Then he went to the Moulin bakery and bought their last apple pie.

Pamela and the other riders had already left when he reached the stables, but Hector was still in his stall with Balzac. Having seen the dog there, Pamela knew Bruno would come when he could. A note was stuck to his saddle: "Short climb to ridge. Remember only canter. Pxx."

When he reached the ridge, he saw them at the far end, about to ride through the firebreak in the woods. He cantered after them, Hector again showing unusual patience with this slow pace. His friends were walking their horses now, presumably after a good gallop along the ridge. He caught up with them before they turned off down the bridle trail. The welcoming smiles of Pamela and Fabiola told him he was forgiven, or maybe they were just enjoying watching Balzac's headlong efforts to keep up.

"Bonsoir," he called. "Thanks for letting me catch up."

"How was the rugby practice?" Pamela asked.

"Very impressive. That new Polish woman who's working at Ivan's is a born player and, Fabiola, your new tenant is a natural athlete. We might even get them onto the team this winter. I'm sorry about this morning," he went on. "It was a grim way to start your day."

"It wasn't a very professional reaction on my part, but they were just so young . . ." Her voice broke off.

"It's not as though plenty of French girls weren't raped in that war, or sent off to concentration camps," said Gilles. "Bruno and I saw a lot that was just as bad in the Balkans, and it will be repeated in Ukraine." He paused. "I haven't seen this story of an Italian and two German bodies become public yet, but I'm sure it will, and *Paris Match* won't be pleased that I missed news like that on my doorstep. Is it a problem for you if I write about it, Bruno?"

"I think the story is going to break today, so go ahead. We have German and Italian diplomats coming down tomorrow or the day after, so their papers will probably carry it. And I've had half a dozen calls from Philippe Delaron that I haven't answered. I can give you some background, if you like."

Gilles took out his phone, set it to record, and they rode on together, Bruno recounting the details.

"The two women are skeletons, so there's no hard evidence of rape," Bruno said. "Since there were no clothes found with them it looks probable but we can never confirm it. And let's not forget the context, the executions of civilian hostages, some of them just boys, that had been taking place in Bergerac and Périgueux that week. And don't forget that special SS squad of young Arabs recruited from the slums of Toulon and Marseille. They had been burning and raping and looting their way through this country-side on suspicion that the farmers were feeding the Resistance. It was war, Gilles."

He pulled out his notebook to give Gilles the names and details of the dead, described the way the grave had been con-structed, the bodies hidden under a false floor in the tomb to make it look like the burial of a family dog.

"We're planning to let the diplomats repatriate the bodies, but the mayor wants to put up a separate memorial at the site with the names of the dead," Bruno went on. "The town is going to buy the land between the grave and the memorial to the dead FTP guy and create a small garden of remembrance to all the dead. I don't know what more we can do."

"Can I quote you, not your name, but as a town official?" Gilles asked.

"I don't see why not, but please quote me saying that once we found them, we treated the remains as if they were our own, with dignity and respect, and with due regard for the tragic time shared by all Europeans as well as Americans, Australians, Canadians and Asians. At least sixty million people died in World War Two, more than half of them civilians. It's important that we never forget that. That's why we want to create this memorial."

They had come in sight of the stables and rode on, dismounted and unsaddled the horses in silence.

"I'd better go write this up and send it in so it will be on the website tonight," Gilles said. "Thanks, Bruno."

"Thank you, Fabiola," Bruno said as she turned to leave with Gilles.

She came back, gave Bruno a hug and said, "I heard what you told Gilles. Thank you for what you said to him. It reminded me that this is about something much bigger than just another grave in St. Denis. I'll make sure he puts it in his article because it needs saying and we need reminding."

Bruno and Pamela stood watching them go, and Pamela said quietly, "You lead a charmed life, Bruno. Would you like to stay for supper?"

"I'd have loved to, but I agreed earlier to have dinner with the baron and Jack. I'm sure you'd be welcome to join us. The baron said he'd caught a lot of fish."

"I'd like to, but Félix, Miranda and the kids are having dinner with me." She reached up and kissed him on the cheek. "Give Jack and the baron a hug from me."

Bruno fetched Balzac and drove on to a *lieu-dit,* a hamlet

too small to be a village with its own postal address, known as La Terrasse, where he'd been the previous day to visit Joe. The baron's *chartreuse,* a building too small to be a château but too large to be a mansion and known as a *gentilhommière,* dominated the tiny square at the heart of the place. New buildings that were steadily filling the surrounding fields had made the area almost a suburb of St. Denis. The baron's place was separate, with a walled garden and an avenue of walnut and apple trees that led to the wooded hills that flanked the road up to the village of Audrix. Back in June, Bruno and the baron had collected the green walnuts to make their *vin de noix* that would be ready for drinking before the end of autumn.

Jack Crimson was there already, his vintage Jaguar parked beside the baron's old Citroën. Together with Bruno's ancient Land Rover, the three vehicles represented close to two hundred years of automobiles. Bruno released Balzac and let himself in through the iron gate. Jack and the baron were sitting at a garden table, a bowl of mixed nuts and a bottle of what looked like scotch between them. As he drew closer, he saw it was a Talisker from the Isle of Skye, a malt for which the baron had developed a particular affection. Bruno liked it, too, yet another of the many versions of fine Scottish malts to which Jack had introduced them.

Bruno placed the wine and the apple pie on the table, and the two old men rose to embrace him, the baron first as the host. He then poured a good three fingers of scotch into a third glass on the table. Jack then added two fingers of his favored Malvern water, imported from England.

"Well, *mon vieux,* I hear that another grave of our Nazi occupiers has been found here," said the baron, raising his glass. "My father will sleep a little more easily this night."

Bruno knew that the baron's father had been a Resistance leader, and one of the few who had survived arrest and detention in the Mauthausen concentration camp. He had also heard the baron's tale that as a boy he had been pinioned by a Gestapo thug with a knife held to his throat as his mother was told that either his father came out from hiding or the boy died. The father had appeared and fixed in his memory the face of the French traitor who had denounced him. When he'd returned from imprisonment, the father had taken his son to the jail where the informer was held. The traitor was brought out and, with his son's hand in his, the man who had survived Mauthausen had pulled out a pistol with his other hand and shot the traitor between the eyes. The baron had on one well-lubricated evening shown Bruno the bloodstained shirt he claimed to have worn that day.

Bruno had also known that his friend, in the grand tradition of the troubadours of the region, was not the type to let the truth get in the way of a riveting tale, so he had done some private research and found that the baron's father had indeed been a Resistance leader and had been betrayed to the Gestapo and sent to Mauthausen. But he was not surprised to discover that there was no historical evidence for the final chapter of the story, although Bruno did learn that the informer had been arrested after the war and, in the phrase of those dreadful times, had been "shot while trying to escape." The story Bruno most enjoyed was that the baron's father, who had become president of the French society of gastronomes, had been invited by General de Gaulle in 1960 to join him on the official delegation to sign the treaty of friendship and reconciliation with West German president Konrad Adenauer.

"Never, *mon général,* did I think I could say no to you," the baron's father had supposedly said, "but you must excuse me. As president of the gastronomes, I swore a solemn oath never to return to a place where I had eaten badly."

"Did I tell you of the pilgrimage I made to St. Julien de Crempse?" the baron asked, clinking his glass with Bruno's. This was a former commune near Campsegret, on the borders of the

Pécharmant wine region. "It was the fourth of November 2003, and they were exhuming the graves of seventeen Nazi soldiers who'd been taken at gunpoint by the Resistance from the POW camp in Bergerac. They were shot in retaliation for the Nazis' murder of seventeen men and boys of that village, every living male they could find, a month earlier. There was more publicity about those Nazis being sent back to a German war cemetery than there ever was about the slaughtered French villagers. So I don't mourn those dead Nazis, even if they were officially prisoners of war, just as I don't mourn those in the grave you found, Bruno, even if they were women."

Bruno sighed, nodded and sipped his drink. He had no idea how to respond to his old friend, who had also known the brutal realities of the Algerian War, just as Bruno had known those in Bosnia. There was nothing to say, except that he murmured the old French saying: *À la guerre comme à la guerre.* In war, that's the way it is.

"Of course, in that context, my dear baron, you are entirely right," said Jack. "But we now live in a different reality, nearly eighty years on from the dreadful time of the occupation. Your British, American and Canadian friends came to help the Resistance liberate France. I think we need to bear in mind the new context, when a different generation of Brits and French, Germans and Italians and a score of other countries are all allies under NATO."

The baron shrugged, poured himself another drink, rose from the table and said he should start the barbecue.

"Are we eating out here or indoors?" asked Bruno.

"Wherever you like," came the grumpy reply of a master chef, too preoccupied with the immediate demands of his craft to concern himself with such petty issues.

"Just squeeze me a couple of lemons and add some salt and a touch of black pepper and paprika to the juice, then slice two more lemons very thinly and bring them to me," the baron said after a pause. "Then kindly peel three cloves of garlic, one for each of us, put them through the garlic press and bring me the results. I'll also need some of the broad-leaved parsley from the garden, enough cherry tomatoes for the three of us and whatever else you need to make us a decent salad."

Bruno went off to obey his host's commands as the baron filled his little *cheminée,* a perforated metal cylinder into which the charcoal was poured. At the bottom of this chimney was a large inverted dome into which paper could be stuffed and ignited, making the heat rise up through the coals remarkably quickly. This device had been a Christmas present from Pamela to each of her male friends—Bruno, Jack, the baron, the mayor and Gilles. Everyone had marveled at the ingenuity of the cylinder, which halved the time of preparing a barbecue. It also meant no lingering scent of gasoline from artificial fire starters.

Bruno returned from the vegetable garden with his modest harvest, completed his minor chores in the kitchen and took the lemon and garlic to the baron and his barbecue.

"What happens next?" Jack asked.

For a moment, Bruno assumed that Jack was asking about the preparation of dinner, as any sensible Frenchman would. Then he realized that as an Englishman, even one who had developed an enthusiastic taste for the cuisine and wines of the Périgord, Jack was ignoring the priorities of dinner and asking about the grave and its implications.

Bruno outlined the arrangements for the arrival of the diplomats, the prefect and other guests. Then he explained the plan for the transfer of land and the memorial garden. Since Jack had been a diplomat as well as the chairman of Her Majesty's Joint Intelligence Committee and would therefore appreciate such arcane questions of procedure, Bruno went on to describe the added complication of the confusion among the Italians whether their dead submariner was a fallen war hero or a renegade who had thrown in his lot with the Nazis.

"Do you know, Bruno, I think that in another life you might have made an accomplished diplomat?" Jack replied, a note of respect in his voice.

Bruno ignored this, knowing Jack well enough to have learned that whenever the wise old Englishman needed a moment to think, he bought time by deploying a plausible but unconvincing compliment.

"And do we know yet who was responsible for the dead bodies?" Jack then asked. "Were they killed by local people?"

"It seems to have been a squad from the Lot, FTP militants who called themselves the Kursk group, a name that honored a Soviet battle," Bruno replied. "One of them was killed at the same spot and at roughly the same time, so it seems more than likely that they were connected. And just to complicate matters, apparently there were some members of the Kursk group who were Spanish veterans of their civil war, dedicated antifascists with a reputation for being ruthless."

"That sounds as if you're going on supposition rather than hard evidence," said Jack.

Bruno nodded wearily and went on to describe the existing memorial to the *résistant* from the Marty clan and his link to the Kursk squad from the Lot. He made a mental note to visit Alphonse Marty in the morning and warn him what was coming. *Merde,* he thought, he should have done that this evening, since the members of that large and politically influential family were going to be directly involved once the press got hold of the connection between them and the new grave.

"An unhappy situation, and I must say I'm rather relieved that I'm not involved, so we'll leave it in your capable hands, Bruno," said Jack. "We're going to need more plates and tiny glasses. I brought some of that excellent local caviar from Neuvic to begin, and I put a bottle of Stolichnaya in the freezer."

"In that case, I think I have to plead that I'm still supposed to be on convalescent leave, so I won't be drinking much more tonight," said Bruno as the baron, at the barbecue, opened a bottle of local Chardonnay from Château Briand and poured himself a glass. "I wasn't feeling too well earlier, and there's a lot more work for me this week with this business of the grave."

He declined the vodka with the caviar and took only a single glass of the Chardonnay with the fish, despite teasing from his friends. Then he changed the topic by asking the baron if he had any recollection of the peak flood of 1944 that had reached almost the top of the stone archway at Limeuil.

"Not personally," the old man replied. "I was in Paris with my mother, and my father was still in a German concentration camp, but I heard the stories after the war. The river rose so high that in the village here we were cut off from town, and the approach to the railway bridge was flooded, so there were no trains. In St. Denis, the main square was flooded, and all the roads were closed except the one to Périgueux, and the water came about halfway up the columns that support the *mairie*."

Bruno tried to imagine how St. Denis had coped with such a challenge as he drove home. When he came to the bridge over the Vézère River, he slowed down to look at the *mairie* and see just how high the water must have risen back in that winter of 1944. There was no traffic behind him, so he stopped.

At that moment someone came quickly from the rue de Paris and crossed the road in front of him. It was Colette Cantagnac. Fishing in her shoulder bag for the keys, she headed to her car, parked in one of the spaces in front of the *mairie*. As she moved to open the door of her Renault, a large figure dressed in black jumped out from the shadows to grab at her. Bruno leaned on his horn and swiveled the wheel so his headlights could illuminate the scene and opened the door to let Balzac leap out. Then he grabbed the police whistle that he kept in the ashtray and followed his dog, blowing hard.

Balzac jumped to grab one ankle of the attacker, who punched at Colette and hurled her into Bruno's path, then kicked Balzac to free his leg. As Bruno fell sprawling over Colette, her attacker limped away. Suddenly, with the flare of a new single headlight and the roar of a high-revving engine, a dirt bike braked beside the black-clad figure. He clambered onto the pillion and was driven away on the road to Les Eyzies at a speed Bruno could never have matched.

"Are you all right?" he asked, helping Colette to her feet. She seemed more stunned than hurt, but her shoulder bag was still gripped firmly in one hand and her car keys in the other.

"I'm fine, just startled," she said, gasping. "Thanks for the rescue. They didn't get my bag. His hand was diving into it, maybe to grab my money."

Bruno pulled out his phone and called the gendarmerie to report the attack. Then he called Juliette, his counterpart in Les Eyzies, in the hope that she might be able to stop the bike if it came through her town. But when she answered, she was having dinner with friends in Périgueux.

"He seemed to be waiting for you, along with the motorbike," Bruno said to Colette. "Were you somewhere your attacker could have spotted you and then followed?"

"I was having dinner at Ivan's with Roberte, from the *mairie*. I suppose we could have been seen through the window. But does this happen often in St. Denis?"

"It's never happened before, as far as I know," Bruno said. "Did the guy say anything?"

"He swore in English when Balzac bit him. 'Shit' is an easy word to recognize," she said.

"Where are you going now?"

"Home, to Périgueux. Why?"

"In your bag, is your phone hot to the touch?"

She looked at him oddly, but then plunged her hand in, brought out her mobile and said, "Yes, it's very hot."

"Someone could be running spyware to keep track of you," Bruno said. "You have an Android? Go into settings and put your phone into airplane mode. That shuts off cell and Wi-Fi. Or from settings select Privacy and then Location Reporting and turn that off. Then delete Location History and that will delete previous tracking data."

"Why would anyone be tracking me?" Colette asked, her fingers tapping at her phone as she did as he suggested. "And how do you know this stuff?"

"I was taught it, and I don't know why someone would be tracking you or want to steal your phone or purse. You may have a better idea about that than I do."

She looked at him coldly. "Interesting coincidence that I get attacked right after you report back for duty and you just happen to turn up to rescue me."

Bruno ignored this and asked, "Did you book your table at Ivan's by phone? Might you have been overheard?"

"No, we just decided to go there at the last minute."

"So how would I have known where you were? I was just coming back from a dinner with friends."

"I'm sorry, Bruno. I'm just upset; it must be the shock. Who the hell would do something like this?"

"That's what we'll try to find out. In the meantime, if you have enemies who are this intent on grabbing your purse or your phone, they'll probably know your address in Périgueux. Why don't you stay in my spare room for the night?"

"Thanks, I'll do that. And thank you for the rescue, Bruno."

Chapter 15

The next morning, after a run with Balzac and a shower, Bruno fed and gave water to his chickens and checked the internet for Gilles's story on the *Paris Match* website. There were links attached to Italian and German papers, to a short piece in *Figaro* and a longer one in *Sud Ouest* by Philippe Delaron, which Bruno couldn't access without a subscription. Fauquet's café would have a copy and he would read it there later. He heard Colette moving in the spare bedroom upstairs and then heard the shower going, so he left her a note in the kitchen before driving to Alphonse Marty's house. He told him of the mayor's plans and accepted another cup of coffee, this time with a slug of Alphonse's homemade eau-de-vie, before heading to Lespinasse's garage.

It was the expertise of his son, Edouard, that Bruno sought. The young man had made a success of selling trail bikes and other off-road vehicles, and Bruno asked him whether any big and burly English-speaking foreigner had rented a trail bike in recent days. Not this time of year, came the reply, but there's a place in the shopping complex at Trélissac that might be worth trying. At Bruno's request, Edouard called a friend who worked there, who said there had been an Italian who bought the oldest serviceable trail bike in the store and paid in cash, nine hundred euros. The guy had shown an Italian passport and driver's license. The salesman hadn't bothered to take note of the details. He'd just been happy to get rid of a battered old wreck. At least he could give Bruno the bike's license plate.

Bruno thanked Edouard and went to the gendarmerie to give Sergeant Jules a statement on the previous evening's attempted mugging of Mademoiselle Cantagnac. He suggested that the file should include the possible license plate number and to note that the attacker may have been using an Italian passport and driver's license. He would certainly have the marks of a powerful dog bite on his right ankle. Bruno added the bike salesman's details.

Bruno then strolled to Fauquet's for a coffee and croissant and to read Philippe's story in the café's copy of *Sud Ouest*. It was unusually restrained by Philippe's standards. He led with the diplomatic descent on St. Denis to view the new grave and then described the plan for a garden of remembrance to connect the grave site with the existing memorial. Farther down in the story he wrote that the absence of clothes on the female corpses suggested brutal mistreatment, but with unusual sensitivity he did not deploy the word "rape." The story concluded by quoting the Englishman, Monsieur Birch, who said that the grave would not upset his plan to restore the long empty hotel of the Domaine de la Barde. That was good to know, Bruno thought, handing Balzac a corner of his croissant and turning to the sports pages. A shadow fell over them as someone came to his table and sat down.

"Bonjour, Philippe," he said. "Your story today was good, not sensational and with some useful local news. We all want to see the Domaine de la Barde back in business."

"Thank you. But why have the forensic experts of the Police Nationale not been called in?" Philippe asked. "That would be the usual procedure."

"That may happen, but we need to hear what the German and Italian diplomats say first," Bruno replied, feeling proud of himself for coming up with a plausible explanation on the spur of the moment. "They may want to send their own forensic teams. After all, it's not as though this is an urgent murder investigation."

"Have you been to the grave this morning?" Philippe went on.

"Not yet." Bruno felt a sense of foreboding. "Why?"

"Fabiola called me to say that she and some other women would be laying flowers there this morning in memory of the two dead German girls—"

"Very nice of them," said Bruno.

"—and to commemorate rape victims in general," Philippe concluded. "Fabiola said she'd done an initial autopsy and that her conclusion was that the two women, who were at the time prisoners of war, had very probably been raped. So she called the members of her women's group, and there are dozens of bouquets there now, and two of them call for justice for—I quote—'all victims of male sexual violence.'"

Bruno considered the implications of this development for St. Denis. "Of course," he said, "it's sadly very possible that these women were raped. But there's no clear evidence of that, and given that they are now skeletons, there probably never will be."

"So why were these teenage girls stripped naked?" Philippe asked. "Fabiola is a doctor, so her opinion carries weight."

"Indeed it does, and she's right to make the point about the lack of clothing and what it might mean, although given the time that's passed, we can't be sure." Bruno's imagination was conjuring up the prospect of women's groups lining up on one side of the grave, confronting male French nationalists on the other carrying banners saying that these foreign invaders deserved their fate— and himself in the middle, trying to keep them apart.

"Once I've finished my breakfast I'll go and take a look," he went on. "But you know I'm not back on duty yet."

"So, you wouldn't be the anonymous town official who was quoted in the *Paris Match* article?" Philippe asked.

"Me? Anonymous? Come, Philippe, you know me better than that." Bruno put three euros on the table and rose to go.

"Oh, one more thing," said Philippe. "That tent you erected at the grave. Somebody has spray-painted a big swastika on it with the words NAZIS OUT! I thought you'd like to know."

"Thank you, Philippe. Always good to see you." Bruno nodded genially and, with Balzac at his heels, set off to the memorial. Colette beeped the Renault's horn at him from the roundabout. He waved back, continuing on his way, stopping often to greet and be greeted while Balzac pretended not to notice the occasional cat arching its back at him. At the memorial, long rows of flowers lay heaped around the plinth, dozens of them, as Philippe had mentioned. Indeed, Bruno had never seen anything like it since the images of the railings of Buckingham Palace almost obscured by floral tributes after the death of Princess Diana.

There were bouquets from Fabiola, Pamela, Miranda, Madame Brosseil, Commandant Yveline of the gendarmes, Madame Fauquet at the café, Marguerite at the Crédit Agricole bank and another from Antoinette at the dress shop. There was a small bouquet from Marta, three from different women bearing the name Marty, two from the checkout women at the supermarket, one from Sergeant Jules's wife, another from Nathalie at the wineshop, two from the women at the Moulin bakery, a big one from "Suzette and all the girls at the retirement home" and one from Colette Cantagnac.

Bruno strolled along the line of flowers, noting lots more names. There was even a bouquet from Florence, who must have been called, probably by Fabiola, and had arranged the bouquet by email from where she was visiting her parents. The largest tribute came from Jacqueline, the mayor's partner, who was teaching at the Sorbonne in Paris, so she, too, must have ordered flowers on the internet.

Bruno realized that the women of St. Denis had made an

overwhelming statement of their views. Their menfolk had better take careful note. As he stood there, thinking, a tractor heaved to a stop beside him, and Nicole, a farmer's wife and the neighbor of his friend, Stéphane, a cheese maker, jumped down. She threw her arms around him in a hug and said, "Bonjour, Bruno, welcome back!" before depositing her own bouquet, then clambering back aboard and setting off again in a black cloud of diesel fumes.

It seemed somehow symbolic. He looked across at the tent, and he could see the fluorescent swastika from where he stood, at least forty meters away. He walked briskly to the Bricomarché, where Abby had bought her locks and bolts, and bought a can of fluorescent red paint, another of blue, a third of white and a pair of rubber gloves. He returned to the tent, donned the gloves and transformed the offending swastika into a giant French tricolor.

He had just finished when he saw the mayor walking toward him with a thoughtful look on his face that suggested to Bruno that he'd just seen Jacqueline's bouquet.

"Well done," the mayor said. "How much did you pay for the paint?"

"Twelve euros and two ninety-nine for the gloves," Bruno replied. "A fraction of what the women have spent on floral tributes."

"Yes, I saw." The mayor paused before he spoke again. "What do you think we should do?"

"You mean what we should do after you and the town council lay an even bigger bouquet than Jacqueline's and persuade Father Sentout to hold a service of remembrance?"

"Good ideas. I was thinking in more modest terms, but you're absolutely right, Bruno. We have to arrange something very special. The more grandiose our display the better, and I don't think we should stop at flowers."

"I agree. I was at Fauquet's earlier when Philippe Delaron came by and told me about this, which means it will be all over the radio this afternoon and on the TV news this evening. I imagine it might even make German TV. Looking on the bright side, I suppose that could be good for tourism."

The mayor nodded. "All the TV coverage will come just in time for the diplomats to turn up. Maybe we could arrange a religious service here at the memorial. Let the dead rest in peace, that sort of thing. Do you think Father Sentout would cooperate?"

"He will if we tell him we're looking for a Protestant preacher because the two German girls are Lutherans. But why don't we get ahead of *Sud Ouest*? You could call France Bleu radio and TV3 in Bordeaux, and I'll tell Gilles, who can run something new for *Paris Match* with a positive spin: 'St. Denis to Salute All the War Dead.' All these flowers make for a great picture, and the TV news outlets will certainly be sending cameras for the diplomats' visit. Yveline can arrange for the gendarmes to turn out, and we can get a bugler to play the 'Sonnerie aux Morts' followed by a minute's silence. Rollo could get all his schoolkids to come along, so long as your budget can handle a small bouquet for every child."

"That would be great for television," said the mayor, looking much more cheerful. "I suppose we can use the tourism promotion budget."

"No problem there," said Bruno. "Mademoiselle Cantagnac already added her own floral tribute. She strikes me as the kind of woman who knows how to make our civic budget stand up, salute and give a song and dance."

"I'll form a committee to run this," said the mayor. "Mademoiselle Cantagnac, Commandant Yveline, Father Sentout, Rollo and you."

"Not me," said Bruno. "I'm still on convalescent leave, and I don't even have an office. Best if you make this committee entirely of women, don't you think? But certainly include Yveline and Cantagnac, plus Fabiola and a member of the council."

Chapter 16

As the mayor debated with himself which councilor to choose, Bruno's phone gave the special buzz that meant he was being called by someone on General Lannes's secure network. Bruno rolled his eyes. A call from Lannes was usually the prelude to some special duty for the interior ministry's security service.

"Bruno," came the general's familiar voice. "Somebody is trying to hack into that special phone we gave you. Colonel Morillon's team sent us the alert. They won't succeed, but I thought you should know. You might want to get another phone for your civic duties or personal calls. Let me have the numbers, and we can monitor them, too. Have you made any new enemies lately?"

"Not that I know of, sir," Bruno replied politely. "Are you able to trace who it might be?"

"Not yet. He or she is very good, routing things in and out of the dark web, so I'm told. And I don't understand it either, so don't ask, but you've been warned. Take care, Bruno."

He ended the call.

"Was that who I think it was?" the mayor asked.

"Yes, General Lannes. It seems that somebody is trying to hack into my phone."

"The secure phone he assigned to you?"

"Yes. They can't get into it, but I've been warned, which I suppose is useful."

"Who is it? Does he know?"

"Not yet. It's somebody very good, apparently, using the dark web. Lannes suggests I get another phone for day-to-day use while they track down the hacker. I suppose I'm entitled to one through the *mairie*'s account."

"See if you can get it through Mademoiselle Cantagnac," the mayor said with a chuckle.

"I'm sure she'll be helpful," said Bruno. "Somebody was after her phone last night." He explained the evening's events. "I'll try to have a watch set on her phone, too."

"Fine," said the mayor. "But don't forget to call on Father Sentout and exercise your persuasive skills, get in touch with your various journalist contacts and make sure that Commandant Yveline organizes a gendarme to guard our town's generous floral tribute around the clock. We've been set a challenge, Bruno, and we have to rise to meet it."

"I agree," said Bruno. "I remember that American woman, the one from the FBI who came here during that difficult business with Momu's adopted son, and she taught me an American saying, that when life gives you lemons, it is the moment to make *tarte aux citrons*."

"Bonjour, Monsieur le Maire; bonjour, Bruno; et bonjour, Balzac," came a familiar voice, and the impressive bulk of Sergeant Jules heaved into view, accompanied by a rake-thin young gendarme. Side by side, they had the appearance of the digits 0 and 1, thought Bruno. Jules and the mayor shook hands and made approving comments on the impressive bouquet that Jules's wife had donated to the pile.

"That's why I'm here," said Jules. "My wife thought we should mount a guard, and then Commandant Yveline said the same, so here he is. Allow me to introduce our latest recruit, *gendarme-*

aspirant Roland Montfaucon, direct from training school with excellent results, not least in marksmanship."

"Welcome to St. Denis, young man," said the mayor grandly. "I'm confident that you'll fulfill our trust in the gendarmerie."

Having greeted the newcomer, Bruno and the mayor strolled back into town, heading first for the *presbytère* where Father Sentout lived. Before they reached it, Bruno's phone vibrated again on the pouch on his belt. He looked at the screen, saw it was his friend, Detective J-J. Bruno excused himself to the mayor, who walked on.

"Bruno, you have a problem," J-J began. "Our tech experts tell me that somebody adept at this kind of thing is trying to break into our police computer, and he's coming through your email account. Do you know anything about this?"

"Bonjour, J-J. No, I have no idea. Except that General Lannes called me a few minutes ago to say that somebody was trying to go through the dark web to break into the special phone Lannes issued me. He hasn't succeeded, but Colonel Morillon of the army's cyber-warfare center is investigating. I'd better let him know of this new development. We also had an attempted mugging and phone theft from the new executive assistant at the *mairie*, Mademoiselle Cantagnac, queen of the public employees' staff association."

"Better bring the phones and laptops in, or the tech guys say we might have to cut your access to the police computer," J-J replied. "And how are you, back in harness yet?"

"Not quite," Bruno replied. He filled him in with all the latest news from St. Denis, the overwhelming flowers, the diplomats arriving.

"Yes, the boss isn't happy about having to provide a police escort for the prefect and assorted diplomats."

"I've been dragooned into helping out. I'm off to persuade our village priest to provide us some kind of religious commemoration. Seriously, J-J, I'd better call Colonel Morillon and tell him about this attempted break-in to the police computer. He'll know what to do. What's the name and number of your computer expert?"

"I'll text it to your phone, but you'd better bring your tech in for a thorough check. Why not drive up with it, and I can take you to lunch and we can catch up."

Bruno agreed with pleasure. Then he sent J-J's warning to General Lannes, with a copy to Colonel Morillon and a note about the attempted theft of Cantagnac's phone, before knocking on the priest's door.

"My dear Bruno, how good to see you again, and with dear Balzac," said the plump cleric with a smile, dressed as usual in his black soutane. "Do come in and tell me what I can do for you. Are you fully recovered from your wound?"

"I'm mending, Father, and I wanted to thank you for your special prayers on my behalf," Bruno said as the priest led him into the study, the largest room in the house, and showed him to a chair beside the large desk. "But there is something else I wanted to discuss with you. No doubt you've heard about this wartime grave that we found by the Domaine de la Barde, and the arrival of the various diplomats with the prefect tomorrow."

"Yes, very sad, and I was preparing to visit the grave and say a few words of commemoration, since I doubt that a funeral ceremony would be appropriate in the circumstances."

"Perhaps not, but I've persuaded the mayor that it would be fitting if you were to say a few words at the grave. We're expecting TV cameras and various journalists, and the mayor agrees that your and the choir's presence would be a welcome addition to the town's act of remembrance of these unfortunate victims of war."

"The mayor has agreed to this?" the priest said, in tones of surprise that verged on disbelief. The mayor was renowned for his fervent support of the traditional French division between church and state, and jealously guarded his right to perform marriages.

"We think that the whole town, church and state, choir and schoolkids, should be seen to take part in this solemn moment," Bruno said. "The mayor did think of asking a Protestant pastor, since the German women were Lutherans, but I reminded him that the Italian officer would most certainly have been a Catholic, may God rest his soul."

"I agree, of course," the priest said, his expression shifting from horror at the word "Lutheran" to relief when Bruno mentioned the Italian. "France is a Catholic nation, and such an act of solemn community would be wholly fitting. I shall be delighted to be there. And my profound thanks, Bruno, for your part in arranging this."

"Five minutes maximum was the best I could get the mayor to accept, Father," Bruno said. "A prayer, a hymn, a benediction and the Lord's Prayer. I think that would be fitting in hands as skilled as yours. And what would you suggest for the choir?"

The little priest looked from his desk across the garden to the gray, stone bulk of his church as if seeking inspiration, and his hand came up to toy with the buttons of his soutane. For a moment Bruno thought he was about to cross himself.

"Perhaps we might sing from Bach's Mass in B Minor, the 'Credo in unum Deum,' I believe in one God," he said. "It's less than five minutes, as I recall."

"Perfect," said Bruno. "I won't take any more of your time, Father, but may I suggest you walk out to the site of the memorial? You will be struck by the sight of the massed floral tributes laid there by the local women to commemorate the two German girls whose lives were so tragically cut short."

"I shall do so this very morning, Bruno, but while you're here I should tell you about an interesting reference to the nearby fighting in that summer of 1944 in the journals of one of my predecessors, Father Rochan from Limoges, who lost an arm and an eye at Verdun as a young army chaplain."

"Could I read it, please?" Bruno asked, restraining his excitement.

"Of course. I was looking at it earlier to refresh my memory." Father Sentout handed Bruno a large old book that looked like a ledger, its pages filled with spidery handwriting. "Here, where I left a ruler to mark the page, under the date, August 1944."

Bruno started to read the cramped, old-fashioned handwriting.

As the news spread of the landings of a new American army near Marseille, we saw in St. Denis the first sign of German flight. A small convoy of three trucks and a staff car, all led by a motorbike, came through town from the west, apparently from Bordeaux but reaching us from Ste. Alvère.

They were mostly from U-boat crews for whom there were no more U-boats, along with some female personnel and a small Wehrmacht escort. They were not aware that they were about to run into a Resistance column, coming fresh from the liberation of Cahors and driving through St. Denis to help liberate Périgueux, via Belvès and St. Cyprien. Unlike the Germans, the men from Cahors had sent ahead an advance guard that was able to warn their comrades, who thus had time to prepare a successful ambush of the German column.

The shooting lasted less than three minutes and none of the Germans escaped, except for two young women in the staff car, a Lancia that was driven by an Italian naval officer who was also killed. I and other townspeople who went to help any wounded were warned off at gunpoint, and the Resistance men's celebration went on late into the night. It was fueled, I later learned, by cases of wine and schnapps from the staff car. The following morning I went to offer last rites and arrange burials but was again ordered at gunpoint to return to town. This instruction included various insults from the godless Marxists about my faith being so much "mumbo jumbo in the service of capitalist exploiters." Late that night, a young man, one of the Resistance fighters, came secretly to see me in great distress and under seal of confession described to me the shameful events that had taken place. I gave him penance and absolution. The next day one truck filled with Resistance men and the Lancia staff car drove off to the north, presumably to Périgueux. The remaining Resistance men were joined by two trucks and some workers from the rail depot at Le Buisson who cleared away the two burned-out German vehicles and the motorbike and left a stone to mark where one of their comrades had fallen. The bodies were disposed of in the river.

Father Sentout gave a discreet cough, and as Bruno looked up, the priest said, "In a later entry, in October, after the Germans had been evicted from France, Father Rochan notes that he sent a copy of his entry to his bishop and to the new prefect, asking for their comment. There is no record that he received any reply. He does note that another priest, who later became an archbishop, was asked to give a benediction at the formal unveiling of the memorial to the dead Resistance fighter once peace was declared."

"Are you surprised?" Bruno asked, not looking at Father Sentout. "After four years of occupation?"

"Not really, but perhaps at last we can put the souls of those poor girls to rest, and indeed of them all." He paused, then added, "Including Father Rochan."

"May I make a copy of this?" Bruno asked.

"I already made one for you." The priest handed Bruno an envelope, and went on, in a more cheerful tone, "It's a pity that

Florence isn't here this week to sing the solo part of the *credo*. She has such a fine voice, and such faithful parents. I enjoyed meeting them when you were in the hospital. And I must say that it's a blessing to see you so well recovered, my dear Bruno. Bless you and thank you for your part in arranging this with the mayor. The Lord does indeed move in mysterious ways."

Chapter 17

Reluctant as he would be to admit it to Colette Cantagnac, or to anyone else, Bruno found that she had made his office much more pleasant than it had been when he had simply taken over the furniture and placings from his predecessor. There had been little that was personal in Bruno's time, except for a framed photo of his previous basset hound, Gigi, and another of a much younger Bruno in camouflage uniform with members of the squad he'd commanded in Bosnia. Those photos remained in their place, although dwarfed by a framed vintage poster advertising a May Day parade of several trade unions from 1937. The furniture had been shifted so that the light from the window fell onto the new desk, making room for an easy chair that had not been there before. A large sisal rug covered the floor in front of the desk, and a vase filled with fresh flowers that he could not identify filled the room with their scent. Now, as he entered, he admired her changes but realized that he reluctantly thought of the room as her office.

Colette thanked Bruno for his hospitality, adding that she had given a statement to Sergeant Jules on the previous evening's attack. Then she shifted her attention to Bruno's dog. "Balzac, I have a very small dog biscuit, just for you." She let the dog take it from her hand, saying to Bruno, "When I realized that he was likely to be a regular visitor, I got him a box."

"That's very kind of you," he said, and pointed to the wall. "I like that poster, but why 1937?"

"The poster was to celebrate the rights of workers that had been enacted by the socialist government of Léon Blum. He was elected the previous year. It included a forty-hour week, twelve days of paid annual leave, the right to strike and a fifteen percent pay raise for the lowest-paid workers. A historic time, and my grandfather was a great supporter of Blum, a member of the Socialist Party and a union member. He became a shop steward at the Citroën factory in Paris. My father followed in his footsteps and so do I."

"A family tradition," said Bruno, sitting down in the easy chair, which was very comfortable, and he said so.

"I'm glad you approve. What can I do for you, Bruno?"

"I've just come from the memorial and admired the growing pile of flowers there. I saw your own bouquet among them, so I thought I'd thank you."

"Really?" she asked, an eyebrow cocked and skepticism in her tone. "I'm glad to hear it, although a little surprised."

"Why?" he asked, genuinely curious.

"I don't often see feminist sympathies from someone with your background, a former soldier, a policeman, so it's a pleasant surprise."

"I don't think feminist sympathies are required to honor those who died in war," Bruno replied. "I think it's a very fitting gesture, and it seemed directed at the Italian naval officer and the dead French *résistant* as well as the two young German women. That's partly why I'm here. The mayor asked me to arrange a brief memorial service for when the diplomatic delegation arrives. He would like it to include our choir singing, and for the schoolkids to carry small bouquets, just to make the town's sympathies clear."

"A very good idea," she agreed.

"The mayor also thought you might find a way to pay any incidental expenses from the town budget without trouble with the accountants."

"Not a problem. I'll handle it. But why send you rather than ask me himself?"

"Because I also have a personal request. I need a new phone."

"What's wrong with your phone?"

"It's not a *mairie* phone, but one given to me by General Lannes of the interior ministry. I've just heard from him that there's been a serious attempt to hack it from some very capable but unknown source. So he wants me to get a new one for local use. I also just heard from the Police Nationale in Périgueux that a separate attempt was made overnight to hack into their computer. They've traced it back to my computer here. And whether last night's target was your phone, mine or the *mairie*, some kind of attack seems underway. Where did you put my computer while I was in the hospital?"

"It's here, in the bottom drawer of my desk, which is kept locked when I'm not here."

"Good, may I have it, please? I've been asked to take it up to the police computer expert in Périgueux."

"Of course—make sure you get a receipt from them." She bent down, took the big laptop from the drawer and handed it to him. "Just bring in the receipt for your new phone and I'll take care of things."

"Thank you," Bruno said. "One other thing. I don't know if you've had time to visit the National Museum of Prehistory at Les Eyzies yet, but Clothilde, the curator there, has an old friend and former pupil, an American archaeologist called Abby. She's an interesting woman, recently divorced, who's a visiting lecturer this year at the museum. She's hoping to set up specialized tours for American visitors. There are several links between the United

States and the Périgord which turn out to be much more profound than one might assume. The mayor is sympathetic, but we're not sure how to handle the bureaucracy of giving her guide status without her having the usual *brevet.* Can you advise us?"

"I'll have to think about it. Would this be paid work, charging the visitors for her guided tour?"

When Bruno confirmed that it would be, she said, "That complicates matters. But we could give her an unpaid position as adviser to the town's tourist office, citing her archaeological post at the museum. Abby would have free admission to all public monuments and museums, but her clients would have to pay the usual entrance fees. Let me check, but that should solve it, particularly if she were to write a booklet on the region's American connections. Why not get her to come see me here at the *mairie* and we can work something out."

"Thank you, that all makes sense," Bruno said, rising and turning to look again at the vintage poster. "Those were admirable reforms by the Blum government and well worth commemorating. Did you know, by the way, that he was one of the first male feminists?"

"Léon Blum, really?" She looked startled.

"He was radicalized by the Dreyfus affair and was a friend of the socialist leader Jean Jaurès," Bruno said. "But he became notorious for something he wrote. You might want to look up Blum's first book, *Du Mariage.* It's in the town library. It challenged the traditional Catholic view of marriage. He criticized the conventional wisdom that women should remain virgins until marriage and suggested that women as well as men should be entitled to what he called a polygamic love life before their weddings. He argued that it would help them to build a more mature and stable relationship in marriage."

"A very sensible view," she said. "I didn't know that, but I can imagine it creating a stir at the time."

"Charles Maurras of the extreme right-wing Action Française called him 'the pornographer of the council of state,' since Blum was working there at the time as a legal aide."

She grinned. "I must remember that. I had no idea that you were such a wide reader."

"We old soldiers occasionally like to broaden our horizons, Colette," he said, smiling at her. "As I said, you'll find a copy of Blum's book in the library."

"*Touché,* Bruno. I'll be sure to make a point of reading it, and I won't jump to conclusions about old soldiers again. Since you seem to like history, did you know about the role my grandfather's Citroën factory played in the Resistance?"

"I knew they produced trucks for the German army, but that's all."

"They did indeed, and found a very subtle way to sabotage them: they changed the dipsticks to show there was still sufficient oil in the engine even when there wasn't. The engines conked out after the truck had gone for about a thousand kilometers."

"Brilliant," Bruno exclaimed with a laugh. "I'll remember that."

"I heard it from my father, who was very proud that his father had been part of the team that planned it."

"You should be proud, too," he said, letting himself out.

It was odd, Bruno thought as he set off on the familiar road to Périgueux, the way that people construct their own sense of history, cobbled together from family anecdotes, like Colette's story of the sabotaged dipsticks, and from half-remembered school-books, isolated facts picked up from friends and newspapers and random books they read. Collectively, the people of France probably knew considerably more about their history than the most learned professor could hope to acquire in a lifetime of study. And most history was written by the victors, or by those minorities who could read and write, like the churchmen in the largely illiterate centuries after the fall of Rome. Even now, whole catalogs of the past could be lost. For example, Bruno recalled, the network of single-track tramways that had crisscrossed the Périgord from the late nineteenth century to the late 1940s. Hauled by small steam trains fueled with wood, the trams had averaged around twenty kilometers per hour, but the passengers had to get off and walk when the trains were going uphill. He had learned about it by accident, thumbing through a collection of vintage postcards in the market one day.

What would be forgotten of his own times? Bruno wondered as he drove. Eight-track music systems, tape cassettes and video-tapes; they had come and gone with startling speed, each fueling its own brief microculture of tape decks and video stores. Coal fires had gone, and woodburning stoves like his own would probably be next, he thought, along with gasoline pumps, but bicycles had made a comeback.

"Dogs like you will go on," he said aloud, taking a hand from the wheel to scratch Balzac's neck as he slowed for the roundabout that led to Périgueux, the nearest to a big city the region could boast, with its population of thirty thousand.

Chapter 18

Balzac stayed in the Land Rover in the garage as Bruno took the phones and laptop to the computer room at police headquarters. He was about to introduce himself to the woman who was the only staff member there, but she seemed to be engrossed in comparing something on two computer screens. Unsure about interrupting her concentration, Bruno waited. She was young, in her early twenties, he guessed, and painfully thin. She wore no makeup, and her dark hair was piled into a bun atop her head, secured by a pencil with a well-gnawed end. The door was on some kind of slow automatic closing system, and when it finally clicked itself shut behind him, she appeared to register his presence and looked up.

Bruno gave his name and explained that after an attempted hack he'd been asked to bring in his official laptop by Commissaire Jalipeau, adding that he's expected to give it to Raymond, the tech who had schooled him in using the police computer.

"He's at lunch and I'm the new aide," she said, and held up for his inspection the official ID card that was hanging on a chain around her neck. She introduced herself as Gabrielle Teyssier, asked to see his police ID and entered the details in a new logbook. That had never happened before. Bruno turned on the laptop and entered his password. He explained that his special phone from the interior ministry had been attacked at the same time and was being investigated by Colonel Morillon's team at the French military cyber-warfare center near Rennes. The technician's eyes widened, and she asked if Morillon knew about the attack on his computer. Bruno told her that he did, and described the attack on Mademoiselle Cantagnac, apparently to get hold of her phone. Might Mademoiselle Teyssier take a look at the computer system of the *mairie* in St. Denis?

"I'll try," she said. "Sounds intriguing." She said he could retrieve his laptop later that afternoon. Bruno went downstairs to get Balzac from the garage and took the stairs up to J-J's office. He found his friend on the phone, rolling his eyes and being unusually polite and patient, and murmuring "*Oui,* madame," at regular intervals, occasionally interspersed with "*Merci,* madame."

Finally the call ended, and J-J rose, greeted Balzac, stretched out a hand and said, "My new dentist, telling me all the treatments I need, while explaining that my old dentist had retired just in time to save me from a complete set of false teeth."

"So, better enjoy your lunches while you can," Bruno said. "I delivered my laptop to your tech wizards, and the cyber-warfare experts are trying to discover who's attempting to hack the special phone I got from General Lannes. Have you heard about our new floral mountain in St. Denis?"

"Yes, Philippe Delaron was talking lyrically about it on the radio news," said J-J. "It sounded like he'd just been given a management lecture on the need for sympathy to female concerns or some other woke fashion."

"Let me fill you in on the other development, last night's attack on my new colleague at the *mairie,*" said Bruno as J-J led the way across the main square to his favorite restaurant, L'Atelier, on the corner of the rue Voltaire. The restaurant knew him so well that without asking they took it for granted that J-J would have the foie gras with a black-currant sauce followed by *ris de veau,* with a chocolate-caramel concoction for dessert.

Bruno, knowing he was in for a grand meal that evening, chose the *retour du marché,* a main course and dessert from whatever had caught the chef's eye in the market that morning. In this case, it was lamb's liver in sage with baby onions and new potatoes, followed by a perfect individual lemon tart, topped with a tiny half globe of crème brûlée that left Bruno envying the pastry chef's skill with a blowtorch.

They shared a bottle of Château Mondazur from the Pécharmant, a wine made by Bruno's old friend François-Xavier de Saint-Exupéry. Pressure from the rest of the sprawling de Saint-Exupéry family had required the sale of the ancestral Château de Tiregand, for whose wines François-Xavier had built an international reputation. They had been one of Bruno's personal favorites, a wine he liked to serve at special occasions. Now François-Xavier was maintaining the grand tradition with the much smaller Mondazur, and Bruno made a point of telling the waiter how pleased he was to see it.

"It's excellent," J-J pronounced after tasting it and smacking his lips. "It looks as though you've helped me find a new favorite, Bruno." He put down his glass and leaned forward as if determined to change the subject. "So, let's get serious. Who do you think is trying to hack into your phone and computer? Could it have something to do with that Russian business that put you into a hospital bed?"

"I've no idea, but I think Colonel Morillon's team will track it down. Of course, it could be somebody thinking that my computer could be the weak link that allowed them to break into your big mainframe. All I know is that the hacker was apparently skilled in using the dark web, about which I know very little, except that it's heavily encrypted and used for drug dealing, porn, ransomware and the dark arts in general."

"I had to sit through a briefing on the dark web that made me feel like a dinosaur about to go extinct," said J-J. "All I could follow was the image of an onion, because there was a cartoon drawing of one up on the screen. The expert said that it was like an onion because every time you peel off one layer there was another one underneath."

"That's more than I know about it," said Bruno. "But that new expert you have in the computer room, Gabrielle, seems to know what she's doing."

Their talk drifted on to the newfound grave in St. Denis, the arrival of the diplomatic delegation, presumably with accompanying TV cameras, and the prospect of a mounting scandal over the presumed rape of two German women prisoners of war by Resistance fighters.

"I wish people were more concerned about how many of our own women were raped by those Nazi bastards," J-J declared grumpily. Bruno nodded, knowing that similar sentiments were being expressed in bars all across the Périgord.

"Maybe that's the point," Bruno said. "The fact is that we haven't had an honest national conversation about how many of our own women were abused or driven to sleep with pro-Nazi Frenchmen from the Milice as the only way to get ration cards to feed their kids."

"That was wartime, Bruno," J-J said. "A completely different time, different context."

"You'd be as surprised as I was by some of the women from St. Denis who laid those flowers. There were farmers' wives, women who work in the *mairie* and the banks, upstanding bourgeois matrons, checkout girls from the supermarket, Yveline from the gendarmes and Sybille, Sergeant Jules's wife, women you've met at my table, women who've fed you in their homes. This isn't some group of woke Parisian feminists, J-J. It's local women whom you know. I suspect they are taking this opportunity because they want to make a point about sexual violence that we've pushed under the carpet for too long."

J-J sat back and stared at him in surprise, obviously taken aback by Bruno's words.

"We haven't pushed it under the carpet, Bruno," he replied after taking a swig of his wine. "What about that rotten apple we had, the bastard you beat the shit out of when he tried to rape that girl from Paris who was reconstructing those skulls for us? We got rid of him and he's still in jail."

"I'm glad I stopped him, J-J. But I wonder what would have happened if I hadn't turned up, and he had raped her. He might have gotten away with it because it would have been a cop's word against hers. You know what a tiny proportion of reported rapes lead to convictions."

J-J nodded. "I'm with you there. It pisses me off that we work hard to get a rape conviction and some clever lawyer persuades the court that she was no virgin and dressed as though she was asking for it. And so the bastard goes free. Bruno, I'm probably in the minority in the *commissariat* who'd even go that far to agree with you. But you're right to say that some of those flower layers are fine women; Yveline is the best head of gendarmes I can recall in St. Denis."

"You know that joke guys like to tell, that rape is impossible because a woman with her skirt up can run faster than a guy with his trousers down? Next time I hear it I'm going to say, Not if he slugs her in the jaw first, because we both know that's the reality, J-J. It's not just the forced sex, it's the violence and intimidation that make it possible."

J-J nodded, his face grim. "Yeah, you're right. I can't think of a rape victim I've seen who hadn't been beaten up." He sat up, leaned back and said, "After that, I think we need a brandy with our coffee."

"Not for me, thanks," said Bruno. "I'm driving. But that was a very good lunch. Can't we split the bill?"

"Not when I invited you, and the number of times you've fed me. And that reminds me, you remember Goirau, the guy from the financial police, we had lunch together at the Hercule Poireau. He's coming up next month to give us the benefit of his financial skills, a two-day course on this credit card fraud that's been going through the roof."

"Great, I'd like to see him, and I owe him a dinner after some very useful advice he gave me. We'll make a night of it at my place. I'll cook, and you two can stay the night in my spare rooms. I'll roast a shoulder of lamb with Monbazillac and make that *tarte Tatin* with apples that you like."

"Jesus, Bruno, you're making me hungry again. It's a date."

Chapter 19

Back in the *commissariat,* Bruno collected his laptop from Gabrielle, who said with a shrug that Raymond was still at lunch.

"Don't you get a lunch break?" Bruno asked.

"I never eat lunch," she said, briskly. "And Raymond has a new girlfriend, so I imagine his hunger is not just for food. Anyway, I like working with this stuff, which is why I applied for this job."

"What's the attraction?" Bruno asked. "Is it all the imaginative ways we cops find to break your precious computers?"

"No, you'd be amazed how utterly predictable the problems are. Laptops are either dropped in the bath, run over by a car, fall off a desk, become overloaded with movies, or wine is spilled across the keyboard. That gives you ninety-nine percent of what causes the problems, at least with police computers. Yours was an interesting challenge."

Gabrielle assured Bruno that his laptop was only clean because it had been unused and turned off since his injury. The moment she had turned it on, it had started loading a vast queue of assorted emails, and one of them had set off an alarm. It had been sent two days earlier, a thank-you message in the form of an animated musical greeting card. But it contained a virus that could have given the sender access to the hard drive of a less professionally protected computer.

"It's a Hive system, state of the art in its day, a virus program developed secretly by the Americans—the CIA, to be precise—and it was made embarrassingly public by WikiLeaks in 2017," she said. "It has a public-facing HTTPS interface to transfer information from target smartphones and desktops, while leaving access open for further commands. It had a really elegant concealment system, hiding behind innocent-looking public domains through a masking interface known as LP, for listening post, something the CIA also developed."

"I didn't understand a word of that," Bruno said. "Apart from the bit about the CIA."

"Of course, it's old hat now," she went on, ignoring his comment. "Even with the xdr33 tweak they put into it a couple of years ago. But it's interesting that they're still using the basic Hive source code."

"What I want to know is who sent it. Can you tell who it might have been?" Bruno asked.

"Ostensibly it came from someone signing themselves Abby, but there was another clean and apparently genuine thank-you note from her that came from a local address ending in orange.fr. The poisoned greeting card came from an American university address ending in edu-dot-com. So I think you should warn her that it looks as though both her phone and laptop have been compromised by somebody who knows a lot about computing but is not quite up-to-date with the latest stuff."

"Is my laptop vulnerable?"

"No, you're clean and protected. Raymond put some pretty robust defenses on all our gear, and I've now added some extra stuff on yours, including an automatic alert to me if some new mole starts burrowing."

"Could you clean and protect Abby's phone and laptop and Colette Cantagnac's phone if I brought them in?"

"Yes, if they are *mairie* phones, but no personal phones unless they are cops. Anyway, the hacker would just try something else. The name of the game is not just to stop them but to find out who they are and what they want. Then you give them something that they think they want but which infects them so you can find out everything else they're doing."

"If I asked you nicely, Gabrielle, could you make my laptop do that?"

"Probably, but I'd need a work order from someone authorized, that means of *commissaire* rank or above."

"So that would include J-J?"

"Of course," came the reply. So Bruno pulled out his phone to call J-J, who gave the requisite work order.

"What do you want to feed your intruder and what do you want to know?" the tech asked.

"I don't want to feed the bastard anything, but if I must, my work schedule, perhaps? And I want to know who and where the intruder is, who else he is targeting and what he is planning to do."

"So you want to know his location, targets, travel plans, contacts, bank accounts and cash flow, would that do?"

"That would be great, Gabrielle."

"Go and have a cup of coffee and come back in half an hour."

"Can I bring you a cup when I return? Anything to eat?"

"Sure, double espresso, no cream, no sugar, no eats."

Thirty minutes later Bruno returned to hand Gabrielle her coffee, received his laptop in return and was told that Gabrielle would inform Bruno when her traps had revealed something useful about the intruder. Bruno thanked her, loaded Balzac into the Land Rover and was driving back, pondering the cyberattack, when his special phone gave its familiar vibration at his waist. He pulled over to the side of the road and answered, to hear the cheery voice of Colonel Morillon.

"Bonjour, Bruno. I was hoping that this interesting challenge of your phone being hacked might give me the excuse to come down and see you in the Périgord, but no such luck, I'm afraid," Morillon said. "We have narrowed your hacker down to two possible numbers, each of them new this week on your call log. One is a woman called Abby, and the other is calling from a phone linked to the *mairie* of St. Denis who signs herself as Cantagnac and also as Colette. What can you tell me about them?"

Bruno explained about the two women, and that the attack on Colette Cantagnac had targeted a woman of long service in the administration of Nouvelle-Aquitaine, currently attached to the *mairie* of St. Denis to manage the new policing reform. He had first made contact with each of them that week.

"Is Cantagnac her family name or a married name?"

"I don't know, but she calls herself mademoiselle, so I assumed she is unmarried. I could be wrong."

"And Abby?"

"Abby Howard, American born, on a year's sabbatical from her teaching job in the United States."

"I thought so. She's using a new French phone, sometimes uses it to check emails on an academic server in California. I suspect the attack is coming via her phone. If somebody is hacking her just so he can piggyback on her device she may know nothing about it."

"You might want to discuss this with the police tech team in Périgueux," Bruno replied, and went on to explain what he'd just been told of the attack on his police-issued laptop.

"Christ, an animated greeting card, the oldest trick in the

book," said Morillon. "The good news is that your phone was well protected, so you weren't compromised, but you should warn Abby that she needs to install a really good protection system against malware. Meanwhile, we're still checking on Colette Cantagnac."

"I can tell you that Colette's last job before being assigned here was to run the regional government's committee to create a new diversity policy, so she's a serious player in administrative circles. She's also one of the top people in the Syndic staff union, and last night she was the victim of an attempted mugging, apparently aimed at stealing her phone. You have two highly intelligent women, but neither one of them strikes me as particularly adept in the dark arts of the internet, although as you know I'm not remotely qualified to judge."

"It's not much of a problem, since neither attack succeeded in breaking into the police computer nor into General Lannes's network—at least not unless they were able to cover their tracks, which would mean the hackers are very much better at this than I thought. However, it's theoretically possible, given the skill the hacker is showing with the more arcane tools of the dark web. Do you know if either of the two women is involved in cryptocurrency?"

"You mean Bitcoin, that sort of thing? Not that I'm aware, but I don't know either of them that well. I can try to find out."

"Right, do what you can discreetly and leave it with me. We're treating it as a training exercise, but I'll keep you and Lannes informed. It's going to be useful for my team to learn from it."

"The police tech has set up a trap on my laptop to track who is targeting me and why. Her name is Gabrielle Teyssier and she seems pretty good. She talked about some updated version of CIA software called Hive."

"Really? Maybe she should be working for me. I'll check her out. Thanks, Bruno. We'll keep an eye on your phone. *Au'voir.*"

Bruno drove on, trying to remember how many calls he had made or received from the two women. Abby had texted him to confirm the Vieux Logis dinner at eight that evening. He couldn't remember any calls to or from Colette, except that just before lunch he'd forwarded to her a copy of the receipt he received for his laptop. He pulled in again and looked at the log on his phone, knowing that he was less than assiduous in checking his overnight text messages. He found one from the *mairie,* dated two days earlier, saying, "Alternative office space available," which must have come from Colette, since that was after he'd first met her. It was timed just after midnight, which was odd. The second was from Abby, again late at night, to thank him for the rugby practice. He shrugged. Morillon had access to all his phone history, so he'd know about each text. But it was odd that Colette had never mentioned that alternative office space again. He called her.

"Hi, Colette," he began when she answered. "I was just checking my messages and saw I hadn't replied to your note about an alternative office for me."

There was a silence. "I don't understand, Bruno. I didn't send you any message and certainly not one about office space."

"That's odd. It came from the *mairie,* timed just after midnight."

"I occasionally do overtime but never that late. Perhaps somebody was playing a joke on you."

"That must be it. Sorry to have bothered you."

Bruno ended the call and sat thinking without driving off. Balzac put a paw on his arm and gave him a quizzical look, so Bruno patted him and told him he was a good boy and watched his dog lie back down on the seat and curl up. Then he phoned Morillon and reported what he'd just heard.

"Does that mean the intruder hacked into the *mairie* switchboard and took it from there?" Bruno concluded.

"Could be," Morillon replied. "I'll get the team to dig into the switchboard log for activity after midnight, but it may take a while. A lot of internal stuff happens then, heating controls and routine backups. Thanks, Bruno, we'll check it out."

Back in St. Denis, Bruno parked in front of the gendarmerie and took Balzac on a stroll past the cemetery and along the road that led to the memorial, where the heap of flowers was at least twice the size it had been that morning. The tent still sported his tricolor but was otherwise untouched, perhaps because the young gendarme Montfaucon was standing in its shade. He came to attention and saluted as Bruno drew near.

"At ease, Montfaucon. I trust all is well."

"Yes, thank you, sir. Lots of visitors, the women laying flowers, the men just looking and lots of photos taken, selfies mostly. Two TV cameras and some reporters."

Bruno had spotted some distant figures moving through the trees on the far side of the bridge, on the grounds of the *domaine.* Curious, he moved closer, recognizing Birch, the Englishman with the interesting plans for the *domaine.* A woman and a child were with him. Bruno strolled across the bridge, calling out a greeting, and Balzac trotted ahead, going first to the child, a boy aged about six or seven. The dog stopped just short of the boy, his tail wagging appealingly, and the moment the child came to pat him Balzac gave his hand an affectionate lick and then rubbed his head against the boy's leg and a friendship was formed.

"Bonjour, Monsieur Birch," Bruno said. "My dog seems to have made a friend. Is this Madame Birch?"

She was a pretty woman with fine eyes and dark hair, a sweet smile and a cheerful look, as if happiness was her usual state.

"This is Bruno, the village policeman," Birch told his wife as she shook hands. "Bruno, meet my wife. Everyone calls her Krys."

"A pleasure, madame, and welcome to St. Denis," Bruno said in English, but she replied in much better French than most foreigners managed.

"The flowers at the memorial are very impressive," she said. "It was quite a surprise to learn that the grave was so important. I hope it won't upset our plans to buy this place and restore it to its former style."

"I don't think so, madame. In fact, the mayor is planning to enhance your surroundings with a small garden of remembrance to link the existing memorial to the grave we opened, which would be on your land. Did he mention that to you?"

"Not yet," said Birch. "What does he have in mind?"

Bruno explained the plan to compensate the Birch family with another adjoining tract of land of their choice, and Bruno saw Birch's thoughtful reaction, probably thinking that he would be in a favorable bargaining position. Bruno turned to look at the land beyond the bridge.

"I think the mayor said something about your plan to host weddings here," Bruno said. "That would probably mean erecting big tents so you would require some flat land and room for parking, access for caterers and so on."

"The ceremony would take place on the steps of the *domaine,* or at least that's where guests would want to take the formal photos," Birch explained. "If we erected marquees on that land across the stream, I'd have to replace that flimsy bridge. And we'd need to create a path to the marquee suitable for the bride and women guests to walk in high heels. Maybe I'd also have to build a bathroom block, since I can't see women in heels wanting to trek back to the bathrooms in the *domaine,* least of all after dark and a few drinks. And putting up a couple of Portaloos doesn't fit the image we want for this place."

"You could always use the tennis court for the marquee," said Bruno. "It's flat, and then your guests could use the bathrooms of the swimming pool, or that restaurant you mentioned."

"Then we'd need flat land across the stream for parking, and we'd still have to fix that bridge," said Madame Birch. "How much land would we have to give up for this garden of remembrance your mayor wants?"

"He will be your mayor, too, madame," said Bruno politely. "It's forty meters or more from the old memorial to the grave, and I'd imagine that a formal garden would have to be at least ten or so meters wide. You would be compensated with a similar amount of adjoining town land, and our local public works department should be able to help with the bridge. It's all to be negotiated, but the mayor likes your plans, and he always prefers a deal where everybody wins."

"It sounds like he's already committed to this garden of remembrance," Madame Birch went on coolly. "He'd certainly need our land for that. And I'm not sure that some fancy tomb is quite what we had in mind as a neighbor. This is supposed to be a happy place, vacations, parties and weddings."

Bruno smiled at her. "All the publicity and the garden of remembrance may well attract new bidders for the *domaine,* madame, although you know that the mayor and the judge in the bankruptcy court look favorably on your very attractive project, with the jobs and the tourist trade it would bring. And so, of course, do I, since I have the extra incentive that my dog has clearly found a new friend in your son."

Birch looked fondly down at the boy entwined with Balzac, laughed and said, "It promises to be an interesting negotiation."

"And tomorrow's event will certainly help your project with publicity," Bruno told him, before taking his leave, Balzac following reluctantly behind, glancing back as the boy waved goodbye to his new friend.

Chapter 20

Bruno drove home to change, wondering if he should dress formally for dinner. He knew ties and jackets were not required at the Vieux Logis, but he took a shower and decided to dress in a clean shirt, gray slacks and a dark blue blazer. He checked his watch, crossed to the bookshelf in his sitting room, pulled from the shelves the Henry Miller book he'd mentioned to Abby and copied a brief paragraph into his notebook. Then he went for a leisurely stroll along the ridge with Balzac to work up some appetite. He checked on his chickens before leaving Balzac on guard and heading to the restaurant for what he knew would be a splendid meal.

He pulled into the parking lot just as Horst and Clothilde were emerging from Horst's VW, and to Bruno's relief, Horst was also wearing an open-neck shirt. Clothilde looked magnificent, her red hair piled high and wearing an emerald-green dress. He recognized Abby's car, which was empty. Her guests were on time, but as hostess she had arrived early and was waiting for them at a table in the bar which bore a bottle of champagne in an ice bucket. She rose to welcome them with an embrace for Clothilde first, then Horst and finally Bruno. With his usual perfect timing,

Yves, the maître d', appeared to greet the guests by name and to open and pour the champagne.

"I'm so glad to see you all. I only just arrived, barely had time to look over the menu," Abby said, clinking glasses with her guests.

"I think you have good timing, Abby," Bruno said. "You arrive in St. Denis just in time for a moment of history that has put our town onto the front pages. Thank you for the flowers you laid at the grave, and you also, Clothilde," he went on, before turning to their German companion. "And Horst, my sympathies on those two young women we found."

Horst acknowledged the words with a slight bow, and Clothilde asked, "So what exactly happens tomorrow?"

Bruno explained about the short commemoration service to be held at the memorial after the diplomats arrived at eleven. He went on: "The mayor will then make a brief statement on the sadness of war and the blessings of the peaceful unity of Europe. Then the diplomats will lay flowers and go into the tent to view the remains. When they emerge, the schoolchildren will lay their flowers and then everyone can sign a book of condolence. The diplomats go to the *mairie* to see the plan for the garden of remembrance and to put in writing whether they want the bodies shipped home. After that they'll have lunch and be driven back to the fast train to Paris."

"Have you seen the mayor's statement?" Horst asked.

"Only in outline."

"He might want to add some phrase in German and another in Italian, to the effect that we all now live in peace in Europe. This will be going on German TV. I'll write something for you now, if you like."

"Good idea," said Clothilde. "And maybe Horst should be invited to the lunch at the *mairie.*"

"You are both already on the list," Bruno said. "Sorry this is all coming together so late, but we've been scrambling. Diplomacy is not my thing, but thank you for the good advice."

"I think your diplomatic skills are coming along pretty well," said Abby.

"Since you are the resident American, Abby, perhaps you should attend the lunch as well," said Horst.

"That's a great idea," said Bruno. "Jack Crimson is coming, so the Brits will be included, too."

"No Russians available?" asked Clothilde.

"Not that I know of, and no Canadians, who were also part of D-Day," said Bruno.

"As my first diplomatic statement," said Abby, "I think we should reorder our priorities and consider what we're going to eat. I suggest we order their *balade,* the recommended menu of the season, but if it looks like too much to eat, we could cancel the fish course. And Bruno, I've been told of your expertise on the local wines, so perhaps you would make a selection. What do you think of a bottle of white and another of red?"

Bruno chose a Cuvée Mirabelle white wine from Château de la Jaubertie and a 2018 Pécharmant red from Château de Tiregand, a splendid year when his friend François-Xavier was still in charge of the vineyard.

The waiters entered with a tray of complimentary amuse-bouches: a small croquette of minced duck, a tiny roll of smoked salmon on a skewer, smeared on the inside with honey mustard; and a bite-size baby pizza. Yves came to refill the champagne glasses and to describe the *balade* menu. They agreed to cancel the fish course, which left them with a duet of goose and duck foie gras, a soup of chanterelle mushrooms, roast lamb with apricots and a small pilaf, salad, the cheese board and a gooseberry pudding with meringue.

"This will be a feast to remember," said Bruno as a young waiter approached with an assortment of different rolls, white and whole wheat as well as yellow corn bread. "By the way, Abby. I looked up the full version of Henry Miller's remarks about this region, which were penned right here in this courtyard." He handed her the note he had made, adding, "You read it, your American accent is just right."

" 'I believe that this great peaceful region of France will always be a sacred spot for man and that when the cities have killed off the poets this will be the refuge and the cradle of the poets to come,' " she read. She looked up, smiled at her companions and then went on, " 'This visit to the Dordogne was for me, I repeat, of paramount importance: I still have hope for the future of the species and even our planet. It may be that one day, France ceases to exist, but the Dordogne will live on, just like the dreams that fuel the human soul.' "

She looked up. "Thank you, Bruno. I will treasure this. Funny, but I made a note for you today, something I came across in one of the letters Thomas Jefferson wrote while in this region. It was to Lafayette, the general revered by Americans for his help in winning our independence, and he and Jefferson had discussed—this was the late 1780s before the fall of the Bastille—whether France was in a prerevolutionary situation. And Jefferson wrote that Lafayette should research the living conditions of the people."

She took a notebook from her purse and read, " 'You must ferret the people out of their hovels . . . look into their kettles, eat their bread, loll on their beds under pretense of resting yourself, but in fact to find if they are soft. You will feel a sublime pleasure in the course of this investigation, and a sublimer one hereafter when you shall be able to apply your knowledge to the softening of their beds, or the throwing a morsel of meat into the kettle of vegetables.' "

Into the silence that followed, Horst dropped a lame joke about the kettles of their restaurant being well supplied with every variety of food, and Clothilde hurried to his rescue.

"Vincent is a great chef, classic but inventive," she said. "That dish of his on the menu tonight, lamb with apricots, reminds me of a meal we had in Isfahan, Horst, during that conference we attended on the archaeology of the Zoroastrians."

"I recall only having eyes for you that evening, Clothilde," Horst replied, as their first course came, the foie gras accompanied by a glass of chilled Monbazillac.

"That was long before we were married, Abby," said Clothilde. "Talking of marriage, I only met Gary twice, each time briefly, and I never understood why you married him, but I'm glad for you that it's over."

Abby looked down at her plate and then up at Bruno before switching her gaze to Clothilde.

"It was not a good marriage, but I tried to make it work," she said, toying with a fork. "We both did. He hated my being away on archaeological digs, which was what my job involved. After the novelty wore off, he disliked the discomfort on the few times I persuaded him to join me."

She looked up at Clothilde and Horst, grinned and said, "I guess that's why you two each ended up with another tent freak."

Clothilde reached across to take Horst's hand and winked at Bruno. "Sex in tents is intense sex—the secret charm of archaeology," she said as Horst raised her hand to his lips. "There's nothing quite like it."

"Yeah, but maybe I should have picked a real digger rather than Gary," Abby replied. "He liked archaeology but hated the digs, liked writing the reports but never wanted to get his hands dirty."

"I thought you met Gary at a dig," Clothilde said as their plates were cleared for the next course.

"He was the archivist at the Black Mountain petroglyph site in the Mojave Desert where I was working," Abby replied, and glanced at Bruno. "That's rock art to you, Bruno. Gary was a real computer nerd, very good at digitizing and classifying the images. But it was so hot that it would have turned most people off archaeology for life."

"I remember that report, he did a great job," said Clothilde as the soup course was served. Bruno mentally tucked away the information that Abby's ex-husband was a computer nerd and therefore possibly capable of the hacking attack.

"To be fair, I equally disliked the big tech fairs Gary loved to attend," Abby said. "They usually took place in cities I didn't much want to visit, like LA, Las Vegas, Atlanta and—heaven help me—the Baltimore convention center. I tried, and almost enjoyed the web summit in Lisbon, but Helsinki in the dead of winter for the Slush conference was grim. So, I went off to my digs and he went to his conventions and we met for breakfast and evenings in my teaching time, and then he got the blockchain bug and started working through the night."

"Blockchain?" Bruno asked, recalling something that Morillon had said. "Is that the computer currency?"

Abby nodded. "Gary was an early adopter, mainly out of curiosity at first, but he became serious after Bitcoin fell from over eleven hundred dollars to less than four hundred in 2014. He began buying, and as Bitcoin revived, he made a lot of money, enough that we were able to purchase a small house in San Francisco—and small in that city starts at a million bucks. I was teaching at Berkeley, and soon Gary was making enough cash to give up his day job and began getting into other cryptocurrencies. He made some big bets after the Korean crash of 2018 that triggered all those suicides. Then suddenly, it began to be respectable. Central banks started studying the prospect of a digital dollar or yuan or euro. Lots of new investors got into the game, and suddenly Gary was worth tens of millions, more than fifty million, at least on paper. He bought himself a fancy mansion in Pacific Heights. And then he began going seriously crazy and I filed for divorce."

"Crazy in what way?" Clothilde asked.

"He became a hermit, sitting all day and half the night in a room with his banks of computers," Abby said, with a grimace of distaste. "He almost never bathed, hardly ever slept, just dozed in his chair in front of his screens and lived on peanut-butter-and-banana sandwiches. And sodas. He didn't contest the divorce. I got the little house and two million bucks. He kept the mansion and the tens of millions and I was happy to be asked to join the team studying the Ancestral Pueblo cultures of the Southwest. We were trying to nail down the theory that climate change triggered their decline."

"We read your paper on their Great Drought," said Horst as the plates were cleared. "Impressive work."

"And what happened to Gary?" asked Clothilde.

"The first crash—Luna went from one hundred twenty dollars to less than ten cents. Something like forty billion dollars evaporated, and that wiped Gary out. He lost his mansion, his millions, his computers, pretty much everything. At least, that's what he claimed when he tried to get back some of my divorce settlement. That was when he came to my doorstep, asking for two million to help him start again."

She paused, sipped at her wine appreciatively.

"So what did you say?" Clothilde asked.

Abby again raised the wineglass to her lips.

"Abby," said Clothilde. "You're keeping me in suspense. What did you tell him?"

"I said no and closed the door."

"And then?" Clothilde demanded.

"He tried to kick my door down and then began to trash my

car that was parked in the driveway. I called the cops first, and then my lawyer to get a restraining order to forbid him from coming near me ever again. He was arrested and held in jail overnight because he looked like a hobo and was carrying no ID. That was when I called you, Clothilde, and took the sabbatical year the college owed me. I rented out my house for a year, booked my flight to Bordeaux via Paris, boarded the plane, and hello, Périgord, here I come."

Clothilde, Horst and Bruno looked at her, stunned into silence by this blithe and casual revelation of fortunes worth tens of millions made and lost by a half-mad recluse with poor hygiene and a worse diet; of Abby's homeland abandoned and connections severed.

Bruno put together in his head the hack of his phone, Morillon's reference to cryptocurrency and Abby's nervous tension since he had first met her.

"Is it possible that he is still trying to contact you?" Bruno asked. "Does he know you're no longer in America?"

"That wouldn't be difficult," Abby replied. "I told you he was a computer nerd when I first met him. My sabbatical has been posted on the university website, and he probably has ways to see my emails and social media posts, although I tried to block him. Why do you ask?"

"Because the Police Nationale warned me today that somebody was trying to hack into their computer through my email," he said. "The attack failed because as a cop I have strong security systems. But did you by any chance send me an animated greeting card to thank me for my help in finding you the house to rent?"

"No, I sent just an email of thanks," Abby said, putting down her knife and fork with a clang that had other diners turning to look at their table. "Why, Bruno?"

Bruno lowered his voice. "The card seemed to come from you. It contained a sophisticated little mole that tried to burrow into the police computer via my official laptop, but it was caught by the police computer experts."

"Does that mean my computer is compromised?"

"Yes, and almost certainly your smartphone, too."

"Where did this attack come from, France or the United States?"

"From your American university email, the one that ends in edu-dot-com, but I think your husband might have followed you here."

"Surely if he came to France the police can check that from passport records," said Clothilde.

"He could have landed anywhere else in Europe and then come to France without being checked," said Horst. "And I don't think the European system is sufficiently advanced to check the passport records of all twenty-seven countries."

"Worse than that," said Abby. "He might have used his Italian passport. His father was born in Italy and came to the States as a baby, so Gary was able to get Italian citizenship."

"What's his full name and place and date of birth?" Bruno asked, taking out his notebook.

"Giuseppe Garibaldi Barone, born July 19, 1983. That's why he was known as Gary in the States, from his dad giving him that middle name." Abby swallowed hard and blinked, as if fighting back tears as Bruno scribbled down the details. "Does that mean he's tracking me here?"

"Very possibly," said Bruno. "If you give me your phone, I can get it checked. You'd better turn off your laptop when you get home. He may already have its location, but I can get it cleaned. You might want to buy a cheap phone for local use."

"*Mon Dieu,* Bruno," said Clothilde. "You've got me worried."

"I'm worried, too," he said. "In the meantime, Abby, we ought to think seriously about your security. Do you have a copy of that restraining order against him that you got in the States? I can try to get you something similar for France. Did that American court order say anything about his using violence?"

"Apart from trying to break down my door and trash my car? Yes, when I told him I was leaving and wanted a divorce, he threw a pot of hot coffee at me, and then he hit me and kicked me when I was down. I got up and hit him back, kicked him in the balls and left. I'd already packed, so I went straight to my doctor's, still soaking wet with coffee, and got a medical report with photos of my bruises. Then I went to the police to swear out a complaint and then called my lawyer. That was part of the evidence we presented for the divorce, but we used it again for the restraining order. And to think I went easy on the bastard. Under California law I could have demanded fifty percent of everything he had."

"You'd better come back and stay with us again," said Clothilde. "But he may already have that address. Could she stay with you, Bruno?"

"Of course, but for obvious reasons it might be better if you came, too, Clothilde, as a chaperone. Or if you prefer to stay where you are, Abby, I could move in with Gilles and Fabiola to be on hand, just in case."

"Just a minute, all of you," said Abby, firmly. "I'm not frightened of him, not physically. I have strong bolts on my doors and windows. I admit that I am worried about his internet skills, sabotaging my plan to set up as a guide, making trouble for me here in France and so on. I will take the precautions Bruno suggests, and maybe I should talk to a French lawyer, see if I can get the equivalent of a restraining order against him."

"Leave that with me," Bruno said. "We have a good friend, Annette, a magistrate at Sarlat. We'll see what she can do. And the FBI man at your embassy in Paris is a reliable friend. I'll talk to him. If the techs can trace this online attack on a police computer to your ex-husband, we may have cause to arrest him. Do you know if he has any French friends or contacts or speaks the language?"

"No to both. He speaks Italian but not French, and I know of no French friends."

"Right," said Bruno. "We know the problem, we have a plan, we have friends, so let's enjoy this dinner. In the meantime, please send me any good photos you have of your ex-husband that might help us recognize him."

"Doing it now," said Abby. Clothilde added that she still had some of the wedding photos on her phone and began looking them up.

"And now, on with the feast," said Bruno.

Chapter 21

Showered and shaved, his horse exercised and Balzac happy to be left with Hector in the stables, Bruno arrived at the *mairie* in full-dress uniform shortly before nine the next morning, having already informed Morillon and General Lannes of the strong possibility that Abby Howard's ex-husband was behind the attempt to break into his phone and office computer. He had forwarded to them the photos and passport numbers Abby had sent him of her ex-husband. He also emailed the details to Annette, the magistrate based in Sarlat. She was a good friend, and he knew she would be sympathetic to Abby's problem. He asked her to check whether the restraining order in the United States had any legal force in France. Then he called his friend Hodge, legal attaché at the U.S. Embassy in Paris, who was also an official in the FBI. Bruno had worked with him on two previous cases, trusted him completely and knew him to be an early riser. After their usual greetings, Bruno asked if Hodge knew whether an American restraining order on a possibly violent ex-husband would have any legal standing in France.

"It would almost certainly have been a ruling by a state judge, and that might not have much impact in the other forty-nine states, let alone abroad," Hodge told him. "Which state was it?"

"California," Bruno said. He explained Abby's divorce and her husband's rise to riches, his obsession with crypto and his sudden fall.

"Give me a name and some details, and I can check it out," Hodge said, and Bruno gave Abby's name, her university, her useful possession of an Irish as well as an American passport and what little he knew of her ex-husband, including the Italian passport and his computer skills that he'd applied to enhance the rock art in the California desert. He also sent Hodge Abby's photos.

"One more thing. Somebody tried to break into our police computer in Périgueux through my office laptop and also into my special phone from General Lannes. Our cyber experts say it is someone using the dark web who seems familiar with its secretive cryptocurrency systems. So if it is Abby's ex-husband, and we find him on French soil, he's in serious trouble."

"So, you're offering me a chance to do a favor for General Lannes while helping you persecute an American-born citizen," Hodge said in his laconic way. Bruno smiled. He had a mental image of Hodge as a lanky, slow-talking character in an old Western film, a cowboy wearing a white hat. During one case when Bruno had called in the baron to help him, Hodge had referred to the baron as Bruno's deputy, much to the delight of the old man for whom the Western was still the greatest film genre of all.

"If you want to see it as winning favor with one of the most powerful men in France, it could be useful all around. And given the Italian passport you can hardly call Gary a hundred percent American. If this turns into a penetration attempt on police computers, it could be so serious that it might even give us the pleasure of your company down here in the Périgord again."

"Leave it with me, Bruno, you silver-tongued devil, you," Hodge said with that lazy laugh of his, and hung up.

Bruno parked his police van and picked his way between the puddles left by the overnight rain. The sky looked clear, as if the rain might hold off long enough for the morning ceremony. He stepped across to the parapet overlooking the river and saw the water now lapping across the quayside. That was unusual, although he recalled that the high-water mark at the town gate in Limeuil was for November 1944, and it was almost November now. The skies overhead were clear, but there were dark clouds far to the west. He shrugged and entered the *mairie* to find everyone, including the mayor, wearing their Sunday best. The long table in the council chamber was set for twenty, to seat the three diplomats, the prefect, the mayor of Castillonnès, assorted town councilors including Brosseil, the elders of the Marty family, Commandant Yveline, Monsieur and Madame Birch, the judge of the bankruptcy court, the regional bank manager who was expected to offer a donation to help finance the garden of remembrance and not forgetting Bruno and the mayor—and after a discreet chat with the mayor about the usefulness of Clothilde, Horst and Jack Crimson in providing him with German and English phrases to insert in his official speech at the grave site, four more places were squeezed in.

"Perhaps we should ask Father Sentout, who spent time at the Vatican, if he could provide a similar phrase in Italian," Bruno suggested. "The American archaeologist, Abby Howard, could serve as another representative of the wartime alliance, which would take us to twenty-three, and there's bound to be someone we've forgotten."

The mayor agreed and Bruno set off for the church, and heard the choir practicing as he approached, wondering who would sing the soprano solo with Florence visiting her parents. As he opened the side door he saw, to his great surprise, that her place had been taken by Flavie, the lead singer of Les Troubadours, the local group that specialized in medieval music. Her sweet clear voice suddenly soared above the chorus to proclaim her belief in one, single God. He stood, transfixed and enchanted by Bach's music and the miraculous transformation of the very ordinary farmers and shop assistants, boatmen and bank clerks, into a magnificent instrument of voice.

The others of Flavie's group were also there. Vincent stood below the choir, playing the rebec, which looked like a very narrow fiddle, and his partner Dominic was playing the gemshorn, a medieval flute, while Arnaut kept time with the tabla, a doubled-ended drum. Beside them Maurice the church organist was playing a harmonium, his legs pumping to drive air into the miniature but portable organ.

Father Sentout's readiness to bring anything into his church in the name of music was one of the many reasons that explained Bruno's affection for the priest. This was daring even by his standards, and yet the result was splendid. As the last chord faded, Bruno applauded with enthusiasm and went up to greet his friends.

"My congratulations, Father," he said, embracing the little priest, and then exchanged *bises* with Flavie, exclaiming his pleasure at her presence. Then he asked Father Sentout if he could write some words in Italian for the mayor's speech, and showed him the phrase Horst had put into German. The priest swiftly wrote an Italian version in capital letters in Bruno's notebook, *Ora che siamo tutti amici e partner in Europa, è giusto e doveroso ricordare tutti i morti di quest'ultima, spaventosa guerra.*

He left them to their rehearsal, returned to the *mairie* to give the mayor Father Sentout's Italian phrase and handed him the German one that Horst had written for him the previous evening—*Jetzt, da wir alle Freunde und Partner in Europa sind, ist es richtig und angebracht, der Toten dieses letzten schrecklichen Krieges zu gedenken.*

Bruno then asked if Les Troubadours might be added to the lunch table but was told that twenty-four was the maximum, so there was but one seat spare. And the mayor had already filled it by inviting the owner of the town funeral parlor who was providing the hearses that would take the remains of the two German women to Bergerac airport, to be loaded onto a German air force transport plane. The table was nearly full.

"They should be there, I agree, but there's no room," the mayor said. "Why not invite them all to dinner at your house tonight, and I'll come along with Jacqueline? The town can pay for the food and provide the wine. And invite that singer-magistrate friend of yours, Amélie. She is coming down by train with Jacqueline from Paris to join us."

Four Troubadours, the mayor and Jacqueline, himself and Amélie would make eight, and he could invite the baron and Colette to make ten, Bruno thought. That was as many as his dining table could handle. His brain clicked into menu mode. It would have to be simple, since he'd have little time to prepare. Foie gras to begin, or perhaps a light soup of young pumpkins from his garden. And then because these autumn nights could turn cool, he'd offer a hearty dish, maybe *boeuf bourguignon* with *pommes de terre sarladaises,* some cheeses, and he could get a couple of fruit pies from the Moulin.

"Good idea," he said. "Should I get some foie gras and a bottle of Monbazillac?"

"The town is not made of money," the mayor replied, giving Bruno a look that combined reproof and reproach with the faintest touch of guilt.

Because of that hint of the mayoral conscience, Bruno held back the obvious retort, that the mayor's catered lunch for twenty-four with wine was likely to cost the town at least a thousand euros. Instead he said, almost innocently, "Anyway, I suppose we're already having foie gras at lunch."

"Diplomats, the prefect, other mayors," the mayor replied vaguely. "They all expect it in the Périgord. And I persuaded Jules Polidor to join us, from the bank's main board."

"Of course, you were *énarques* together," said Bruno, recalling that the mayor had built his career, like all graduates of the elite École Nationale d'Administration, on those old classmates who could call one another *tu* forever after.

"Think of it as an investment, Bruno. We have to finance this garden of remembrance somehow."

"The diplomats should be with us by eleven. Will they go straight to the site for the ceremony?"

"Oh no, that would never do, Bruno. For diplomats, you're expected to provide access to a toilet every two hours or so. They'll come here first, and Mademoiselle Cantagnac is taking care of the restrooms, arranging flowers and setting out little soaps, fresh towels, that sort of feminine touch."

"I hope she's providing soft toilet paper," said Bruno, a little hesitantly. The mayor would happily admit that the town's usual offering was obviously a close cousin of sandpaper, but always added that he could lose the next election if the voters learned that he was spending their money on such personal luxuries. Bruno wondered how best to justify his suggestion. "I think the voters would agree that we should offer a generous welcome to our diplomatic guests."

"Good thinking, Bruno, and quite right. It's a matter of civic pride. But I don't think she'll need reminding. Perhaps you might have a word before you head off to make sure that all is in order at the site. Expect us at about eleven-fifteen."

Bruno made a quick trip to the bathroom, and his eyes widened as he noticed that the mirrors were sparkling, the taps polished and pots of flowers placed behind each sink. And this was in the men's lavatory. He knocked on the door of the ladies'. There was no reply, so he peeked in to find the white walls had been repainted in pale blue; the rubberized floor was now carpeted and the white plastic seats of the toilets had been replaced with solid mahogany. The light was somehow softer, and he saw that the old bare bulbs had been changed for pink ones, discreetly encased within spheres of parchment.

"Admiring my work?" came a familiar and slightly amused voice from behind him.

"I'm reminded, Colette, of the Emperor Augustus, who is said to have found Rome made of brick and transformed it into marble."

"You are very kind, Bruno, but I've barely begun," she replied.

"So, we poor males can also expect one day to find carpets in our bathroom?"

"No, or at least not until your masculine hygiene, or perhaps your aim, improves."

Game, set and match, Bruno thought, nodding and smiling in appreciation and retiring swiftly to the refuge of the gendarmerie, to find Sergeant Jules in a brand-new uniform.

"Have you seen the grave site yet?" Jules asked. "You can't move for flowers and it's all roped off, crowds are gathering already, and there's a big panel with an artist's impression of how the garden of remembrance will look. It means a lot more work for the town gardeners. That reminds me, have you been told about the firing squad?"

Bruno gaped at him. "The what?"

"Like a guard of honor. Alphonse Marty arranged it with the mayor. Six members from the hunting club will fire a salute over the grave after the mayor's speech, and then the bugler will play the 'Sonnerie aux Morts,' then the minute of silence followed by the bugler playing the German version, 'Ich hatt' einen Kameraden.' The poor devil has been practicing all night."

"Is that it?" Bruno asked.

"Not nearly." Jules sighed. "The mayor and the German and Italian diplomats are supposed to lay their wreaths. Then either the hunters or we gendarmes carry the coffins to the hearses, and they drive off to the airport, and the grandees all stroll off to lunch. We practiced it last night, with Mademoiselle Cantagnac presiding like a sergeant major."

"This guard of honor, I presume they'll be firing blanks, but the question is where do they aim?" Bruno asked. "It must be somewhere where the hot wads don't fall onto the crowd. Have they thought this through?"

Jules shrugged. "You'd better have a word with Alphonse, but he usually knows what he's doing."

"Is Yveline in her office?" Bruno asked.

"No, she's out on the site somewhere."

Bruno found her in the tent that carried his crude tricolor, where the body bags rested on a trestle table. Two coffins, one large and the other standard size, stood ready to be filled once the diplomats had seen the skeletons.

"I can't find the tin that's supposed to hold their identity papers and badges," she said. "Do you have it?"

Bruno shook his head. "It was supposed to be kept in the mayor's office. I'd better check."

He called the mayor but only got a recorded message. He called Colette Cantagnac and got the same result. He then called Roberte, who ran the social security office, and asked her to have the mayor to call him back urgently. Bruno checked his watch. It was almost ten. The diplomats should have arrived at Libourne by now and would be on their way by car. Bruno excused himself to Yveline and began walking quickly back to the *mairie*.

He found the place in chaos, the mayor ransacking his own office, his secretary looking under desks and Colette searching the storage room, since the essential cookie tin had disappeared.

"I'm sure I brought it back here," said the mayor.

"I remember that you left with me to fend off Monsieur Birch at the bridge, and we left the tin there at the grave with Brosseil and Michel," Bruno said, already punching in Michel's number at the works office. No reply. He then tried Brosseil, but the notary said he recalled Michel taking it.

Bruno informed the mayor and asked him to keep trying Michel while he walked swiftly to the public works office near the cemetery. Or rather, he dodged in and out of what seemed like the entire population of the retirement home walking very slowly or rolling their wheelchairs and blocking the pavements. Fending off endless greetings and proffered handshakes, he arrived at Michel's office at 10:20.

Michel was not there, nor were any of the public works staff except for the trainee who had left school that summer and was still finding his way around the place. There was no sign of the tin in Michel's office nor anywhere else. The trainee said that he thought Michel had gone to the grave site to check that the ropes were doing their job of managing the crowds.

At 10:30, a very worried Bruno found himself blocked by half the population of St. Denis and hundreds more from nearby towns and villages, many of them demanding that he sort out their parking problems. The diplomats were due at 10:45, but only if their car could navigate the road that was half blocked by lines of parked cars on both sides, reducing the traffic flow to one way and filling the air with the sound of angry car horns.

Chapter 22

This is your own damn fault, Bruno, he told himself. He had left the traffic management to the gendarmes, but most of them were tied up managing the crowds and preparing for their part in the parade. Finally, at 10:50 he found Michel, standing by the grave itself and scratching his head.

"Where the hell is the biscuit tin with their papers?" Bruno asked breathlessly.

"We left it in the grave before we closed it up again," Michel replied. "It should still be there."

Bruno stared at the solid concrete block at his feet that protected the grave. The last time it had taken the mechanical digger to lift it and that machine would never get through the crowds. And Bruno's shoulder was far from healed.

"We need all the men we can get," he said, and as he spoke he saw Alphonse Marty and the men from the hunting club, shotguns over their shoulders, pushing their way through the crowd from the direction of the cemetery while the choir and Les Troubadours and Father Sentout were crossing the bridge from the Domaine de la Barde.

With the hunters, musicians and the choir, Bruno finally managed to get eight men plus Michel and Monsieur Birch to start heaving at the concrete lid with muscle power alone.

"One, two, three—lift," he cried, and the lid inched upward until it toppled back, rainwater sluicing over their shoes, leaving the grave open to reveal the still wrapped skeleton of the dog.

"I left it under the dog," said Michel. He lay flat on the ground and reached his arm in to push aside the bag of dog bones to reveal the missing tin. Between them, Bruno, Michel and Alphonse managed to haul it out. Bruno opened it and gave a sigh of relief when he saw the papers, badges and paybooks inside. He shook hands all around, asked Michel to help the gendarmes with crowd control, and took the tin to the tent, where he phoned the mayor with the good news.

"I just had a call from the prefect," the mayor said. "She says they can't get through the traffic jam. Can you clear their way, Bruno?"

Once again Bruno summoned what gendarmes he could find and Alphonse's band of hunters and organized them to block the roads from Campagne and Le Buisson, leaving a clear single lane for the cars coming from the road to Périgueux. At 11:10, with the choir and musicians in place, Bruno spotted the prefect's black limousine, which contained the diplomats, followed by a large Peugeot carrying Prunier, police chief of the *département,* its blue lights flashing and escorted by two police motorcyclists.

He called the mayor, suggested that they were now running so late that they had better cancel the trip to the *mairie* for a toilet break and that he should leave at once for the grave. Bruno then steered the official cars into the Domaine de la Barde. As the prefect and the diplomats clambered out of their vehicles, he greeted them, apologized for the extraordinary number of cars and people coming to pay their respects and led the party across the bridge to the tent. Luckily, the mayor arrived at the same time.

But after that inauspicious beginning, the ceremony unfolded as precisely as clockwork. The mayor made a short speech of welcome, included the phrases in German and Italian, and the microphone and speakers for once worked perfectly and carried his words to a crowd that Bruno estimated at more than two thousand people. Then Father Sentout stepped up to the microphone and announced a short Bible reading in honor of the dead.

"Jesus said, 'I am the resurrection and the life. The one who believes in me will live, even though they die; and whoever lives by believing in me will never die.'

"'And so will it be with the resurrection of the dead. For our light and momentary troubles are achieving for us an eternal glory that far outweighs them all. So we fix our eyes not on what is seen, but on what is unseen, since what is seen is temporary, but what is unseen is eternal.'"

Father Sentout ended the reading, crossed himself and said, "These are the words of our Lord."

Flavie, the choir, the harmonium and the medieval musicians performed Bach's *credo* magnificently, and the priest led the crowd in the Lord's Prayer. Then he backed away from the microphone, and the first pure note of the "Sonnerie aux Morts" rang out from the bugler, standing by the monument to the dead Resistance man. He ended the French army's traditional music for those who died in battle, waited for perhaps ten seconds and launched into the German equivalent.

"We will now observe a minute of silence for our common dead and for all—British, Americans, Canadians, Poles and Russians—who fought and died in what we hope will be Europe's final war," said the mayor. The silence stretched out endlessly, broken only by the sound of weeping, until Alphonse, standing with his hunters by the grave, called out, *"Chasseurs, une fusillade d'honneur aux morts."*

And one by one, the six hunters fired their weapons, with what seemed a perfect five seconds between each shot.

As the echoes of gunfire died away, the German, Italian and French diplomats, escorted by the mayor, each walked to the Resistance memorial and laid a wreath. Then the German, a tall woman in a black suit and wearing a black hat with a veil, lifted the veil to dab at her eyes with a handkerchief before returning to the platform from which Father Sentout had read the lesson. She looked at the enormous crowd, smiling in admiration at the turnout, and then gave a mercifully short speech. She spoke excellent French and thanked the people of St. Denis for their flowers, their kindness and their moving act of respect for the dead.

"There can be no clearer sign of our common European destiny than this, that we mourn together our dead from the tragic times of the past, while we all look ahead together to a lasting peace in this new Europe that we are building together," she ended, to respectful applause.

The Italian diplomat, a young military attaché dressed in what looked like a naval uniform, simply thanked St. Denis for their welcome and their kindness, adding that he and all Italians were honored and proud to leave their lost naval officer to his eternal rest in France. He sat down to applause all the more appreciative for his brevity.

The prefect said only that the government of France joined the representatives of Germany and Italy in thanking St. Denis for this moving tribute and that she was proud that so many people in the department of the Dordogne had gathered to pay their respects in this splendid ceremony with such excellent music. And in the name of the florists of the region, she wanted to thank all those who had contributed to the most impressive display of flowers she had ever seen. This won her the most appreciative applause of all.

The mayor then presented the documents and badges of the

dead to the Italian and the German diplomats. He led them into the tent to view the remains in the coffins and to observe the closure of the lids before the hunters carried each coffin to the waiting hearses. Finally, the mayor led the whole party to inspect the heaps of flowers laid around the monument and for nearly fifty meters along the roadside. The ceremony over, Bruno suggested to the mayor that he and his guests should walk to the *mairie* for lunch because the traffic was still crawling at a snail's pace.

They reached the square in front of the Hôtel de Ville. At that point three figures moved into the square and took position in front of the *mairie,* all wearing black boots, jackets, trousers and gloves. Their faces were concealed by that ever-popular mask of a dark-haired and roguish man with a thin mustache, goatee and a sardonic grin. Their heads were covered by wigs of long dark hair designed to match the mask.

The first of them was holding a small poster, long enough to cover his, or perhaps her, body from chin to knees, that read ET LES 6 MILLION JUIFS?

The next demonstrator's poster carried the old election slogan of the Communist Party, which liked to claim they had been the real Resistance, with the slaughtered prisoners and hostages to prove it. ET LES 40,000 FUSILLÉS?

The third's poster read ET LA FRANCE MARTYRE?

With TV cameras upon the mayor and journalists holding small recorders to catch his every word, Bruno watched him walk calmly toward the three masked people and say to the first, "If you are really interested in the six million Jewish lives extinguished by Nazism, I suggest you visit the town museum where you'll find an entire room dedicated to the dozens of Jewish children saved by the people of this region. The children were hidden in the surrounding farms, where people brought them up as their own. They were also taught by trusted teachers using remote barns for schoolrooms."

To the next two, he said, "Thanks to the Resistance and to our allies, we in France once again live in a democracy. And so today do all the other countries of Europe up to the Russian frontier, including the old enemies, Italy and Germany, now our friends. That democracy includes the right of free speech and free assembly, which you are taking advantage of today. It also means taking responsibility for what you say, rather than skulking behind the anonymity of your masks. And instead of saying what you mean, you hide behind the apparent innocence of those rhetorical questions on your posters.

"So, while I disagree with your meaning, I accept and defend your right to protest. I support even your right to make dumb fools of yourselves in this way and to make a mockery of the essential human rights brave men and women died to win and to defend. Perhaps you wished to embarrass this town before its honored guests? You have failed. All you have is my scorn and my contempt."

The German diplomat was the first to break into applause, swiftly followed by Bruno and all the rest of the luncheon guests and the crowds that had followed them. The mayor opened the main door and bowed his guests into a *mairie* that had never been so proudly his.

Chapter 23

Bruno strolled discreetly around the back of the *mairie* to approach the protesters from the rear. The one in the middle was somewhat shorter than the others and with more pronounced hips; probably a woman. A splash of distinctive red paint on the left shoe of this figure caught his eye, since the color was like that of the swastika daubed on the tent. Having transformed it laboriously into a tricolor, Bruno now instantly recognized the particular shade of crimson. He slipped his phone from his pocket and advanced toward this shorter figure, took a picture of the shoe and murmured into her ear, "Madame Montsouris, does your husband know you've taken up drawing swastikas?"

Startled, the woman before him dropped the placard, bent to retrieve it and straightened up. Then in a harsh, female voice, she snarled at him, *"Vas te faire foutre, Bruno."* And that crude expression of what he should do with himself was all the confirmation Bruno needed.

Madame Montsouris was far more radical and militant than her easygoing husband, who was the only member of the Communist Party with a seat on the St. Denis council. Not that he took his politics too seriously; his membership was more an homage to the memory of his father and to the proud history of the *cheminots,* the traditionally Communist union of railway workers. Bruno was fond of Montsouris, less so of his wife, and had never been able to keep track of her changing allegiances between the endlessly shifting *groupuscules* of the French far left—its Trotsky- ites, militant anarchists and these days extreme Greens.

Shaking hands endlessly and murmuring polite greetings and small talk, Bruno joined those trudging up the stairs to the receiv- ing line of the prefect, mayor and diplomats. With a discreet skill born of experience he sidled past them and went around to the rear door, emerging behind the bar to take a glass of a sparkling wine enlivened with a splash of crème de cassis.

Bruno glanced across and saw Abby chatting to Horst and the Italian naval officer, and again Bruno noticed Abby's habit of glancing nervously to the left and right as if on watch for some kind of danger. But this time it lasted so briefly he could have been mistaken, and she was clearly listening with interest to whatever the Italian was saying. He was a good-looking man, as tall as Bruno but slimmer and flattered by a far more elegant uniform than Bruno had ever owned. None of them had a drink, so Bruno collected and filled some glasses, offered them drinks and thanked the Italian for his speech.

"As so often in diplomacy, it was most remarkable for the things I did not say," the Italian replied. "An Italian war hero who continued to work with the Germans after Italy had changed sides is a delicate subject, particularly now that we are getting a new prime minister who makes no secret of her admiration for Benito Mussolini."

"Really?" Bruno asked. "I'm afraid I don't know much about Italian politics."

"That's all right, I'm used to hearing that, but Giorgia Meloni, who is widely expected to become our next premier, is more inter- esting than you might think. Her real hero is not Mussolini but Gandalf, the wizard in *Lord of the Rings.* She used to dress up as a Hobbit, and I've heard her suggest that Tolkien explains everything that conservative nationalists like her believe in."

Abby laughed out loud, and Horst and Bruno joined in, while others in the crowd glanced at them reprovingly, as if merriment was hardly fitting for such an event, until the German diplomat joined them to ask what was so amusing. The Italian, who evidently knew her from the diplomatic circuit, explained, and she allowed herself a modest chuckle as the Italian introduced her to the others. "Please call me Erika," she announced, and they were all still chatting when Colette and Roberte began circulating with trays of drinks.

"Do you know anything about the dead Italian officer?" Bruno asked the attaché. "He was carrying the papers of Captain Salvatore Todaro. But thanks to Abby we've learned that Todaro died nearly two years earlier. He was a *capitano di fregata* and commanded a submarine called *Comandante Cappellini,* which apparently sank five Allied ships in the Atlantic."

"Thanks to Abby?" the Italian repeated. He raised his glass to Abby and said, "Your research skills are as striking as your beauty, mademoiselle." Then he turned to Bruno. "I think you'll find Todaro did rather more than that. You might also be interested to know that his middle name was Bruno. Perhaps we could meet later to discuss it, since your archaeologist friends convinced me to spend the weekend exploring your region."

"Great," Bruno said. "I'd like to hear more about Todaro and to learn the real identity of the man carrying his papers."

"I'll be glad to help, but I was hoping to meet here the expert on your Resistance movement from the Centre Jean Moulin. I spoke to him by phone when I was assigned to this event, and he told me he would be here. I gather he's a friend of yours."

"He is, his name is Julien and I've been looking for him," Bruno replied. "I assume he's been delayed in the traffic."

The Italian gave Bruno his business card. "Call me when you have the time. I know something of Captain Todaro. He was a comrade in arms of my grandfather."

Bruno's eyes widened in surprise, but the Italian had turned to talk to Abby, leaving Bruno to stare at the card and read "Capitano di Fregata Lorenzo Felipe Borghese, Addetto Militare, Ambasciata d'Italia," followed by a French mobile phone number and his title as Military Attaché.

Then the mayor began calling people to their seats, and Bruno was jostled as they all seemed to move at once. The German diplomat and the Italian were steered to the center of the table, close to the mayor's place as host. The prefect was already standing opposite the mayor, beside the banker, the bankruptcy judge and the mayor of Castillonnès. Bruno and Abby found themselves with Father Sentout, Yveline, Monsieur and Madame Birch and Horst and Clothilde, all together at one end. Assorted councilors, Brosseil and the Marty clan were at the other.

Bruno felt hungry after all the running around that morning. He passed along the bowl filled with healthy portions of bread and looked up to see the mayor standing to glare at him before he said, "And now, Father Sentout, the blessing, if you please."

That was a decent gesture, thought Bruno. Always conscious of the division between church and state, the mayor seldom allowed the priest to officiate at any civic event. Perhaps this was the priest's reward for the choir's successful performance that morning. Father Sentout, deftly secreting his chunk of bread in the sleeve of his soutane, rose and with his other hand made the sign of the cross and intoned a brisk *"Benedictus benedicat"*; he had long since learned not to stand too long between the people of the Périgord and their food. He sat, retrieved his bread and cut a generous slice of foie gras before handing the serving plate to Abby.

"Thank you, Father, but I'm on a diet," Abby said, passing the plate along.

"Are you a Catholic, my child?" the priest asked her.

"No, Father, I'm an Episcopalian, which is the American version of the Church of England, but I'm not a regular churchgoer. Only Christmas, christenings, weddings and funerals, I'm afraid. But I enjoyed the music you arranged this morning."

The polite and somewhat strained chatter of strangers, of people with little in common except the invitation that had brought them together, flowed on around Bruno as he thought once more about Abby's way of casting nervous glances around her. The only threat that he could imagine might trouble her in St. Denis was the ex-husband, after her intriguing tale of his sudden rise and fall from riches. He was far more concerned, though, about the threat to Colette Cantagnac, to her phone and to his own.

The plates were cleared and the next course, roast breast of duck with orange sauce, was served by young trainees from the *collège* who were planning on careers in hotels and restaurants. Bruno knew them all, not only from his tennis and rugby lessons but because he had guided them and their mothers and later their younger siblings across the road to school for the past decade and more.

He returned his attention to the talk around him. Monsieur Birch was also praising Father Sentout for the choral music, and Madame Birch was asking Yveline about life as a gendarme. Clothilde had turned to the center of the table where she had engaged the prefect about an archaeological site called Combe Grenal, where the oldest human remains in the region had been found, a child who had lived some 130,000 years ago.

"You're an easy man to read, Bruno," said Horst quietly. "You overhear Clothilde chatting about archaeology at Domme and you're wondering if she's trying to charm some extra funds to let her explore further."

"Quite right," said Bruno with a smile as he laid down his knife and fork on his empty plate. "And I was thinking that with the glorious view down the valley Domme could be a natural place for human settlement. What about you, Horst, do you think it's worth digging?"

"We're spoiled for choice, Bruno. You can dig almost anywhere in this valley and find something. And now, tell me, did you recognize any of those masked demonstrators at the door?"

"I'm not sure, I was pretty far back," Bruno replied, which was not entirely true. "I think the mayor handled it very well."

"As chief of police of the whole valley, you must go to events like this all the time."

Bruno laughed. "This is the Périgord, Horst. We have communes here of just two hundred people, so every adult will probably have to take his and her turn on the council, and probably serve a term as mayor. If I'm invited, it will be to a feast of the local hunters' club, or to a meal at the mayor's home, cooked by him and his wife, and I'll bring a bottle of decent wine."

As he spoke, Bruno felt the familiar vibration on his phone, looked at the screen and saw it was General Lannes. He excused himself and left the council chamber as discreetly as he could before answering. Seeing the door to his old office was open, he slipped inside.

"Your FBI friend Hodge said you'd asked him to do me a favor," Lannes began. "There's new information on this American with an Italian passport, Giuseppe Garibaldi Barone. Hodge has learned that he's a person of interest to the FBI regarding a big fraud inquiry into one of the top cryptocurrency groups. But he left his last known address in California before they could question him. We're also interested in this blockchain business, mainly because of similar concerns in our finance ministry. I'm focused on the Russian crypto exchange called Garantex. It seems to be one of the routes Moscow has been using to get around our sanctions efforts."

"So, am I back under your command, sir?" Bruno asked.

"Not yet. This is a potential criminal matter rather than national security. Morillon's team will be trying to get into his phone, if he's in France. The operation is being coordinated by the fiscal police. I believe you know Goirau, its chief in Bordeaux?"

"Yes, sir, I've met him before with J-J—I mean Commissaire Jalipeau. He's always been very helpful."

"He's asked for you to be assigned to his command for this operation. It's sensitive because apparently the European Central Bank had been considering getting involved with this blockchain money. It's all way above my head, Bruno, but if Garibaldi is in your neighborhood, I'd like you to make the arrest, but don't mention anything about funny money. You can charge him with fraud or under the telecommunications legislation, and then once he's in custody, Hodge will apply for extradition. Is that clear?"

"Yes, sir, arrest him for anything except cryptocurrency, inform Hodge and wait. Hodge will have to move fast. We can only hold someone for twenty-four hours without the public prosecutor's agreement. Goirau may be able to help with that."

"Or you'll need to charge him with something else. Day one, you charge him with phone tapping; then computer fraud on day two, and so on. Report to me once a day and let me have your new mobile number. Morillon's team is monitoring this network to ensure we're not penetrated, and Goirau is waiting to hear from you."

Lannes hung up. As Bruno was putting his phone back into the pouch at his waist, he felt a tap on his shoulder. He turned to see Colette, holding her own phone.

"A Monsieur Goirau from the financial police has been trying to reach you," she said. "I promised you'd call him back. Apparently, you're being temporarily placed under his authority. I checked the regulations. You'll have the titular rank of *commissaire,* with a considerably higher salary, while it lasts."

"What about my convalescent leave?" Bruno asked.

She gave him a look that was becoming familiar, blending an amused glance with a cool smile. "Working for the *fisc,*" she said, "you'll probably be in a bank all day."

Bruno rolled his eyes and called Goirau's number. He answered at once, saying, "Bruno, we get to work together. Any idea where this Italian American might be?"

"Not at all. Except that his ex-wife is here, and I imagine he's hoping to get some money from her, even though she got a court order against him in California after he was arrested for attacking her house and car."

"Does she have photos? The passport photo the Americans sent us could be anybody."

"I'll forward what I have and try to get more. Are you staying in Bordeaux? Where do you need me to be?"

"So far, we don't have a clue as to the man's whereabouts. But we do know he's interested in St. Denis and in his ex-wife. He seems also interested in you, Bruno, for a convenient way to gain entry into police databases."

"The same with my colleague Colette Cantagnac," said Bruno. "She was waylaid coming out of a restaurant the night before last by somebody with an accomplice on a trail bike. They were after her purse or her phone. Luckily I was driving by at the time and was able to help. The gendarmes filed a report."

"Yes, I've seen it, and it may have nothing to do with our Garibaldi guy."

"Sure, but if he comes here I can probably find out," Bruno replied, and went on to explain the mailing list Florence's computer club had created for him. He could reach all hosts of hotels, campsites, *gîtes,* bed-and-breakfasts, holiday farms and other accommodations with a single query.

"Good. And make sure you ask them about any bank or credit card he may be using," Goirau said. "In the meantime, we'll try to track his whereabouts through his phone connections to cell towers. We'll have an online conference at nine and six each day, starting tomorrow morning. And we need any information his ex-wife may have about his banks, insurers and so on. Now, what do you know about cryptocurrency?"

"Almost nothing. I don't understand it and certainly wouldn't trust it."

"That's not a bad start. I'll send you a simple report on it I was asked to draft for a Senate committee."

"I can't say I look forward to it, but thanks," said Bruno. "Meanwhile, you should get J-J to put you in touch with Gabrielle Teyssier, the new computer expert at police headquarters. She was really good on the attempts to break into their computer system."

"Noted. And Mademoiselle Cantagnac from your *mairie* has already talked to my office about the administrative details of your transfer. She seems committed to your best interests. We'll talk tomorrow morning."

Chapter 24

Still in his old office, Bruno plugged in his laptop and drafted an email to the long list of local hotels and tourist lodgings. He gave Barone's full name, date of birth and passport details, added a copy of the American passport photo and one that Abby had sent him and asked for all sightings of the man to be discreetly reported, along with any information on credit cards, vehicles and so on. He sent it off, with copies to Colette and Goirau, and emailed Abby to ask if she could send him any information on the banks and credit cards of her ex-husband. He then returned to the luncheon table, where he found his place taken by Julien, his friend from the Resistance archive in Bordeaux, who had arrived late. He slipped in, trying to be inconspicuous, and knelt at Julien's side.

"Glad you made it in time for some lunch," Bruno said quietly. "The Italian naval officer wants to see you, says the papers on the Italian corpse were those of an old friend of his grandfather."

"Sounds interesting," Julien replied. "I couldn't find much about him in the archives."

"When lunch is over, bring him down to the café behind the *mairie.* I'll see you both there."

Julien nodded and Bruno left the room, noisy with chatter

and the sounds of cutlery in busy use. He retrieved his laptop and went down to Fauquet's café. It was still almost full, mostly strangers who had been at the ceremony. At a corner table he saw Jack Crimson, reading a newspaper propped against a carafe of wine as he tucked into one of the salads that Fauquet offered for a light lunch.

"May I join you?" he asked.

"My pleasure, Bruno," said Jack, putting away the newspaper. "I presume you've had your lunch upstairs. I gave up my place to some banker who was an unexpected arrival. Happy to do so—I've had more than enough of these official luncheons."

Bruno smiled in response and said, "Julien from the Resistance archive arrived late because of the traffic jam, so he took my place when I was called away on police business. You met him once when we had lunch together in Bordeaux."

"Of course, I remember him, a very bright man and a scholar," Crimson replied. "He knew more about Roger Landes than I did; you remember, the Frenchman who became one of the finest agents of the SOE."

Bruno nodded. He knew that Britain's Special Operations Executive, formed by Winston Churchill's wartime order to "set Europe ablaze," had been the mainstay of the French Resistance. They had furnished the parachute drops of more than ten thousand tons of weapons, the lavish funds, medical supplies and the military advisers who had organized and supplied the Resistance and built it into an ever-growing menace to the Nazi occupiers. By giving the French the tools to fight back after the humiliating defeat of 1940, the SOE had done much to restore France's self-respect.

Fauquet silently placed a second wineglass on the table and another carafe of the town's white wine. He offered Bruno a menu, but Bruno shook his head. He'd eaten enough of the foie gras and the duck.

"The Landes family left France before the war and came to London," Crimson went on. "Young Roger joined the British army, and because he could pass as a Frenchman he was recruited by the SOE and trained to be a wireless operator. Then when half the network was rounded up by the Gestapo, he took over the leadership of what was left and did a brilliant job, even organized the execution of Grandclément, the other Resistance chief who was turned by the Gestapo."

Julien came in, followed by Captain Borghese. Curious glances followed them as they took seats at Crimson's table. Bruno made the introductions and Borghese shook hands, thanked Bruno for the invitation to meet and then asked if he or Julien had ever heard of a man called André Grandclément.

Bruno and Jack Crimson exchanged startled glances at hearing the name they had just been discussing. Then there was a pause while Fauquet arrived to place two more glasses and another carafe of wine on the table before returning to his post behind the bar.

"You're referring to the Resistance leader who was turned by the Gestapo and betrayed the arms dumps of his network?" asked Julien.

"Yes, the leader of the Organisation Civile et Militaire. Until 1943 it was the most important Resistance group in southwestern France," said Borghese.

"Why are you interested in him?" Julien asked, his voice neutral.

"Because the dead Italian in that grave was carrying the military identity papers of Captain Salvatore Todaro, who knew Grandclément well and who was also a friend and colleague of my grandfather. But Todaro had been dead for eighteen months when that ambush took place in St. Denis. He was killed on a trawler that was strafed by a Spitfire while supporting attacks on British shipping on the North African coast."

"Do you know who the man in the grave was?" Bruno asked.

"Yes, I think I do, but first some background," said Borghese. "Do you have any idea how big the Italian presence was in Bordeaux? We ran thirty-two submarines, lost half of them but sank more than a hundred Allied ships. Todaro was one of the heroes of that flotilla, one of the Italians most respected by the German allies."

"Why do you say that?" Julien asked.

"Because he and my grandfather together planned the midget-submarine attack against the British fleet in Alexandria in December 1941. They damaged two battleships so badly they were out of service for most of the next year."

"Good God Almighty." Jack Crimson was so shocked he responded in English, and every head in the café turned their way. He took a deep breath and then continued, much more quietly, in French. "Because of that attack we lost control of the Mediterranean for most of 1942, so we could no longer stop tankers and supply vessels taking fuel and munitions to reequip Rommel's army in North Africa. That was how he recaptured Tobruk and stormed through the Egyptian frontier all the way to El Alamein. If we hadn't stopped him there, we'd have lost the Suez Canal and maybe even the Iraqi oil fields. And if that happened, Rommel could have joined up with the German armies closing in on Stalingrad, which would have blocked the Caucasian oil that kept Stalin's armies alive. We could have lost the whole damn war!"

The table fell silent until Captain Borghese said quietly, "I am honored to hear an Englishman say this, because my grandfather was also involved."

"Would your grandfather have been Prince Junio Borghese?" asked Crimson. "The man known as the Black Prince, whose forces blocked Tito's attack on Trieste in 1945? If I'm right, he remained a passionate Fascist all his life, even launched a failed coup d'état against the Italian government in 1970."

"I regret to say that you're right. But for the Italian navy my grandfather was the hero who commanded the submarine *Scirè* that took the midget submarines into the harbor of Alexandria to attack your battleships. He died in exile in Spain in 1974 but left all his papers to my father."

"That doesn't explain who the Italian was who died in St. Denis, and why he stayed with the Nazis even after Italy joined the Allies," said Julien.

"From the many letters exchanged between Todaro and my grandfather, I believe the man in the grave who carried Todaro's papers was a friend of theirs. I think he was Capo di Prima Classe Alonso Luca Barone, a top warrant officer who was a legend in the navy. My grandfather claimed Barone was both a logistics genius and the finest of frogmen. It was with Alonso that my grandfather planned the Christmas Day attack on the shipping in New York harbor, which had to be aborted when Italy switched sides in the war. Even after that, Alonso decided to remain in Bordeaux until every last Italian submarine had been accounted for. And he certainly would have been able to equip himself with Todaro's identity documents."

"So who did he report to after Italy changed sides?" Julien asked. "To the Germans, or to Italy's new pro-Allied government?"

"To my grandfather. He'd sworn an oath of loyalty to Mussolini, and he remained faithful to him."

"Is there any way to identify this man Alonso from his skeleton?" Bruno asked, wondering if the name Barone meant any connection to Abby's ex-husband. "Any broken bones?"

"He lost the ends of two fingers from his left hand in an accident. That's what I looked for on the skeleton and that's what I found. It's Alonso, I'm sure."

"So why are you interested in Grandclément, who was seen in both France and in Britain as a traitor who sold out to the Gestapo?" asked Julien.

"I'm not sure 'sold out' is the right term," said Borghese. "Grandclément certainly did a deal, giving up the Communist-controlled arms dumps to the Gestapo in return for the release from prison of his own men. Grandclément thought the real war would come later, against the Communists. A lot of Germans, Gestapo as well as military, agreed with him. I know my grandfather did. And of course, they were right. Less than five years after the war ended, Britain, France, Italy and America were all in the anti-Communist alliance of NATO, and Germany was soon to join them."

"It took some brutal acts by Stalin to impose communism in Poland and Czechoslovakia, and the blockade against West Berlin, for the British and Americans to realize Stalin's threat," said Crimson.

"I agree," said Julien. "There was no way they'd have been ready for that in the summer of 1944."

"You're probably right," said Borghese. "But I'm struck by the way that so much seemed to be triggered by the Hitler bomb plot on the twentieth of July. There was the American offensive to break out of Normandy five days later, to be followed by the British and Canadian offensive to cut off the German retreat at the Falaise gap. And Grandclément was executed by British agents at a landing strip outside Bordeaux on the twenty-seventh of July."

"But what is the significance of the dates?" Bruno asked Borghese.

"We know that Alonso and my grandfather were in touch with some of the German Abwehr and naval officers around Admiral Canaris who supported the military plot to assassinate Hitler in July '44. There are letters to my grandfather asking if he could influence Mussolini to join the grand design of eliminating Hitler so the Wehrmacht leaders could reach a negotiated peace with the British and Americans. Then they could all combine to defeat the Soviet Union and crush communism forever."

"I know that was Canaris's dream, along with that of half the German high command, but it was a complete fantasy. Churchill and Roosevelt would never have agreed," said Crimson. "They'd already declared their war aim of an unconditional surrender."

"Perhaps, but let's get back to Alonso," said Borghese. "I think he was worried that his connections to the conspirators were too well known. Like my grandfather, he was also a friend of a well-connected German naval officer, Lieutenant Commander Alfred Kranzfelder, a close friend of von Stauffenberg, the ringleader of the plot to assassinate Hitler."

"So you think Alonso was fleeing Bordeaux to avoid arrest by the Gestapo?" Julien asked.

"Perhaps. But I don't think he was fleeing to Germany, but to northern Italy, where Mussolini's Republic of Salò was nominally in power."

"What about the two Luftwaffe women who were killed with him?" Bruno asked.

Borghese shrugged. "I don't know. But after the July plot failed, he could no longer use the German naval communications links through Kranzfelder. Maybe he had Luftwaffe contacts, maybe one of the women was his girlfriend. Who knows? But as well as the failure of the July bomb plot against Hitler, he must also have known that his friend Grandclément had been killed by the Resistance. He was in danger from both sides, from the Gestapo and the Resistance. I think that's why he fled."

A silence fell over the table, until Julien said, "I suppose it makes sense. Bordeaux wasn't evacuated by the Germans until the twenty-eighth of August. Alonso got out two weeks before that."

Bruno felt like an underqualified student attending a high-level seminar on the history of the Second World War. He focused on the obvious point.

"I don't understand," he said. "If Grandclément had turned

traitor and started working with the Gestapo, why did he not betray Alonso before he was killed?"

"Grandclément believed he was a good French patriot all along," Julien explained. "He was turned by a very clever Gestapo man, Friedrich Dohse, who had already arrested Grandclément's wife. When Dohse finally arrested Grandclément, he put the married couple together in their own suite in the Gestapo's Bordeaux headquarters. He treated them with respect and told Grandclément he was honored to meet a brave French patriot who was also a devout anti-Communist. Dohse even put a radio in their room that could receive the BBC, along with fresh flowers and a well-stocked bar."

"And Grandclément fell for that?" asked Bruno. "Deluded by his own self-image."

"He thought he was acting honorably," Julien replied. "And in a way, he was. He reached an agreement with Dohse that if the Gestapo released the three hundred or so *résistants* they had arrested from Grandclément's network, he would take Dohse to all the arms dumps he knew, hundreds of tons of weapons and explosives. He thought he was only giving away Communist Resistance cells and their arms dumps. He was so convinced of his own rectitude that he even agreed to be flown back to England to plead his case. That was when Landes carried out the death sentence on him and Madame Grandclément."

"And that was that?" asked Crimson.

"No, eight years after the war ended, Dohse was tried by a French court, accused of torture, mass deportations and being responsible for the killing of more than twelve hundred hostages. He was found guilty and sentenced to seven years' hard labor. Since he'd already served eight years, he was released, went back to Germany and lived until 1995, making a comfortable living importing French wines through his old contacts in Bordeaux."

"He got off lightly," said Bruno.

"You are missing the point," Borghese said. "Dohse and Grandclément both understood that Hitler was losing the war. They were looking ahead to the war that would come next, against communism. Dohse persuaded Grandclément that he should carry on recruiting his Resistance network and stocking arms so that he would have a conservative Resistance—he called it the Maquis Officiel—capable of defeating the Communist-controlled Resistance in France. And then Britain, France, America, Italy and a post-Hitler Germany would combine to defeat the real enemy—Soviet communism under Stalin."

"That's crazy," Bruno said.

"No, not crazy, but perhaps premature," Borghese said, smiling. "The point that I am making is that my grandfather and Alonso did not simply remain Fascists too long but that they were anti-Communists too soon."

Chapter 25

"Bonjour, Bruno," came a cheery female voice, and he looked up to see Marta, in sports gear, waving at him from behind the fence that ringed the rugby field, Abby standing at her side. He gave them a wave back before they trotted off to join the other women on the pitch, passing a rugby ball back and forth between them as if they'd been playing the game for years.

The meeting at Fauquet's café had broken up while some of the guests at the *mairie* were still lingering over the last of their lunch. Following the mayor's suggestion, several of the guests would be at Bruno's that evening for dinner. Bruno had included Julien, who would in any event be staying at Bruno's home overnight, and had extended the invitation to Borghese, who'd already booked himself a room at the Hôtel de Paris.

While he was changing into sports gear, Bruno's phone vibrated. It was the baron, to say that he'd heard about the mayor's plan for dinner that night.

"When I knew that you would still be doing the rugby practice, I thought that the mayor was asking you to bite off more than even you could chew, Bruno," he said. "You can seat eight, maximum ten, at that table of yours, and by my count the mayor has already committed you to seventeen or even more. We're therefore shifting the location to my place where there's a table long enough. I bought four kilos of veal and a couple kilos of dried morel mushrooms for a very large *veau aux morilles* for you to cook. I also bought three kilos of strawberries, and a liter of crème fraîche. I have a sack of my own potatoes in the larder and lettuce and tomatoes in the garden if you need them, and we'll start with those rillettes of tuna that I like."

"That's more than kind of you, Baron, thank you. Make sure you save the bills because the *mairie* is paying," Bruno said. "But how do you get seventeen?"

"Four troubadour musicians plus Joël, Flavie's boyfriend; Fabiola and Gilles; Michel, who dug up the grave, and his wife; Monsieur and Madame Birch; the mayor and Jacqueline, who has come down from Paris with Amélie, my favorite jazz singer. And we can't have her without your friend, the rock singer."

"Rod Macrae."

"That's right. That makes seventeen, plus you and me."

"So, nineteen. Right, I'll be there in just over an hour, after the practice."

"Anything I can do to help?"

"Set the table, hull the strawberries and open the cans of tuna. Before anything else, pour enough boiling water over the dried mushrooms to cover them and leave them to plump up for an hour, then simmer them for ten minutes so they are fully softened. Drain them and their liquid through paper towels, then set the morels and their liquid aside in separate bowls," Bruno said, closing his eyes to concentrate as he envisioned the various steps. "Then trim the veal and cut it into chunks and brown the meat in duck fat, then transfer it all to your biggest casserole. Stir in the morels and their juice and bring the casserole to a simmer for three or four minutes. Then add a large bouquet garni, season with salt and pepper and a bottle of white wine. One from the town vineyard will do fine. Cover the casserole and stick it in the oven to bake for forty-five minutes," he went on, "by which time I should be back. Then chill more white wine, open some bottles of red and pour yourself a large glass. You deserve it for what you're doing."

"You'd do the same for me, Bruno. In fact, you have, more than once. See you later. I understand how much you enjoy being out there on the pitch, the only male and surrounded by a score and more of young women."

"You're just jealous, my friend, because there was no women's rugby around here back in the days when you were a coach," Bruno replied with a laugh.

"I keep asking myself why we never thought of that in my day. But at my age, my dear Bruno, the saddest memories are the might-have-beens. See you soon."

By the time Bruno arrived at the baron's *chartreuse,* armed with three large *pains* from the bakery, the hard work had all been done. Taking the casserole out of the oven and switching it off, he lifted its lid, sniffed with appreciation and congratulated the baron. He stirred in the crème fraîche and set the casserole over a medium flame to reduce and thicken the sauce. Meanwhile he sliced the bread and stirred together the contents of the cans of tuna with a little mayonnaise, salt and pepper and a touch of paprika. He sprinkled sugar over the strawberries and began peeling potatoes while enjoying sips of the Château Bélingard dry white wine that had been a favorite of the baron for as long as Bruno had known him.

Discarding the bouquet garni, Bruno ladled the meat and *morilles* from the casserole into two of the baron's largest lidded tureens and put them back into the warm oven until it was time to eat.

As he heard the first guests arrive, Bruno turned on the kettle, chopped the peeled potatoes into quarters and dropped them into a large saucepan of salted water and set them to boil. He saw that the baron had already taken a tray loaded with small plates and the toasts and tuna out to the large table in the courtyard. Bruno had quartered half a dozen lemons so that the juice could be squeezed over the tuna rillettes. A small cheer went up when Bruno emerged, and Amélie was the first to reach him.

"Some very fine smells wafting in from the kitchen," she said, presenting her plump cheeks to be kissed. "And Rod has written a wonderful song that has given me some interesting ideas, but it's a secret until Flavie gets here with her band. I thought her singing this morning was just sublime. And how are you, my dear Bruno, after getting shot and scaring us all?"

"Your visit makes me feel almost as good as new, Amélie," he said, and reached out to hug Rod Macrae, who had loomed up behind her, wearing the high-heeled western boots, bandanna and leather cowboy hat that had been his hallmark at the rock concerts of an earlier generation. Still as lean and cadaverous as he'd been thirty years ago, Rod had made a new, late career with his haunting ballads full of an old man's regrets and ancient Celtic wisdom, somehow blended with Amélie's crooning voice and Caribbean soul.

"I wrote it in English and Amélie has put it into French, and I was wondering if Horst might put it into German for us," Rod said. "I gather he's coming tonight with Clothilde."

"News to me, but they'll be very welcome," said Bruno. "I just hope the food doesn't run out."

Then everyone else seemed to arrive at once—Michel and his wife with Tim and Krys Birch, then came Flavie with Joël and Les Troubadours. To Bruno's surprise, along with the mayor and Jacqueline came Colette Cantagnac. Then Clothilde and Horst arrived with Fabiola and Gilles, and they had brought Pamela and Abby. At this rate, thought Bruno, even the baron's ancestral table would be too small. Bruno ducked back into the kitchen to drain the potatoes and mash them with butter into a puree. Then he brought out more wine bottles and slices of bread to go with the fast vanishing tuna spread. As he came out, he was passed by the baron coming in, saying he'd had to add more settings and find five more chairs.

The fact that they were not all friends had, to Bruno's surprise, benefited the gathering. Only Bruno, Michel, Colette and the mayor knew the Birches, so there were introductions to be made, followed by explanations about the Birches' plans for the Domaine de la Barde. Colette had to be introduced to those who had yet to encounter this éminence grise of the town hall, and Abby had to be presented to the baron and to Rod and Amélie. Everybody wanted to congratulate Flavie for her singing that morning, and the mayor preened when everyone assured him that the service of remembrance had been a great success.

"We have plans to make an even bigger success of it," announced Amélie. "But that will wait until after dinner, and we may need Horst to be sure it really happens."

"Time to eat," announced the baron, and beat a sonorous chime on the bronze gong some ancestor had brought back from French Indochina. Bruno threw up his hands in despair when people asked him where they should sit. There was no time to make seating arrangements, he told them; they should just find a seat.

He left the baron to organize matters and went to the kitchen. First he brought out two dishes loaded with pureed potatoes, then he disappeared once more to reappear with two enormous tureens, this time filled with the *veau aux morilles*. He placed one at each end of the table. He eyed the baron, who stood, and simultaneously they lifted the lids from the bowls with a flourish. The unique aroma spread and triggered oohs and aahs and bursts of applause from around the table.

There was more applause as the baron placed magnums of Pécharmant from Château de Tiregand 2019 at either end of the table. He asked the mayor to open one while Gilles attacked the other. The baron brought out two more bottles of Bélingard for those who preferred white wine. Without being asked, Colette, who was sitting next to Bruno, quickly organized a chain of plates being passed up to Bruno, each to be filled with veal and potatoes and then handed back down the chain. The baron, with Fabiola's help, did the same from the other end, and Bruno trusted him to ensure that every plate was filled. He was relieved when the last plate, his own, still held a decent portion.

"I think we can declare the meal a social success, and the veal is delicious," said Colette, clinking her glass of red wine against his. "I foresee a promising future for you in a restaurant once I succeed in driving you out of the *mairie*."

"Is that your plan?" Bruno asked, not entirely sure that she was joking.

"Some people in the *mairie* think so, the mayor's secretary for one. I sometimes think she won't be happy until you and I fight a duel to settle matters, pistols at dawn on the bridge, you firing gallantly into the air while I plug you right between the eyes."

"Are you that good a shot?" Bruno asked.

"Who knows?" she countered with a broad smile. "Even if I'm not, don't you believe in beginner's luck?"

At that point, the baron rose, tapped his spoon against his glass, waited for silence and then said, "Thank you all for coming. It's a pleasure to see this great table filled and I'd like to raise a glass in salute to our friend and chef and guardian of the law, Bruno, and his *veau aux morilles.*"

When the applause had died down and the toast had been drunk, Bruno waited until everyone had taken their seats again before he rose to reply. "What you don't know," he said, "is that I had no choice in the matter. Once the baron knew how many of you there were likely to be, he bought the veal, the tuna and the strawberries that are yet to come and laid down his orders for the menu. And I was happy to obey, because with the ceremony this morning, the mayor's lunch, a sudden burst of police business and then the women's rugby practice, you would probably have ended up with takeout pizza."

He paused for the laughter, mixed with cheers and affectionate jeers, to die down and then raised his glass. "A toast to our host this evening, as so often before. Here's to our wonderful and generous friend, the baron."

Fabiola on one side of the baron and Pamela on the other planted smacking kisses on the cheeks of their old friend, and Bruno left Colette to organize the clearing of the plates as he darted into the kitchen to bring out the strawberries and cream. He returned to hear the mayor asking Amélie about the surprise she had suggested was coming.

"Still a secret until the meal is over and we all get comfortable, and then I'll leave it to Rod," she said.

"So, it's a new song?" Bruno asked.

Amélie shook her head and stayed silent.

"Might it perhaps be a song that has something to do with the ceremony we observed this morning," the mayor wanted to know.

"I won't tell you, I won't tell you, *je te dis rien, je ne chante pas,*" Amélie sang, to the tune of Rod Stewart's "Sailing."

Finally, the plates all emptied, Rod pushed his chair back and went to his car for his guitar. Amélie came to stand beside him as he took his seat again, now some way back from the table.

"The mayor asked if this might have something to do with this morning's ceremony for the dead girls," Rod said. "It does, of course, because like so many others I was touched by all the flowers that began to pile up and then the way the whole town wanted to mark this as an event of unusual importance. So this began as a poem, I guess. But then music started to come, as it often does with me, and I played it for Amélie this afternoon, and with her fabulous voice it took on a new life. But it's really about two teenage girls, caught up in a war."

He began playing a gentle, rhythmic riff. It was very simple, almost like a nursery rhyme, but Amélie's voice gave it depth, but only in crooning notes, not words. Then Rod started to speak the words, rather than sing them.

> *Three bodies in a single grave,*
> *Two girls, a man, from different lands*
> *In a war that's almost history.*
> *Strangers that we've come to know,*
> *Though all we have for them are flowers,*
> *As we now reap what they did sow.*
> *They pull us back to that grim track*
> *Our elders shared and we were spared.*
> *Remembering is what makes us real.*
> *That vicious war, its floods of gore,*
> *Its tanks, the camps, its bombs and tombs.*
> *Remembering is what makes us feel.*
> *But if you'd known those long gone girls,*
> *Their youth and hopes, their smiles, their jokes,*
> *The lives and loves and kids they missed.*
> *We've come to know it's our loss too.*
> *Though all we have for them are flowers,*
> *Remembering is what helps us heal.*

In the silence that followed, Amélie said, "I've made a translation into French, which I will sing now, and we hope that Horst can eventually give us a version in German. Rod hopes that this song can be released in all three languages, but now we want you to be the first to hear it as Rod wrote it this afternoon."

She nodded at Rod, and he began again to play the melody,

but this time she spoke the song in French with a gentleness that came through the grimness of the words. Amélie's voice became a keening, an age-old lament of waste and loss and regret, and behind it Rod's hoarse and humming voice became a gaunt, almost savage bass line. The silence when she ended, despite the quiet sobs from some of the women, became a presence, almost a voice in itself.

"Now we'd like you to hear it as we recorded it this afternoon in Rod's studio, in English with my vocal backing," Amélie said, after a long, long moment. "We hope we can get the choir and Les Troubadours to repeat the hymn they sang this morning, with the solos, so we can record it and blend it into the song, which we hope to release in France and Germany as well as in Britain. And Rod has asked me to say that we want all the royalties from this song to go to the fund for the garden of remembrance here in St. Denis."

This time, having heard the words in French, Bruno was able to understand Rod's English, except that he realized it was not simply English that he was singing, but something much older. His Scots accent was much stronger, in a way that made Bruno think of Celtic bards, perhaps even of an older people, not unlike those remote ancestors, the cave artists of the prehistoric Périgord, singing age-old human chants of grief and loss.

When he had finished, the silence was even longer, broken at last by the mayor, who said, "Thank you, Rod and Amélie, for putting into words and song the emotions that I think we all felt this morning at the grave. Horst, we rely on you to bring a German voice to this remarkable song. And I pledge to you all today that I will move heaven and earth to get the TV footage of today's memorial service and blend it with the song and send it out across France and across all of Europe."

The baron rose, went to the cupboard by the door and took

out two old bottles, each of them an Armagnac of 1939, removed the seal and stopper, then emptied his wineglass and refilled it with the spirit. He raised his glass to Rod, and said simply, *"Merci, mon vieux, et merci, Amélie."*

He sipped before speaking again. "I've been keeping these two legendary bottles of Château du Tariquet from that last year of peace. Some of you may know that Armagnac is at least two centuries older than cognac, and the Tariquet domain has been in the hands of the same family for more than one hundred years. My father bought these two bottles in the last year of peace, 1939. On many occasions I've considered opening them, but it never seemed the right moment. But now I think we should all drink in memory of those who fell in the most terrible of all Europe's wars. And I'm honored that this song was first heard at my table tonight."

He passed the bottle along the table, opened the second and passed it in the other direction. One by one they finished their wine and poured in the Armagnac that was more than eighty years old and raised their glasses to Rod and Amélie.

Bruno sipped at his Armagnac, thinking that in this age of computers and smartphones and social media, something as ancient as song could have such power to mold and shape emotions, to bring into vibrant, living shape the confusion of memories and grief that still echoed from that global conflict that was now so remote from anyone younger than eighty. He thought of Joe, the only survivor he knew who could claim to have played some modest role in that extraordinary conflict that had sucked in most of the human race. Bruno's own concept of that war came from the memories of others, filtered by the skills and research choices of countless historians, by the memoirs of the long dead who had taken part, or been helpless victims of the horror.

Bruno thought to himself that he had played a minor walk-on role in this day's extraordinary act of collective memory and mourning. He, by chance, had introduced Rod to Amélie, and both of them to the baron and to Flavie and Les Troubadours.

He looked down the long table and saw Horst, pausing over an open notebook, doubtless trying to put the Anglo-French versions of the song into German. Horst's own father had fought with Rommel's Seventh Panzer Division that had broken through the French line at Sedan in 1940. Bruno looked at Gilles, scribbling down notes that would doubtless appear in next week's *Paris Match*. He glanced at the baron, who could still summon some personal memories of that war.

He thought of Florence, who was only French because her grandfather had somehow escaped Poland, reached England and fought his way back into Europe in a British uniform. Flavie and Joël and each of the Troubadours doubtless had some family memories of it all. He looked at Abby, whose grandparents had lived through it, probably taken part. He looked at Birch, whose grandfathers must have fought in that last hurrah of the British Empire.

And what of the other people here, Fabiola and Gilles, Clothilde, Colette, the mayor and the others? They would have family memories, perhaps of Resistance fighters, or possibly of collaborators, or simply people who tried to survive the humiliation of being occupied by the most brutal regime Europe had known since the Enlightenment. Bruno could claim no such heritage. He was an orphan, abandoned not only by his parents but also by history, who grew up knowing nothing of his family's part in that monstrous historical drama. And yet somehow that war was a part of him, a cataclysm in whose echoes he had grown up to become, in his turn, a soldier, one of so many among the postwar generations who wanted to expunge the shame of 1940 and restore something of that *gloire* that remained an essential feature of the French soul.

Mon Dieu, how that war lives in us, its heirs, Bruno thought. How much it gave the Americans the conviction that they had a duty to save the world. And how it gave the Russians a mission to save, not socialism, but the historic sense of Russia as the land that had saved Europe from the Mongol hordes in medieval times and saved them again from the Nazis in the twentieth century. We live still in the shadow of that war, seek to learn its lessons, talk of a better world in which such grief and loss and torment can never return.

So, he concluded, he would do what he could to support the song and spread the message that Rod and Amélie had composed.

Chapter 26

Harsh flares of lightning, peals of thunder and the lashings of a downpour on his windows woke Bruno before dawn. He found his phone on the pillow next to him and recalled that he had fallen asleep while failing to comprehend much of Goirau's report on cryptocurrency. He understood that it was about something called Hydra, the biggest remaining market on the dark web, and Goirau noted that its revenues had soared from less than $10 million in 2016 to over $1.3 billion in 2020. Based in Moscow, Hydra offered its clients software for ransomware and hacking services, counterfeit currency, stolen crypto funds and illegal drugs. Germany and the United States were each about to outlaw it, and Goirau recommended that France do the same. There was also something called Garantex, which Bruno remembered General Lannes mentioning, a Moscow-based exchange where various cryptocurrencies could be traded. "Analysis of known Garantex transactions demonstrates that more than $100 million in transactions are associated with illicit actors and dark-net markets," Goirau had noted.

It made little more sense to Bruno when he read it again in the light of day. Since the rain had stopped, he took Balzac for a muddy trot along the familiar ridge and was in St. Denis before eight, just as dawn was breaking. It was his duty to monitor the placement of the market stalls and adjudicate the inevitable minor disputes. He usually resolved such arguments by the traditional method of telling the two opponents that he'd ensure that they swapped places the following week. And he made a point of ensuring that they saw him write down in his notebook whose turn it would be and where.

It was the small Saturday market for locals, covering the square around the *mairie,* rather than the big market of Tuesday. Although he'd already made the tour, greeting each stallholder, Bruno barely needed to patrol it, since he could see most of the stalls from his usual table on Fauquet's terrace. This was where he had arranged to introduce Julien, his houseguest, and Borghese to the best croissants in the region. Julien was on time; Borghese followed a few minutes later carrying the previous evening's *Le Monde,* that day's *Sud Ouest* and the weekly *Paris Match.* Even before Fauquet came out with a basket of pastries and coffees, their table had been joined by Rod Macrae and Amélie, who let the Bruce off his leash as they approached. The basset puppy almost pounced on his father, Balzac, who was dozing at Bruno's feet in a timid beam of sunlight.

"Enjoy it," said Rod. "The forecast says this will be the last sun we see for several days. There's another storm coming from the northwest, all the way from Scotland."

"More rain is the last thing we need," said Bruno, before making introductions. He then changed the subject by asking Rod if the floral tributes were still looking good today. His route into town would have taken him past them.

"Even more flowers than yesterday, but some of them are looking a wee bit wan," Rod said. "Once cut, they don't last long in the open air."

"Bonjour à tous," said Abby, joining them from the market, a basket over her arm full of cheeses, fruit and salads. She greeted

Borghese by name. He was not in uniform, wearing civilian slacks and a turtleneck sweater under a leather jacket. Bruno quickly introduced Abby to Julien, explaining her plan to develop specialist tours of the region for Americans.

"What was your man doing in Bordeaux, working alongside the Germans for almost a year after Italy switched sides?" Rod asked Borghese, in his blunt way.

"We think he was involved in the plot to assassinate Hitler, in the mistaken belief that the British and Americans would then make peace and join the war on the eastern front against Stalin, which was very foolish of him," Borghese replied. "But not only that. He was also involved in sabotaging the German U-boats."

"What?" Rod stared at him, and the others around the table turned to listen as Borghese spoke.

"One of the challenges for a submarine was to aim a torpedo, since it had to hit a target in order to detonate," he explained. "So every navy was trying to develop a magnetic trigger, set to explode if it was close enough to an enemy hull. But it's very difficult because magnetic variation changes with geography. Italy's Professor Carlo Calosi developed an excellent magnetic trigger system, so good that the German navy decided to use it, building thousands of the torpedoes during 1943. When Italy signed the armistice in September that year, Calosi gave the Allies a countermeasure which disrupted the torpedo's trigger. The Allies launched a crash program to put these disrupters on their ships, which helps explain the failure of the U-boat campaign."

After a short silence, Rod nodded and then said, "Interesting. I never heard of that."

"It's true," said Julien. "I checked yesterday, after Captain Borghese first mentioned it."

"Glad to hear it," said Rod. "My grandad was in the merchant navy, and he lost a lot of mates to U-boats. I'm glad he wasn't one of them, or I wouldn't be here."

"I think we can all be honored that we're here with such a media star," said Borghese, holding up his copy of *Paris Match* and opening it with a flourish to a double-page spread. It was dominated by a photo of the flowers, with a woman standing by them with bowed head and tears on her cheeks. It took Bruno a moment to realize that it was Abby. It must have been that morning two days earlier when the floral tributes had begun, he thought, wondering if Philippe Delaron had taken the picture, and whether that would get him into trouble with his employers at *Sud Ouest*. But many photographers would risk a steady job for the chance of appearing in the legendary weekly.

"Great photo, Abby," said Amélie, and Rod gave her a quick burst of applause, which brought out Fauquet and his staff to admire the photo. Then other customers and some stallholders gathered around until Abby's face was bright red with embarrassment.

"It's the price of fame," said Borghese.

"I know your name is Borghese," Abby said, deftly changing the topic away from herself, "but is that Borghese as in Pope Paul the Fifth? Does this mean you're related to Junio Borghese, the war hero known as the Black Prince? He was in the navy, too."

"Yes, but I'm from a very junior branch of the family, so I have to work for a living. Junio was my grandfather. He died in exile in Spain, and I never knew him. Why do you ask?"

"He was a hero figure to the family of my ex-husband," Abby said, her voice sounding to Bruno a little too casual to be convincing. "Barone was their name—did you ever come across them? One of them had served under your grandfather when he was in charge of the frogmen."

"Yes, my grandfather was promoted to command Decima MAS, which ran underwater operations, everything from human torpedoes to frogmen. It was a military innovation pioneered by Italy in the First World War," Borghese said. "The name Barone is familiar, but I'd need to check the context."

"Did you get started on that because you had warm water in the Mediterranean?" Rod asked. "We'd never have thought of it in Scotland—the water is far too cold."

"Warm water doubtless helped," Borghese replied, smiling. "But our naval tradition goes back to Roman days, when we fought Carthage for command of the sea."

He turned to Abby. "To reply to your point, Abby, my grandfather was a remarkable figure who inspired great loyalty and affection from his men, in war and also in peace. Several members of his old unit embraced his politics and even backed his quixotic coup attempt in 1970. I don't know many details, but I learned from his letters that he believed his coup attempt would get American support. At the time, the Americans under your president Nixon and Dr. Kissinger were very nervous about Berlinguer, Italy's liberal Marxist who pioneered Eurocommunism and at one point looked likely to win an election."

"Was this the time known as Italy's years of lead?" Julien asked. "A time of assassinations and kidnappings of politicians and business leaders by the anti-Communist extreme left, Trotskyites and Gramsci, the Red Brigades and so on."

"Yes, but with similar outrages, including public bombings by the extreme right. I should stress that my grandfather was always against that," Borghese replied. "And the far right had a lot of covert support from our security police because they were frightened by the wave of strikes unleashed in 1969."

"Just like de Gaulle was frightened by the student revolts in Paris in '68," said Julien, nodding.

"And the Soviets sent tanks into Prague because they were afraid of, what, a moderate version of socialism?" asked Borghese, grinning and evidently enjoying this exchange, while his glance lingered on Abby.

"I thought the Soviets were more worried by Mao's Red Guard

in China," she said. Bruno noticed the way she kept her eyes fixed on the Italian, and the coolly interested way he returned her gaze.

"They were, which was why Brezhnev and Nixon, those two old white men, clung to each other with détente," chimed in Amélie, laughing.

Bruno, who had struggled to keep up with this account of a period before he was born, was not at all sure how much of this banter was serious. There were smiles on the faces of Borghese, Julien, Amélie and Abby. It reminded him of some of the meetings of the local Périgord historical society, when the professional intellectuals, the teachers and researchers, sometimes seemed to wander off into a world of arcane jokes that only they understood. He didn't resent it, suspecting that any member of the public would feel just as lost if trying to understand the mock insults and in-jokes when a bunch of cops got together, or a reunion of old soldiers. Interesting, he thought, how tribal we humans can be.

"I'm supposed to be working this morning," he said, rising and leaving a two-euro coin and change on the table to pay for his coffee and croissant. Balzac rose at once, raising one front paw while looking at his master, as if to announce his readiness for duty. Julien said that he and Jack Crimson were planning to lunch at Ivan's bistro, if Bruno's duties allowed him to join them.

"I'll try," Bruno said, thinking that he'd probably be tied up with Goirau's operation. "But if I'm not there by twelve-fifteen, I won't be able to make it, so please go ahead without me."

"May I stroll with you?" Borghese asked, rising from the table. "I'd like to know a little more about St. Denis before I visit the Lascaux cave with Abby. Perhaps you'd like to join us, Abby?"

"I'd better go home to put some of this shopping into my fridge," she replied, glancing at her watch. "We're booked for the English-language group at Lascaux at eleven-thirty, so we'd better leave here by ten-thirty. I'll pick you up at the bank, just across the bridge. You take a quick look at the town with Bruno, and I'll meet you there in forty minutes."

"Of course," said Bruno. "I'll be taking a look at the flowers and the shrine, and you're welcome to come along, but then I have to call in at the gendarmerie to consult with colleagues."

"I'll find my own way back," Borghese replied, keeping pace beside Bruno on the side not occupied by Balzac. He went on in a different, almost subdued tone of voice. "Julien tells me you were a regular soldier before becoming a policeman."

"Yes, but never an officer," Bruno replied. "If I'd done better in school, I might have tried for the air force, but somehow the navy never crossed my mind. I know you're a military diplomat these days, but were you a seafaring man at first, or did you follow the family tradition in submarines?"

"No, always on surface ships, on a destroyer at first and then mostly patrol vessels. I was about to be assigned to command a frigate but got sick. I hope for another command once my work in Paris is over, but I fear I may be transferred to NATO headquarters in Brussels."

"I'd have thought that headquarters would be a good career move," said Bruno.

"Perhaps, but I'd prefer to get back to sea, if possible, only not in the patrol boats. It almost broke my heart, spending our days on the trail of refugees in the leaking wrecks they took to sea. It wasn't for such sad work that I'd joined the navy. It was the same for my sailors. You know, when we leave port and head out to sea, it used to be a moment full of possibility, a sense of freedom. Not anymore."

"You mean the refugees in their flimsy boats?"

"Of course, and who knows how many died, women and children as well as men. We think around thirty thousand since 2015. Some died in their life jackets, from thirst or hunger, or we found what the sharks had left. We were told not to bring back such human remains."

"It must have been grim," said Bruno, wondering if the illness Borghese had mentioned had been some kind of breakdown. It was one thing for soldiers to see casualties, one's own comrades or the other side's, but he'd learned in Bosnia that seeing what war did to civilians was something much worse.

"But there's another side to the coin," said Bruno as the piled-up rows of flowers came into view and Balzac trotted ahead to sniff his way along the heaped blooms. "There are even more flowers here today than yesterday."

"Laying flowers at a grave is an easy gesture," Borghese replied.

At that moment, on one of those hunches he had come to trust, Bruno focused on a solitary figure among the score or so of people taking photos of the flowers. Most of them were families, and there were two female couples, but one man stood out. He was wearing a big canvas hat and a trench coat despite the sunshine, and he kept glancing around as though watching for something. Bruno pulled out his phone and took a quick photo, although the man was far too distant. Perhaps he'd been alerted by Bruno's swift movement, but the man turned on his heel and strode away toward an anonymous white Renault. He climbed in and drove off rapidly in the direction of Ste. Alvère.

Could it have been Abby's ex-husband, Gary? Bruno looked at the image on his phone, enlarging it as much as he could, but the face was too vague. A second photo he'd taken of the car was too distant for the number of the license plate to be visible. Nonetheless he forwarded both images to Goirau and to the police technician in Périgueux, asking if the face and number could be usefully enlarged. Then he called Sergeant Jules, asking him to put out a local alert to all gendarmes for a white Renault hatchback, heading from St. Denis on the road to Ste. Alvère. The male driver was to be stopped and have his papers checked and delayed until Bruno could get there. It was a long shot, but worth a try.

"What was that about?" asked Borghese.

"It could be a man we're looking for, Abby's ex-husband, an American who also has an Italian passport. He seems to be mixed up in some funny business with blockchain money and maybe in helping Russians get around sanctions. The Americans are interested in him, too."

"This is the guy that Abby mentioned, whose American family made a hero of my grandfather?"

"The very same," Bruno replied. "He's a computer whiz, and Abby met him when he was running the database on an archaeological dig where she was working. She says he made a fortune in cryptocurrency and went crazy in the process, which was when she divorced him. Then he lost all his money, came after her, began to trash her car and her house, and she got a court order to restrain him. It's mainly why she moved here. Now it looks like he may be on her trail again. We think he's been trying to break into our police computers."

"Any indication of Mafia links with his Italian American family?"

"That would be way above my pay grade, but the FBI is certainly interested in him."

"This must be pretty dramatic stuff for a local policeman like you," Borghese replied. "Except that Julien hinted to me that you sometimes work with France's security service."

Bruno was saved from having to concoct some kind of reply when his phone vibrated and the screen said it was Goirau. Balzac trotted back to Bruno, looking up at his master, presumably having made the connection between the sound of vibration and Bruno starting to talk into that strange box beside his ear.

"Excuse me, I have to take this. Police business." Bruno

answered the phone and moved away, toward the bridge that led to the Domaine de la Barde.

"I assume the man got away," Goirau began.

"Probably, but I put out an alert for the gendarmes. We may get lucky. We can check with rental agencies, recent car sales and so on. I'm hoping the tech wizards can come up with a face or at least a license plate number from the photos I took."

"You have a car at your disposal?"

"Yes, about ten minutes away. It's market day so I'm on foot patrol. Any developments at your end?"

"I've been sent a report from *Kommersant,* the Russian business journal, that Russia has just become the world's second-biggest miner of cryptocurrency. The Duma, Russia's parliament, is even proposing opening a state-backed trading center for the stuff. It's their new way of evading sanctions. And we were the world's third-hardest-hit country for ransomware last year, after the United States and Britain."

"Really? I'm surprised. I didn't think we'd come across that here."

"That's where you're wrong, Bruno," said Goirau. "In October last year, just as the COVID epidemic was filling our hospitals, there was a surge of TrickBot malware attacks on hospitals in America, Britain and here in France. It was so serious that the Pentagon's own cyber command was called in, and we and the Brits joined in the counterattack. That was when the Elysée found a billion euros to finance a massive buildup of our cybersecurity. The politicians saw to their alarm that in the international cybersecurity index, France wasn't even in the top ten, way behind the Americans, the British and the Saudis in the top three.

"Behind the attacks was a group we call Wizard Spider, based in St. Petersburg, and one thing they never do is attack any Russian targets—probably because they're very close to Russian intelligence. Their main tools of breaking into computer systems and then blocking them pending a ransom are called TrickBot, Ryuk and Conti, but they developed a fourth system, purely for spying, not for ransomware, called Spidoh. And that's what somebody was trying to insert into the police computer in Périgueux."

"Putain!" said Bruno. "Why have we never heard of this stuff?"

"Probably because it's too complicated for the mainstream media, too specialized and too scary," Goirau replied. "And it's part of this cryptocurrency issue. It's the way the criminals demand that their ransom money is paid because we can't trace the cash back to them. That's why I want you to join me for a videoconference at two this afternoon at the police *commissariat* in Périgueux. It's the most secure spot we have. If this Gary Barone is behind this, we have to find him and bring him in."

Chapter 27

"Important call?" came Borghese's voice from a distance as Bruno closed the phone and looked up. He'd been so focused on Goirau's voice that he'd barely noticed that he was standing just in front of the rickety bridge that led to the *domaine*. His boots squelched muddily, the ground being sodden from the stream that was threatening to seep over its banks.

"Yes, police business, about a meeting later today," Bruno said, stepping up onto the bridge. "Come this way, it's another route back, and I'd like to show you something, a handsome old building that has been disused for years and that we now hope to restore."

He led the way across the bridge and along the path through the undergrowth and into what had once been a formal garden that still stretched out before the building with hints of its former grandeur. The main structure of the *domaine* was elegant despite being run-down. As they approached, Bruno heard Tim Birch calling from one of the windows.

"You're just the man I wanted to see, Bruno. We have squatters. They broke in through the side door at the rear. Come and see, it's wide open."

The ground floor was dusty, with some scraps of furniture,

but upstairs was a mess. Sleeping bags and rucksacks had been left haphazardly on the floor, and amateurish caricatures were scrawled on walls, a few of them obscene but mostly playful. Some windows had been blocked with flattened cardboard boxes, including pizza containers, presumably so that any lights would not show. Pinned to one door was a flyer advertising work by the day, picking grapes in nearby vineyards at ten euros per hour. The bathrooms and toilets were relatively clean, which was rare for squatters. Bruno turned on a tap to see water flow and noted several towels hanging to dry on ropes stretched between various pipes.

"The water system must still be connected to the house next door," said Birch.

"How did you find out they were here?" Bruno asked.

"I look around the place every day or two and this morning I found the side door open. Whose responsibility is it to look after the property and its security?"

"The judge of the bankruptcy court is responsible, and there's usually an arrangement with the local gendarmes to take a regular look, but there aren't enough of them to keep a permanent watch. I'll have a word with them. But it seems that your squatters are a fairly clean and tidy bunch. It could have been a lot worse."

"What will the gendarmes do?"

"If you want to make a fuss with the judge, he could ask the gendarmes to confiscate the belongings and leave a note saying they can be collected at the gendarmerie, but they are unlikely to take any further action. There are always squatters at this time of year, making a few euros in the vineyards, and some of them would do far more damage than this."

Tim nodded, then glanced at Borghese, who'd followed Bruno inside the house.

"Aren't you that Italian diplomat?"

Borghese agreed that he was and shook hands. "I presume

you're the would-be owner, once this gets out of the bankruptcy court," he said. "You're a lucky man—it could be a splendid property once again."

Birch nodded. "Because of finding the grave, it's now going to take rather longer than I'd expected."

As Birch began to explain his plans for the place, Bruno called Sergeant Jules at the gendarmerie to explain that Birch had found squatters. Bruno was asked to stay until a gendarme arrived, which gave him time to call Colette at the *mairie* and ask her to inform the bankruptcy judge.

"Have you thought about the land you might want in exchange for the remembrance garden?" Bruno asked Birch, putting away his phone.

"Yes, I talked to the judge after the lunch at the *mairie,* and he said he'd approve whatever the mayor and I agreed. So I had an idea I wanted to run past you," Birch said. "The remembrance garden is going to be roughly half a hectare, so I'd be happy to take that stretch of woodland alongside the stream. It's not much more than half a hectare. And since the town is going to rebuild my bridge, I'd like to buy some shares in the town vineyard. Once I'm open I expect to be buying something like fifty cases of wine every year, so I might as well source my house wine locally."

"Makes sense to me," said Bruno. "After all, the whole town will benefit if your project is a success. Let me run it past the mayor, unofficially, at first, and if he agrees we'll put the deal to the council and tell them the judge has already approved it. What do you plan to do with that woodland?"

"I'll leave it as it is but make a pathway through it, alongside the stream, with a couple of benches. The birdsong is lovely, but I'll need to clean out the streambed—it looks like it hasn't been done for years. Even with the rains we've had lately, the stream shouldn't be so high."

Bruno nodded agreement, and the two men shook hands.

"When you open, I think I might be one of your first guests," said Borghese, courteously thanking Birch for the opportunity to look around the *domaine*. "I'd like to come back with my father. I want to do more research into the history of Alonso in Bordeaux, with Bruno's historian friend to help. I've already agreed to send him copies of all my grandfather's letters. Perhaps we could erect a plaque at the shrine explaining Alonso's background."

"Good idea," said Bruno. "Maybe we could even learn more about the two German girls. I'm on duty, so we'd better head back to town. You have to meet Abby, anyway."

Bruno planned first to brief the mayor on Birch's proposal before going on to explain that he'd be in Périgueux later in the afternoon for a videoconference. He also thought he'd better give the mayor a brief account of what he'd heard from Goirau about malware, Wizard Spider and cryptocurrency. As he was marshaling his thoughts, his phone vibrated. It was Hodge, at the U.S. Embassy in Paris.

"Hi, Bruno. It's a sad Saturday when a civil servant like me is still working," Hodge began. "It seems that this business with Garibaldi Barone has got my colleagues in the organized crime department in Washington really excited. It turns out the guy is very heavily connected."

"What?" Bruno asked, startled. "You mean Mafia?"

"Sort of, but with a different name, the 'Ndrangheta Calabrese," Hodge replied. "I'm told that these days it's bigger, richer and much more powerful than the Sicilian Mafia, having spread its global connections more widely. They benefited from the cocaine boom and have developed special relationships in South America and more recently with Russia, where they've forged a long alliance with the Solntsevskaya Bratva. That's the organized crime brotherhood that owns Vnukovo airport and controls much of the Moscow Ring Road. The 'Ndrangheta's base is the Calabrian peninsula, but these days they are global, big in Canada and Australia. Barone's grandfather, who went to New Jersey when he was just eighteen, never got much of an education and fell into bad company. Barone's father did the same, and while young Gary tried to go straight, the collapse of his fortune and his marriage left him with the obvious option of the family business, just when the 'Ndrangheta was getting interested in the whole cryptocurrency game."

"So why is he in France?" Bruno asked. "His ex-wife has made it very clear that the divorce is final and that she doesn't want to see him anywhere near her."

"I don't know, Bruno. Maybe he doesn't want to take no for an answer. Maybe he reckons she owes him something, but whatever it is we seem to have a chance here to scoop him up and extradite him back to the States, where we can make him an offer he can't refuse."

"We just have to find him."

"This may be where we can help," said Hodge. "We have an Italian phone number for him that tells us that he took a flight from Rome to Istanbul and then one that was heading for Moscow before the phone was switched off. We then have the same phone being turned on four days later in Nicosia airport, Cyprus, some forty minutes after a flight landed from Moscow. The phone turns up again in Naples later that day, and I will bet you a lunch that you'll find that same phone number kissing cell towers somewhere near St. Denis this week. You want to take that bet, Bruno?"

"No, I won't take the bet because I suspect that you have ways of getting the cooperation of France Telecom's security office. But I'll happily treat you to lunch if you're right."

"Here's the phone number." Hodge read it off. "Keep me informed, okay?"

Bruno called the security office of the phone network, gave his name and code number and asked for a watch on the Italian number Hodge had given him. Bruno knew that the phone could be tracked to its last location, even if turned off, through its fifteen-digit IMEI (international mobile equipment identity) number, inscribed on the metal SIM tray of every phone. He then messaged Goirau and General Lannes with the information before looking for the mayor.

"Thank heavens you're here," said the mayor as Bruno put his head around the door. He handed Bruno a fax. "We have an emergency. I just received this from the hydroelectric center, a warning that the dams upstream are getting close to capacity and they may have to start releasing water."

"But it's not November yet," said Bruno. "That only happens in winter."

"It was a very wet August and September, and you've seen the amount of rain we've had in the past few days, or rather nights," the mayor said with a shrug. "At the last meeting of mayors, we were all congratulating ourselves that the tourist season was saved because down here it was only raining at night. But up there on the massif, the rain hasn't stopped since mid-August. That's why the dams are filling up."

The ancient volcanic region of the Massif Central covered about one-sixth of France. The prevailing winds from the Atlantic brought clouds to dump their water on the massif and make it the reservoir of France. The great rivers that watered France all the way to the Atlantic coast were born there: the Loire, the Lot, the Tarn, the Dordogne, the Ardèche and the Vézère. And toward the east the massif's high ground also fed rains into the Rhône Valley and down to the Mediterranean.

In Bruno's decade and more in St. Denis, each flood had come because the dams far upriver had been forced to release water or risk being overwhelmed. The fate of St. Denis rested mainly on three big dams farther up the Vézère River, but a far greater mass of water was held back by the ten much larger dams on the Dordogne. The largest one, Bort-les-Orgues, held back a vast lake of water that was twelve miles in length and contained nearly five hundred million cubic meters of water. If that dam ever burst, the surging wave would be nineteen meters high when it hit Bergerac. More alarming for St. Denis, when it reached the hilltop town of Limeuil where the Vézère flowed into the larger Dordogne, the great mass of Dordogne water would overwhelm and block the flow of the Vézère and start flooding back upstream toward St. Denis. Bruno's fellow citizens would have at most ten hours' notice from the breach of the dam to evacuate the town.

"If they are about to release water from the Vézère dams, how long before they start dumping from the Dordogne?" Bruno asked.

"That will depend on the rainfall over the next twenty-four hours, they tell me." The mayor was making an effort to keep his voice calm. "I asked why now, when we were always advised that peak flood risk would come at the end of winter."

"Did they have an answer?"

"They asked if I knew the seas around Britain and our coast were close to five degrees warmer this summer. Apparently warmer water evaporates from the sea's surface more quickly, so the clouds have been much denser than usual, and as a result they dumped much more water onto the Massif Central."

"So, it's climate change, coming a lot faster than we expected," said Bruno.

"Indeed. Still, we're promised twelve hours' notice before they start releasing water from the dam at Viam, which will give us time to organize the evacuation of the camping sites close to the river and maybe some of the more low-lying areas."

"Evacuation?" Bruno repeated, startled. "But that never came up before, except as a hypothetical possibility."

"That's because we only expected flooding to come in winter when the campsites are empty," the mayor said. "Now with the schoolkids on midterm break we still have a fair number of tourists, though they'll be gone next week. I'm going to convene an emergency meeting of the council this evening at six, and I'd like you to make sure the gendarmes and the fire brigade send someone senior."

"I have a police meeting in Périgueux at two, but I'll explain that this potential disaster has to take priority and be sure to get back here by six," Bruno said, jotting down tasks in his notebook as he spoke. "I'll brief the others now. We should also make sure that the schools, *collège* and medical center all send someone. We'll need all available buses and volunteers with cars, so I'd better tell the rugby and hunting clubs, and we should check how much space is available at campsites on higher ground."

"I'll call the prefect," said the mayor, reaching for the phone. "Perhaps you could get Claire to arrange a meeting of all staff in the council chamber in fifteen minutes."

Bruno went straight to his old office, explained the situation to Colette and asked her to help Claire to convene all staff. He also wanted to know what she'd done with his old filing cabinet, which contained the various emergency plans. It was in the room she had been assigned but deemed unfit for human use, she replied.

Bruno called Yveline at the gendarmerie, Albert at the fire station and Fabiola at the clinic to tell them of the meeting at six. He'd have to find time later to call Rollo at the *collège,* Lespinasse at the rugby club and Stéphane for the hunting club. He could do it from his van as he drove to Goirau's meeting. He collected his emergency files, skimming through them as he called his counterparts, Juliette in Les Eyzies and Louis in Montignac, to check whether they'd heard the news from the hydroelectrical team. Neither one had, and Bruno had a brief mental image of faxes being left unnoticed in dusty fax machines. Finally, he called Philippe Delaron and asked him to check whether the radio station and the *Sud Ouest* news desk were yet aware of the problem.

Then he went to the council chamber and turned back to his files, scribbling down reminders in his notebook to inform the local supermarkets of a likely need for emergency supplies, particularly fresh water if the pumping station was flooded. He'd have to find a load of sandbags, and what about the electricity supply? He called Michel at the public works office, told him to attend the meeting and check the waterworks and power on the way. He made a checklist of the people that he'd called and those he had yet to reach, and then went through the emergency plan again. He could remember drafting it, years ago, when the thought of a flood in the last weekend of October was ridiculous. What he should have done, he thought, was to have made just four calls: to Michel, the gendarmes, the firemen and the medical center. Then those four should each have had to call three or four more people, and so on.

Most of the staff had gathered awaiting the mayor, and the hands of the old wall clock were a minute or two short of midday. Bruno asked if anyone had a radio. Somebody had an app on their phone and the room fell silent as the tinny voice of the newscaster announced the flood warning for the Vézère Valley, explaining that unusually high rainfall in the Massif Central had almost filled the dams. The mayor entered and the app was switched off.

"Thank you all for coming, and for staying when I'm sure you all want to get back to your families for lunch, but we're facing the prospect of a real and most unusual challenge—an emergency flood warning for St. Denis and the whole of the Vézère Valley.

"I have just been speaking with the president's team at the Elysée," the mayor went on. "In response to my request of the prefect of this *département* today, the president has authorized the Armée de l'Air to look into cloud-seeding measures using small particles of silver iodide over the clouds crossing our coastline. This should prevent more rain falling on the massif. The amounts of salt being dropped would not be dangerous to human health.

"We expect controlled release of water from the Lac de Viam to begin this evening, and by tomorrow morning a rise in the level of our river here of five to six meters above the usual winter peak," he went on. "That should not flood any major roads in this commune, nor should it affect our water and electricity supply. As a precaution, however, we will begin later today to evacuate three low-lying campsites. There's room available at other campsites on higher ground. We do not expect our police, fire or emergency services to be disrupted by flooding, but in case of any unexpected development we will have reinforcements on standby in Périgueux.

"Some of our neighboring communes upstream may be more seriously affected, so although the *mairie* usually closes at noon on Saturday until Monday morning, I would be grateful for any volunteers prepared to join Bruno, Michel and his public works department team and me in maintaining a skeleton service here throughout the weekend, and being available to help in Les Eyzies, St. Léon, Montignac or other communes in difficulties. We will try to keep an information service going on the town website, and we are holding an emergency council meeting at six this evening.

"One final cautionary point," the mayor added. "Cloud seeding is not an exact science and it may not work as planned. Coastal regions may well block the plan after the damage done to them by last year's floods because of deforestation. So we could be facing a larger release of water down the Vézère Valley than we currently expect. If we're really out of luck and they start releasing water from the big dams on the Dordogne at the same time, we could be in real trouble. The extra water would overwhelm and probably block the flow of the Vézère at Limeuil, where the two rivers meet. The Vézère would then start back-flooding toward us.

"If that happened, I would have little choice but to order an evacuation of all nonessential personnel from St. Denis up to higher ground. Essential personnel means police, fire, all medical services including pharmacists, along with Michel's team. We shall also be contacting all licensed plumbers and electricians in the commune, since we're likely to need their skills. Our priority for evacuation would then be the retirement home, all the elderly who are receiving care at home, the disabled and all families with children under the age of sixteen."

A heavy silence fell as the mayor stared around the crowded council chamber.

"I'm sure you will all rise to the occasion and conduct yourselves in the highest spirit of public service."

Chapter 28

Bruno parked his police van in the *commissariat* parking lot in Périgueux, emptied his pockets before going through the scanner and was escorted to a windowless room with a video screen dominating one wall. Goirau and J-J rose to greet him.

Bruno told them of his conversation with Hodge.

"We know," said Goirau. "General Lannes passed on your message and we've been scanning for what used to be that Italian phone. This guy Barone is an amateur. He changed the Italian SIM card for a French one when he landed at Charles de Gaulle without pausing or changing his location, so we can now track him in real time through the new number."

"Where is he now?" Bruno asked.

"Sharing a *gîte* with a family of Italian tourists near Ste. Alvère and driving a white Renault hatchback, the one I gather that you saw him drive away this morning."

"Do we pick him up?" Bruno asked.

"That's what we need to decide," said Goirau.

"The presence of his ex-wife seems to be the attraction," said Bruno. "And maybe some of the divorce settlement money she got."

"Somehow I feel there's more to it than that," said Goirau, gesturing to the three chairs lined up before the video screen. "We should start the conference."

The screen flashed and then settled into four segments, J-J, Bruno and Goirau visible in one. The second revealed Colonel Morillon, the third was blank, and the fourth featured General Lannes, who seemed focused on the screen of his phone.

"Messieurs," said Goirau, and Lannes looked up.

"What's this about flood warnings, Bruno?" the general asked.

"Unusually heavy rains," said Bruno. "They are having to dump water from the dams on the Dordogne and Vézère, so down here in the valley we're on evacuation watch. This means I have to be back in St. Denis by six."

"We're monitoring Barone's phone," said Morillon. "And we're following two other Italian phones that are in the same location, belonging to a couple who appear to be husband and wife, traveling with a child. Each parent made two calls to relatives who sounded like grandparents, one set in New Jersey in the U.S. and the other in Taranto, Italy. Barone has made no calls and seems only to use his phone to monitor news sites and Bitcoin values, which appear to be rising."

A new image appeared on the vacant panel; the pixels did a crazy dance and then stabilized into Hodge's face. *"Bonjour à tous,"* he said.

Morillon repeated what he'd said, and Hodge asked if anything was known about the Italian family.

"If you can get me an address or a precise location in Ste. Alvère, I'll get their *mairie* onto it, and we should get a name and a bank account number for the tenant if the place is registered for rentals," said Bruno. "Not all of them are, but if not, there's a tax issue that would allow us to pounce."

"Barone rented a car at the Bordeaux airport, showing his

Italian passport and an Italian driver's license, and he has it for another week, so I don't think he's going anywhere," interjected Lannes.

"The extradition request for Barone has been drafted, citing breach of sanctions, conspiracy to commit fraud and tax evasion," said Hodge. "It was hand-delivered to your justice ministry today. Can you charge him with anything under French law?"

"Telecom offenses, wiretapping, attempted breach of police security systems," replied Lannes. "But it's not as though we want to put him behind bars. Monsieur Hodge, am I right to presume you do not necessarily want him back in America to face justice? My devious mind asks whether perhaps you would rather have him at liberty in Russia, working for you from the inside. In that case we'll be happy to cooperate on the clear understanding that you would be sharing the results with us."

"That's the spirit of the deal, yes," Hodge replied. From the screen, Lannes and Morillon smiled in quiet satisfaction, and Bruno sensed Goirau nodding complacently beside him.

"None of us knows this guy," said Bruno, a little alarmed at how quickly this plan was unfolding. "We can't even guess how good or reliable he'd be at working undercover, how much we'd be able to trust him. Has anybody here even met him?"

"No, but we've never had anybody in a position to get into Hydra and Garantex before, not to mention the Russian intelligence connection," said Morillon. "Getting into the FSB communications would be a prize worth taking a few risks for."

"Is there anything to link him directly to the ransomware attacks on French hospitals you told me about?" Bruno asked, turning to Goirau. "We'll need some serious evidence to hold him for more than twenty-four hours."

"In twenty-four hours, we can have him in front of a friendly magistrate who can authorize us to deliver him over to the American authorities," said Lannes, curtly.

A silence fell and Bruno felt compelled to break it.

"Barone is an American, even though he has an Italian passport, and he has a college degree," Bruno went on. "He grew up watching cop shows on TV, so the first thing he'll do is demand a lawyer. If he's then taken to an airport and sent across the Atlantic, where does that leave us when his American lawyer files a complaint? Would that be embarrassing for you, Monsieur Hodge?"

Hodge pursed his lips but said nothing.

"Where are you going with this, Bruno?" Lannes asked.

Bruno spread out his hands. "Let me remind you that I'm an *officier judiciaire,* which means that I'm sworn to proceed with due regard to any suspect's rights under the law, for which I am responsible to the *procureur de la République.* And in an affair such as this we'd all prefer Monsieur Barone to be a willing partner, so I suggest that we should proceed with that in mind."

"Bruno is right," said J-J. "And I, too, am an *officier judiciaire,* with the same legal responsibilities. We should proceed with caution."

"I agree," said Goirau. "We need to do this by the book, or we could have some unpleasant publicity when Barone's lawyer claims his client was improperly arrested by the French cops."

"What do you suggest, Bruno?" asked Lannes.

"That I, or maybe Monsieur Goirau, should call on him and say that we know of the legal order restraining him from visiting his ex-wife and that she has told the French police that she fears he may be planning to visit her while he's in the region. Monsieur Goirau could point out his concerns about cybercrime, the evasion of financial sanctions against Russia and so on. He could then raise the issue of the attempts to break into the police and *mairie* computers and show him a warrant, signed by a magistrate, to examine his laptop to satisfy ourselves that he's not responsible."

"I agree with Bruno," said Goirau. "That would be the legal

way to proceed, and with an inquiry initiated by a French magistrate, our American colleague would be covered against any embarrassment in the American courts."

"How soon can you get this warrant?" Lannes asked.

"With one call," said Bruno. He pulled out his phone, called his friend Annette in Sarlat and explained what they needed and why. Five minutes later, the warrant was being printed out by one of J-J's aides.

"Can you track Barone's phone to locate the precise location of the *gîte* in Ste. Alvère and then email it to my phone and to Yveline or Sergeant Jules in St. Denis?" he asked Morillon. "They can get a gendarme there within thirty minutes."

"Is it that urgent?" Goirau asked.

"It's Saturday, the usual changeover day for rental properties," Bruno explained. "They may be moving on to somewhere else."

"Wait," said Lannes. "You pick him up, take him to the gendarmerie in St. Denis and you and Goirau question him there."

"I suggest we bring him here to Périgueux. There's a smart technician in the *commissariat,* Mademoiselle Teyssier, who'll examine his laptop along with Goirau, and perhaps Colonel Morillon's team would also have access," said Bruno. "That should give us the evidence we need for a charge of attempted hacking of the police computer and also of the St. Denis *mairie.* Each attempt carries a penalty of two years in prison and a fine of thirty thousand euros. If he tried to change any data, it's three years. And we'd share any relevant evidence with our American friends."

"Sounds good to me," said Hodge. "All nice and legal."

"We have the location of his phone," said Morillon. "It's just off the Route du Maquis on the way to Cendrieux, near a small lake. Do you know the place?"

"Not the house, but I know the area. I've hunted wild boar there, in the forest of Les Foulissards," said Bruno. "It housed a big Resistance camp in the war."

"Shall we go?" asked Goirau. "I'll come with you."

"Somebody should call J-J, Commissaire Jalipeau and his boss, Prunier, to make sure they're on board. They should both still be in the building," said Bruno. "And I can call the gendarmes on the way."

"Don't worry," said Lannes. "I'll call upstairs and brief Commandante Yveline in St. Denis."

"Wish I could join you," said Morillon. "We'll keep monitoring the phones."

"And call me as soon as you have him in custody," said Lannes. He was looking suddenly rather lonely, just him, Morillon and Hodge now on the screen, each in his own office, separated by space and united only by electrons.

In the parking lot, Bruno paused to open the back of his van, used the separate key to open the weapons safe and took out his SIG Pro handgun. He checked the action, the magazine and the safety, then put the holster onto his belt.

"Do you think Barone might be armed?" Goirau asked eagerly, like a boy going on an adventure, and Bruno wondered how many armed raids Goirau had joined.

"I have no idea, but I'd rather be armed and not need it than the reverse," Bruno replied, before driving out of the police garage into heavy rain. It was midafternoon but felt like dusk. They had just left the city when Yveline called; she was near the house.

"We did a discreet drive-by, and the rented white Renault hatchback is still there," she said. "Should we wait for you to arrive?"

"Yes, since I have the warrant," Bruno replied. "We'll be there in about ten minutes. Goirau, from the *fisc,* is with me."

"*Ça va,* we'll only move in if someone looks like they're leaving in that car." She ended the call.

"Tell me about the ex-wife," said Goirau.

Bruno explained Abby's arrival, her connection to the prehistory museum and her plan to be a guide, followed by the background of her ex-husband. He then recounted the story of the Italian naval attaché who had come to St. Denis for the ceremony of the three bodies in the grave, the history of the submarines of the Second World War, the tale of Prince Borghese and the failed coup of 1970 in Rome that had sent Barone's grandfather into Spanish exile.

"It's the grandson we now want, the ex-husband of Abby, the American who wants to be a guide," Bruno said.

"That reminds me of Mark Twain, who once said that history does not repeat itself, but sometimes it rhymes," Goirau said, laughing.

"And here we are, heading back into the Second World War and the Resistance camp of Durestal," said Bruno, passing the ruined tower of the Ste. Alvère château and turning onto the Route du Maquis. "History seems to be rhyming again."

He took a left before the lake and into a relatively secluded part of the forest, then up a track to what had probably been a woodsman's cottage. It had been modernized with an extension, a small covered swimming pool and an old barn that had become a garage. A white Renault was parked in front of it. Bruno pulled in close behind the Renault to prevent its departure. He could dimly see figures behind the glass panes of the enclosed pool. The condensation on the glass suggested the interior was probably heated. He called Yveline and asked her to bring her vehicle, with blue lights flashing, in exactly two minutes to block the entrance road.

Bruno stepped out from his van, the gun's weight dragging at his waist, and took the warrant from his breast pocket. A big, almost plump man of middle age wearing trunks and flip-flops stared at him from beside the pool, an uncertain smile on his face, before he slid aside one of the glass panels.

"Monsieur Barone?" Bruno inquired, politely, noticing that

the man had a bandage around his right ankle, with his entire foot wrapped in a plastic bag so he could swim without getting the bandage wet. From the size of him this looked very like the man whose ankle Balzac had savaged.

"He's in the house making drinks," said the man, in stilted French, as a woman in a swimsuit standing behind him draped herself in a large towel and clutched a little boy to her side at the sight of Bruno's uniform. Behind the covered pool and to the side of the house was a small shed, its door open to reveal a lawn mower and an elderly trail bike.

A slimmer man in his mid-to-late thirties in flip-flops and a white terry-cloth robe came from the house carrying a tray. He was balding, but what Bruno could see of his body was remarkably hairy, almost like the pelt of an animal, and he had one of those half beards that left his upper lip bare. No such beard had been on the passport photograph, but beards can be grown, and there was enough of a resemblance to the photo to persuade Bruno that this was their man.

"That's him, all right," said Goirau, looking down at a printout of the passport.

Understandably, Barone looked bemused at the sight of an armed policeman in uniform. On the tray were three glasses of what looked like kir and one of orange juice, presumably for the boy.

"Monsieur Giuseppe Garibaldi Barone, I have a warrant for your arrest on a charge of attempted hacking of official computers," Bruno said politely, proud of the English phrases he had memorized. "Please don't be alarmed. I am sure this is just a formality, but I must ask you to get dressed in my presence and give me your passport, your phone and whatever other electronic devices you may have in the house. You could be back here in time for dinner with your friends.

"Sorry to bother you, madame," Bruno called to the nervous

woman wrapped in a towel who was watching from the open door of the enclosed pool, her child huddled against her. She turned and put her hand nervously to her mouth at the sight of Sergeant Jules in uniform coming ponderously up the drive, a pistol in his hand.

"What do you want with my brother?" she asked, in English simple enough for Bruno to understand.

"Just a formality, madame, probably some mix-up," Bruno replied in the same language and smiled at her, delighted at the confirmation that this was indeed Barone's sister, traveling with her husband and child. So that meant that the man with the bandage on his ankle was her husband, who could therefore be identified as the owner of the motorbike who had been bitten by Balzac while attacking Colette Cantagnac. He was evidently Barone's brother-in-law, and now subject to arrest for assault and attempted theft.

Barone looked down at the tray, more as if confused rather than wondering whether to throw it at Bruno, and saw Goirau with a radio-microphone close to his mouth, prepared to call for reinforcements if required.

"Put the tray on the table, monsieur, and lead the way to where you keep your clothes and computer," Bruno said, and then said to Goirau, "The others are not to come inside, is that clear?"

"*Oui,* Chef," Goirau replied.

And at that moment, Yveline reversed the gendarme vehicle into the driveway close beside Bruno's van, blue lights flashing, blocking any hope of escape.

Chapter 29

Gabrielle Teyssier at the *commissariat* in Périgueux beamed at Bruno as he handed her, wrapped in plastic bags, two MacBook Pro laptops and one Lenovo ThinkPad Extreme, two Apple smartphones and one Android he'd taken after a search of Barone's *gîte*. He handed four passports to J-J, each in a separate evidence bag. There were two each, Italian and American, for Gary Barone and for his brother-in-law.

"Bonjour," said J-J, shaking hands with Goirau first, then Bruno. "General Lannes already called to say you were coming and that Goirau would brief me."

"I want a lawyer," said Barone loudly in English from the reception area, and then he repeated the words in bad French. He had changed into slacks, a jacket and a polo shirt.

"I also demand a lawyer," said Barone's brother-in-law, the man with the bandage around his ankle.

"Désolé, messieurs," said J-J, giving Barone a broad smile, but speaking French. "Saturday afternoon, you know how it is."

He led Bruno and Goirau from the reception area into a small side room and closed the door. "The first bad news is that we have a bunch of trainee magistrates visiting with their professor and they are aching to see a genuine booking, so we'll have to do everything by the book. The second bad news is that I thought this guy had an arrest record, but the paperwork I was sent by Hodge does not include fingerprints. And the embassy says Hodge seems to have left for the day."

"Merde," said Goirau. "That's just a detail." Bruno was already trying Hodge's mobile, waited for five, six seconds and was about to give up when Hodge panted a reply and an apology. He was heading home and had been in an underground garage. Bruno explained the problem.

"It was a state arrest, not federal, so California has the fingerprints and hasn't sent them yet," Hodge said. "I'll call them again, but they are nine hours behind us, just starting their day."

"*Mon vieux,* you understand that we're here trying to do you a favor," said Bruno.

"I know, I know," Hodge said. "But California—it's like a different country. That's why I'm going through the FBI rather than the locals."

"I'm sure you will do what you can," said Bruno. "I'll call you when he asks to speak to his embassy." He closed his phone and glanced from Goirau to J-J. "We can arrest them both for the attack on Colette Cantagnac. There's what is almost certainly Balzac's dog bite on the guy's ankle, and we can get a positive identification from the guy who sold them the motorbike. If you are really nervous, I could take him to the gendarmerie in St. Denis where there won't be a trainee magistrate in sight."

"Too late." J-J sighed. "The desk sergeant has booked him already, and the other one has to be questioned about the mugging. I'd better get you down into an interview room."

He led them out to the hall, and then Barone was booked, fingerprinted and taken down the corridor to an interview room. His brother-in-law was taken to a separate room. Barone was shown to one of the special chairs, its front legs shorter than the rear so he could never get quite comfortable. Bruno and Goirau took two ordinary chairs facing him with a uniformed cop at the door. Bruno turned on the recording system, gave a rough translation of the warrant and asked, "Why did you hack into the computer of the town hall in St. Denis?"

"I don't know what you're talking about," Barone replied.

"We're talking about your attempts to track down your ex-wife. You know her university email address. Why not send her a message and ask her directly?"

"I'm not married," Barone said.

"We know, you're divorced. We know you broke into an official computer system and sent an email to me, using the mailbox of an employee of the town hall, and thus stealing her identity," Bruno said. "That's illegal hacking and carries a penalty of two years in prison. Even more seriously, you tried to get into the computer of this building, the regional headquarters of the Police Nationale."

"I have nothing more to say until I see a lawyer." Barone glanced at Goirau, who was sitting silently beside Bruno, an open notebook before him.

"If you refuse to cooperate you will be taken to a cell while our computer experts look for any other evidence of illegal behavior," said Bruno. "In the meantime, this is Commissioner Goirau of our fiscal police, who has some questions for you about the breaching of sanctions against Russia, which is also of interest to your FBI."

"I have nothing to say until I can get legal advice and I want to call my embassy."

"Which one?" Bruno asked. "American or Italian?"

"American."

Goirau laughed and then spoke in English. "That's interesting, because the FBI also wants to talk with you. They want your extradition. You might find us more reasonable." He paused. "But it's Saturday afternoon, so you'll get a duty officer who will inform the legal attaché."

Barone looked confused, and Bruno took out his phone and said, making his voice casual, "We can call the legal attaché now, if you wish. Yes or no?"

Barone closed his eyes and then said, "Yes, please."

Bruno called, and when Hodge replied, said, "I have a Monsieur Barone, who claims to be an American citizen, under arrest at the *commissariat* in Périgueux, and he asked to speak to you. He's in possession of an American passport but also of an Italian one."

He handed the phone to Barone, who said, "I would like you to arrange an English-speaking lawyer for me and for my brother-in-law who faces some trumped-up charge about a mugging."

There was a pause as Barone listened, then he said, "I am also charged with illegal hacking of some town hall computer."

Another pause, then Barone said, "I know it's Saturday afternoon, but you must have someone nearer than Paris. I'm an American citizen in trouble with a foreign police force and I want the support of my embassy to arrange an English-speaking lawyer for me who can get me out of here tonight."

Yet another pause, until finally Barone snapped, "Well, as soon as you can, dammit." Then he handed the phone back to Bruno.

"Are you prepared to answer my or Commissaire Goirau's questions?"

"Not without an English-speaking lawyer being present to assist me," Barone said.

"Very well. We'll have you taken to a cell until your lawyer arrives or until you're prepared to talk to us. Do you need medical assistance, and do you have dietary restrictions?"

Barone shook his head, and Bruno asked him to confirm aloud for the recording that he had no such needs and then turned it off. Another uniformed policeman appeared and took Barone downstairs to the cells where his brother-in-law was awaiting the arrival of a police doctor to verify that his ankle injury was a dog bite that could be matched to Balzac's jaw. Bruno was not worried about getting a conviction. The salesman of the trail bike was coming to identify both bike and customer.

"We now have to wait for this computer star to work her wonders," said Goirau.

"She'll be upstairs. I'd take you there, but I have to get to St. Denis for a meeting on this flood emergency," said Bruno. "Ask the desk sergeant to page Mademoiselle Teyssier, and she'll come down to help you in my absence. Meanwhile, if you want to confer with Hodge, here's his private number." He handed Goirau one of his cards after writing Hodge's number on the back.

"That's fine, thank you, Bruno. We have our man and good luck with your flood. I'll be in touch."

Bruno took his van from the *commissariat* garage and set off for St. Denis in heavy rain, with flashes of lightning in the skies to the west. He had just passed the turnoff to Les Eyzies when his old phone vibrated, making Bruno feel guilty that he had yet to get himself a new one for police business. It was J-J, and Bruno pulled onto the side of the road to answer.

"I find this hard to believe, Bruno, but it looks like you've arrested the wrong Barone," J-J snapped.

"That's quite enough, J-J," Goirau's voice could be heard in the background. "Bruno was assigned to my department, so if you have a complaint, please address it to me."

"This isn't the Giuseppe Garibaldi that we want, the one who was born in 1984," said J-J. "The guy we've got in a cell is his elder brother, Luigi D'Annunzio Barone, born in 1982. That's probably why they look alike. I have two passports for him, an American one and a European one."

"I never heard that he has a brother, but I'll check with his ex-wife," Bruno replied, more calmly than he felt. "You could ask Goirau to check with Hodge about any known brother, and double-check the two photos, the one we know to be Gary Barone and the one in the so-called brother's passport."

"Did you do any of these elementary checks before arresting the guy?" J-J demanded in reply. "Did you even ask the man to confirm his first name?"

"He made no objection when I arrested him using his full name, Giuseppe Garibaldi," said Bruno. "And you can hold them both on the second charge from St. Denis, the attempted theft and assault on a woman from the *mairie.* And you have the computers. It should not take long for the tech expert to confirm they were the ones that tried to break into your system and our *mairie.* And have you compared the original photo of Giuseppe and the one on the brother's passport?"

"You know passport photos," J-J shot back. "Could be anybody. You had better come back here and help sort this out before we have trouble. There's an eager young magistrate here to talk to the trainees who's asking questions about the American arrest."

"I can't come back, J-J," Bruno replied. "We have a flood emergency all along the Vézère, and I have to organize evacuations. Get Goirau to deal with this. He has the clout. In the meantime call Hodge. He should have Gary's fingerprints by now, and it's his agency that wants the extradition. If the brother is genuine, the prints will be different. Or call Barone's ex-wife, Abby. She's in St. Denis, and here's her number."

Bruno read it out, but J-J was in no mood to listen.

"You got me into this mess, Bruno. You call Hodge or General Lannes and get them to call me. We're supposed to be doing him and the FBI a favor, aren't we? It's about time they showed some appreciation. *Merde!* Why is it always me left holding the bag while these jumped-up magistrates fresh out of school start bleating about prisoners' rights?"

There was no reply from Hodge's mobile, and the embassy said his office was closed for the weekend. He got Abby's answering service when he called her and left a message. She called back just as he reached the outskirts of St. Denis.

"Your message said it was urgent, and sorry that I wasn't checking my phone. Captain Borghese was so impressed with Lascaux that I took him to the Rouffignac cave after he bought me a late lunch, and we've just emerged," she said. "As far as I know, Gary has no brothers. There was none at the wedding, and I met everybody else in his family, including his poisonous sister."

"Are you still at Rouffignac?"

"Leaving now. Clothilde asked me to help at the museum, checking whether this flood warning means we'll have to move everything from the basement. Where are you?"

"Just getting back to St. Denis for the crisis meeting on the flood. But we arrested the guy I was sure was your ex-husband, who's now claiming to J-J that he's the elder brother."

"I really don't think there's a brother, younger or older. Do you need me to see him and give you a positive identification?"

"That's exactly what we need. Can I call the *commissariat* in Périgueux and tell them you're coming?"

"Why not just give them my number and they can send me a photo of him?"

"I should have thought of that," he said.

"You have enough on your mind. I'll expect a call."

"It will be from Jean-Jacques Jalipeau, *commissaire* and chief detective. I'll call him now. Thanks, Abby."

Bruno called J-J at once, but his line was busy. He tried Goirau. Also engaged. Then he called Josette, J-J's aide. There was no reply, so he left a message and tried J-J again and left another message. Then Goirau called him.

"Barone has been released, along with his brother-in-law," Goirau said, disgust evident in his voice. "J-J didn't fight it after one of the magistrates from the *procureur*'s office intervened, saying that in the absence of a lawyer for Barone, he'd defend the American's rights. The pompous idiot was showing off to the trainees. J-J let them both go after getting the Barones to surrender their passports and promising to return to the *commissariat* in Périgueux Monday morning. They had gone by the time Mademoiselle Teyssier confirmed that it was Barone's computer that tried to break into the St. Denis *mairie* and the police computer."

"Merde," said Bruno. "I was just talking to his ex-wife. She insists her ex-husband had no brothers. If we send her a photo of the guy, she'll confirm if it's him."

"I took several photos at the house in the woods, and there must be one of him," Goirau said. "Give me her number and I'll try."

Bruno gave him Abby's number and wondered why J-J was letting himself be intimidated by a fresh-faced young magistrate he'd normally brush aside. Perhaps he'd done so once too often and the *procureur* felt it was time to make sure J-J abided by the legal rules. He shrugged. It was out of his hands, and he had an insistent new priority.

He turned on the car radio, where France Bleu Périgord was giving blanket coverage to the flood warnings. The release of water had already begun with the lowest of the important dams on the Vézère, at Saillant. There were seven dams in total, but only three that mattered in terms of the volume of water they contained. Two of them were far upstream, close to the river's source on the plateau of Millevaches, where a valiant news reporter was reporting live over his mobile phone that he was sheltering under an umbrella "while looking at a vast stretch of peat that is soaking up water like a sponge."

The biggest volume of water was behind the first dam, at the Lac de Viam, but it produced only sixty-four-million kilowatt hours of electricity. The dam downstream at Treignac, although holding less water, had a longer drop to the turbines and thus produced more power, eighty-eight-million kilowatt hours. But before these dams could start releasing water, all the smaller dams downstream had to start emptying in turn, one after the other, to make room for these discharges from upriver. Saillant, largest of the downstream dams, and the lowest, had to be emptied first to make room for all the water tumbling down the eight hundred vertical meters from the massif.

Bruno could imagine thousands of listeners, who like him had long taken the electricity in their homes and offices for granted, suddenly becoming seriously interested in the hydroelectric mysteries that lay behind it. For most people in the region, the Lac de Viam was a place for boating and water skis rather than electricity. Flooding was an occasional inconvenience, involving the temporary closure of a road in winter or a sudden fuss at a café on a river beach. But then the radio began describing the great floods of March 1930, when some seven hundred people had died about a hundred kilometers to the south, in the *département* of the Tarn-et-Garonne, and around Montauban and Agen. Even the pope of the day had sent a handsome check in sympathy, Bruno heard.

It was becoming a time of extremes, of summer days of record heat, interspersed with and followed by unusually heavy rains. Bruno knew from his wine-making friends that this had been an extraordinarily difficult year in the vineyards. It had begun with hailstorms, then the humid spring brought rampant mildew and black rot to the vines. This was followed by some of the hottest days the region had ever recorded, a double blow so hard that the Bergerac wine federation had called it a climate catastrophe. Their latest newsletter had included a suicide helpline, an ominous sign of the mood among the vines. Winemakers were accustomed to one bad year in five; the last five years had seen only one good one.

Chapter 30

Bruno made it to the St. Denis *mairie* with ten minutes to spare before the meeting. The rain was coming down too heavily for him to see clearly. Unable to find his umbrella in the chaos of his van, he would have been drenched during the few steps from the parking lot had not Jacques, one of the councilors, come to Bruno's aid with an enormous golf umbrella in green and yellow stripes that easily kept them both dry.

"I see you're in uniform. Does that mean you're back on duty?" Jacques asked. A spry man in his seventies with a white beard, Jacques lived in the heart of the old town and took a special interest in anything to do with the arts, which seemed to cover everything from Occitan poetry to folk dancing and watercolors.

"With this sort of emergency, it's all hands on deck," Bruno replied as his phone vibrated. It was still the phone on General Lannes's network; he hadn't had time to get another. He saw that it was Florence and answered.

"I heard from Father Sentout that you're back at work," she said. "I'm on the way down from my parents with the twins and just heard on the radio about flood warnings for the Vézère and Dordogne Valleys. I thought I'd better check with you. Is it safe for us to drive all the way down tonight, and can we sleep at your place? I'm at Orléans, about four hours away."

"You'll be north of the floods all the way, and my place is on high ground, so that should be safe enough," he replied. "I may have to work through the night in case of evacuation. I'm about to go into a meeting on this at the *mairie,* so I can call you back in about an hour. My cousin Alain might also be at my place tonight with Rosalie because of worries that the floods might reach the *collège.*"

"Okay, I'll expect your call, and thanks, Bruno." She paused a moment so that her twins could call out a greeting to him and then hung up.

In the entrance hall Bruno found Albert and Ahmed, the two professional *pompiers* who ran the largely volunteer fire brigade and the fire station that was responsible for the safety of half the Vézère Valley. The *pompiers* also provided emergency services for medical care, disease outbreaks among livestock, droughts and floods.

"Any news?" Bruno asked, shaking hands.

"The bad news is that the coastal *départements* have persuaded the government to drop the idea of cloud seeding, since their own rains are already threatening them with a repeat of the flood they had five years ago," said Albert. "Not that it stops them from chopping down the trees that held back the water."

"The worst news is that the Dordogne dams will start releasing water earlier than they thought," said Ahmed. "Their dams are already close to full, so our river will start backing up at Limeuil tomorrow from all the water coming down the Dordogne."

"What does that mean for us here?" Bruno asked.

"The campsites at risk have all been cleared, and they're already evacuating the town aquarium, including the fish, and the amuse-ment park and some of the houses on the low-lying land at Malmussou," said Albert. "I think we'll also have to evacuate the houses on the Voie sur Berge," he went on, using the local name for the properties whose walled gardens backed onto the quayside. "It's going to depend on the capacity of the valley to soak up water, as it did in the old days when there were more meadows. That's unknown territory these days. And it could mean we lose the rail line from Périgueux."

"The big problem," said Ahmed, opening the door to steer them into the crowded council chamber, "is going to be the trees. That's what Albert wants to talk about."

The buzz of conversation stilled as Albert led the way in, Bruno and Ahmed to each side. The mayor rose to welcome them and asked Albert to report. All council members were present, along with senior staff from the *mairie,* the medical personnel, pharmacists and leading employers, especially builders with access to heavy equipment.

"We've done everything by the book, evacuated the endangered lowlands and set up reception areas on the high ground. So we should be in good shape," Albert began. "Except that it's still raining, and that means they're going to have to start opening the dams on the Dordogne, which will begin to block the outflow we were hoping for at Limeuil. Worst of all, we have the problem of the *cingles* and the trees."

Puzzled, Bruno wondered what was wrong with the *cingles,* the lovely, lazy curves the river made as it meandered through the valley. The U-shaped curves were picturesque and good for fishing and boating, but perhaps they were a hazard whenever the water started to flow in real quantities. Albert made the danger clear.

"When the flow becomes excessive," he explained, "such a bend becomes like a racetrack, and the flow starts eating away at the inside and outside of the curve. That means vegetation can fall into the river and get carried away by the current. With the amount of water we've got coming at us, I estimate we could lose two or three meters of soil on those river bends every day, just eaten away. And that means we'll start to lose trees."

Bruno could picture the trees he was talking about: huge limes and alders, beeches and birches, even some oaks.

"When the river is flowing at fifteen or twenty kilometers an hour," the fire chief continued, "just think of the energy of one of those big trees slamming into our bridges; with that weight and speed it would be like an artillery shell. And that collision will be repeated four or five times an hour for the next two or three days.

"Think of our bridges. Some have arches that are too narrow for a full-grown tree to pass through. So it gets blocked, and every other bit of tree branch or vegetation gets caught up in the branches and, before you know it, our bridge starts to look like a dam—only it wasn't designed for that."

Bruno, standing by the long window that overlooked the river and the town bridge, glanced down and at once had a mental image of what the fire chief had described. The river would back up until it had sufficient volume to flow over the top of the bridge and round the sides. That would flood the parking lot and the town square below them and then flow downhill to flood the big roundabout in front of Hôtel Le Cygne—and the fire station, and the entrance to the big retirement home. And on the far side of the bridge, the river would flow sideways into the medical center and the parking area in front of the bank and then down into what had been the parking area for campers with its shower rooms and toilets.

"We can't afford to let that bridge get turned into a dam," Albert went on, "and there are only two ways to keep it clear. The first is to cut down and clear away the largest trees on the bends before they topple into the river. The other is to have a big winch attached to long chains that can pull the trees out before they get stuck in the bridges."

He explained how they would proceed. Ten trucks had been

commandeered, each with a team of volunteers, to fell as many trees on the *cingles* as possible, working through the night. Separate winch trucks were coming from Périgueux and the chalk quarries at St. Astier, plus hooks and chains from the stone quarries up the valley, to haul away any trees that got stuck.

"It may be that the railway bridge upstream by La Terrasse is the most vulnerable, since the arches are narrower and therefore easier for the driftwood to block," Albert said. "And the ground is so slick with rain that the winch trucks themselves could start sliding. We'll just have to do our best."

Albert stopped and looked around the silent, crowded chamber. He turned to the mayor. "Any questions?"

"Just one, but it's the big one," said the mayor. "What time will the flood hit?"

"It won't be that sudden," Albert replied. "They've been releasing water from the lower dams for hours, and all that's happened so far is that vehicles can't use our quayside, the bandstand is flooded, and the aquarium and the mill are already awash. The flood from the higher dams should be reaching Terrasson in the next hour and a half, and Montignac three hours after that, with another two hours to Les Eyzies. I don't expect it here until midnight or a bit later, so I've instructed all my people to get some sleep while they can, because we're facing a very long night."

"Do you have any idea what time we should expect the Dordogne flood to reach Limeuil?" the mayor asked. "As I understand it, the Dordogne could arrive with a flow so strong it would block our own river and start it back flooding?"

"That's our main fear, but the Dordogne flood won't reach Limeuil before daybreak tomorrow, probably," Albert said. "If we're lucky, we might have passed the peak of the flood of the Vézère by then, but I can't give you any guarantees. We simply don't know at this stage how much floodwater will be soaked up in the valleys upstream."

"What about those of us with no chain saw or grappling hooks or big trucks?" asked Lespinasse. "What can we do?"

"First of all, make sure that your own families are safe. Those with cars, fill up your gas tanks and then go to the Boutenègre campsite, which is to be the emergency reception and first-aid center. You may have to take people to the Périgueux hospital, or resupply the chain-saw gangs who will be felling trees and towing them away. You may even be asked to go onto the ridge road and try and give us some illumination from your headlights if we lose all street lighting.

"As for you sports club presidents, Lespinasse, Joubert and Bouvier, I'd like you and some volunteers and wives to get to the rugby, karate and tennis clubs because they should be high enough to be out of danger. They have water, bathrooms and dry places to sleep, so those being evacuated from the low ground at La Borie can take shelter there. Get whatever emergency food supplies you might need from the supermarket and we'll settle up later.

"Bruno, we want you to organize a team of volunteers to get all the sand from the builders' merchants and as many heavy-duty plastic bags as you can find and protect the front entrance to the supermarket. The rear entrances are all closed off and sandbagged on the inside, but the big glass doors are the weak point. We might need that food as things develop.

"My advice to all of you is get a good meal inside you and then get some sleep and set your alarms for eleven or so. Just be sure that you're ready to help by midnight. And if the *mairie* has to be closed for fear of flooding, go uphill to the Boutenègre campsite or the tennis club."

Bruno had silenced his phone during Albert's briefing, and he had a message from his cousin, Alain, when he turned it back on, saying that he and Rosalie were driving back from Bordeaux and had heard the flood warnings. If their apartment at the *collège* was closed because of flooding they would head for Bruno's house to spend the night.

With Florence and the twins there, his house was going to be crowded, Bruno thought, smiling. But he would need to get some sleep before what promised to be a very long night. He texted a reply to say Alain and Rosalie were welcome, that Florence and her twins might join them, that he expected to be on duty all night, would call them if needed and would hope to see them in the morning.

Then Bruno went to the supermarket, arranged for two trucks to bring all available sand from the two main building suppliers, and directed the volunteers to fill all the heavy-duty plastic bags with sand. He left Simon, the supermarket manager, in charge. He set off for the riding school, which was halfway up a hill and safe from flooding. There was no sign of life, and all the horses were gone. Pamela and Félix must have taken them out. He left a brief note on Pamela's kitchen table to explain what was going on. Then he set his phone to wake him at eleven that night and settled down to sleep under a horse blanket in Hector's stall, with Balzac snuggled alongside.

Chapter 31

Bruno was woken by the touch of Pamela's hand on his shoulder. Then Bruno heard her voice telling him it was five minutes before eleven, that he was welcome to shower in her bathroom and that she would have a plate of toast and eggs ready before he went back to town. He quickly showered and wolfed down two fried eggs with toast and some of the English bacon that Pamela loved. He downed a glass of fresh orange juice and then another slice of toast with her homemade marmalade. One more cup of coffee and he felt ready for anything.

"Take care of yourself," she said. "Don't worry about Balzac, I'll take good care of him." She gave him an affectionate kiss on the cheek and steered him to the door in a businesslike way that made him feel like a boy being sent off to school. He was still smiling at the thought when he pulled in at the rugby club, saw Lespinasse and asked for news.

The flood had not yet reached Les Eyzies, he was told, but the river was already higher in St. Denis than anyone could remember, more than halfway up the stone steps from the quayside to the town square and still rising steadily. Bruno drove down to the supermarket where the river was creeping ominously toward the back road that led to the loading bays. At the front of the supermarket, the stacks of sandbags stood a good meter taller than Bruno's own height. Simon pointed out proudly that it was three sandbags deep up to waist height, two deep for another meter and then just a single layer for the top three rows. And in front of the glass of the window were sliding metal shutters.

"That should keep the river out," Bruno said, admiringly. "Any problems? Have your people been fed?"

"A delivery of pizzas arrived at nine and a five-liter box of red wine from the town vineyard," Simon replied, "all courtesy of the mayor."

"That's the next election sewn up, then," Bruno replied with a grin and headed off to the *mairie,* where all the lights seemed to be on.

"Ah, Bruno," said the mayor. "Bad flooding at Montignac, along with parts of the road to Lascaux. The flood has now gone past Marzac but has yet to reach the Grand Roc, let alone Tayac, so I imagine it will reach us sometime between midnight and one in the morning, and Albert says that the valleys seem to be soaking up more water than he expected."

"Yes, but we have the Beune River flowing in to join the Vézère at Les Eyzies, then two more tributaries flow in from St. Cirq and La Combe before it reaches us," said Bruno. "Even before the flood gets here, the river has almost reached the road behind the supermarket already. Does Albert think you'll have to evacuate the *mairie*?"

"Fifty-fifty, he says. He'll tell me when the flood reaches Campagne." The mayor thumbed through the logbook he, or some colleague, was evidently keeping of the night's events, and said, "Some calls for you. One from your curator friend at the Centre Jean Moulin to say he was heading back to Bordeaux and thanks for putting him up. One from Abby to say she's staying at the museum in Les Eyzies, and another from your cousin, Alain, to say he was at your house with Rosalie and Florence but that he and Rosalie have now joined the tree-felling squad. And there was one from that Italian diplomat, Borghese. Apparently he'd been staying at the hotel and was told they were evacuating, and he called here to volunteer to help. He's been assigned to the teams by the railway bridge."

"Good for him," said Bruno. "Was it your idea to keep that log? Makes a lot of sense."

"No, Mademoiselle Cantagnac suggested it. She's still here and she's a godsend, with contacts in just about every *mairie* up and down the river, so we're getting real-time reports on the flood. She was the one who assigned the Italian attaché to his crew and arranged pizza deliveries to all the teams."

"I was told at the supermarket that the pizza and wine came with your compliments."

"Really?" The mayor beamed. "That woman is worth her weight in gold."

Bruno's eyebrows lifted in surprise. "That sounds as though I've lost my office for good."

"Well, it's not as though you used it that much," the mayor said vaguely. "But enough of that. Have you been assigned to a bridge-clearance team or to tree removals?"

"Neither. I got a few hours' sleep, then helped sandbag the supermarket, so now I'm available again. Where's Albert? I'd better see what he has in mind."

"You'll find him at the fire station, where he's got his own communications system. Let me know what he wants you to do."

Albert was snoozing on a sofa in his office, and Bruno didn't have the heart to wake him, but Albert seemed to sense his presence. He opened one eye and grunted that Ahmed was out in the field with the winch crew. Bruno left him to doze while things were calm and then called Ahmed.

"The flood has just reached Tayac, almost at Les Eyzies," Ahmed said. "I just heard from the dragon lady in the *mairie*."

Bruno had not previously heard Colette's nickname among the firemen but thought it suitable. Ahmed made it sound almost affectionate.

"So another hour or so before it reaches us, is that right?"

"A bit less than that. Did you see the TV news with that guy surfing the wave at St. Pantaléon just this side of Brive?"

"No, missed it. Did he live?"

"Oh yeah, really good surfer. Where are you?"

"At your fire station. Albert is catching a nap and I wondered if you needed help."

"No, we've got lots of volunteers, almost too many, and I hear from Les Eyzies that the flood level is now not much more than a meter. The valleys are soaking up a lot of the floodwater. We've hauled off the biggest trees, and so long as we can keep the bridges clear we should be okay tonight. What worries me now is the Dordogne blocking our flow at Limeuil, but that's for tomorrow."

"It sounds like it's time for you to get some sleep."

"Not quite yet. Let's see our flood pass, and I want to hear how high the Dordogne flood's going to be. If you could check on things at the rugby club and the karate place and up at Boute-nègre, just in case there are problems, that would be great. I'll call you if we have a major issue. But you should rest while you can—tomorrow could be a nightmare."

Bruno set off on foot to the karate club, where Dr. Gelletreau was asleep in an armchair. The pharmacist was drinking coffee and playing some game on her mobile phone and seemed grateful for Bruno's interruption.

"No evacuation tonight?" she asked, yawning. "There's been no siren and no church bells."

"It looks like we'll be okay for the night, so you might want to get some sleep," Bruno said. "The worry is early tomorrow morning when the flooding Dordogne blocks our river."

He walked back to his van and drove to the rugby club where

all was quiet, with Fabiola asleep in one armchair, Gilles asleep in another and Lespinasse snoring. Bruno drove up the hill to Boutenègre and found the campsite almost deserted. Xavier, the deputy mayor, was dozing on one of the loungers that were usually lined up beside the swimming pool. Bruno left for the *mairie* without disturbing him.

"I feel like the boy who cried wolf," Bruno told the mayor. "There's no sense of emergency, no sign of evacuation, and most people seem to be asleep."

"Everybody knows that we'll sound the siren and ring the church bells if need be," the mayor said. "I'm going to have a nap. Ahmed knows to wake me when the flood reaches Campagne."

It all reminded Bruno of his army days, when everyone was tense and excited before an operation, but then there were always delays and frustration. The only sound came from his old office where Colette was checking on teams at the bridges. He waited until that stopped before putting his head around the door.

"I can help you if you like," he told her. "I had a nap earlier."

"So did I," she replied. "It was always clear that not much would happen before midnight."

"I understood you organized pizzas at nine."

"I ordered those before I took my nap. It's called forward planning." She gave him a glance with a raised eyebrow that he now thought was teasing rather than mocking, before she went on, "I heard something about an arrest being made of some Italian who was trying to break into our computer. You were said to be involved. Is that true?"

He nodded. "You have good sources. He's an American citizen who also has an Italian passport, and the Americans want to extradite him."

"What was he looking for in our computer here?"

"I don't really know, sorry."

"Was this connected to that attack on me that you interrupted?"

"Possibly, but I really can't say any more."

"But this all started when I was supposed to have sent you an email, but I hadn't. Is that right?"

Bruno smiled at her and shook his head. She stared at him, and then her phone pinged, she put it on speaker, and Ahmed's voice said urgently, "The railway bridge on the road to Audrix just took a big hit from a fallen tree, and it's too heavy for my winch, so we need the second winch team urgently. We'll want it on the *mairie* side of the river, so best to send Arnaud's team and warn Albert. And you'd better warn the railway that they'll need to inspect the bridge before sending any train through."

"Tell him I'll get hold of Arnaud and wake up Albert," Bruno told Colette. "You call the railway emergency number."

"I don't know that number," she said calmly.

"It was on the list that used to be on the wall beside my desk," he said crisply, already calling Albert, who responded groggily. Bruno explained Ahmed's message and added, "I'm calling Arnaud now, and I'll go with him to the bridge."

He ended the call, then looked up the directory on his phone, read out the rail emergency number to Colette and left at a run while calling Arnaud, a volunteer fireman whose day job was in the local Crédit Agricole bank. His phone was busy, but Bruno was sure his team was stationed at the town bridge, although he couldn't see them on this side of the river. He trotted over the bridge and saw the winch truck in the parking lot by the medical center, Arnaud standing beside it with his phone to his ear.

"Ahmed," Arnaud mouthed at Bruno, and then shouted to his crew, "mount up, we're off."

"Railway bridge, far side," Bruno said. "I'll follow you."

He jogged back across the bridge to where his police van was parked, waited for the winch truck to pass him, then turned on his blue light and followed. The truck turned off on the Malmussou road and then took the rue du Port past the tree plantation toward the riverbank, where several headlamps illuminated the scene. Ahmed's winch truck was on the same side of the river, but on the upstream side of the bridge, maybe ten or fifteen meters from the now flooded riverbank. The water was already lapping at the truck's wheels. The winch cable was lost in a mass of branches that were stuck in the nearest arch of the bridge.

The bridge itself towered above both trucks, carrying the railway track some twenty meters or more above their heads. The land was low on this side of the bridge, obviously an old meadow. The bank on the other side of the bridge was fifteen meters higher. The railway was lifted to reach the bridge by a high, steep berm, evidently man-made. There was no way the truck could climb it. But it was also clear the river had risen so high that Arnaud's truck could not take the usual route along the riverbank.

"We can't make it this way," shouted Arnaud. "We'll have to double back and come to you along the other side of the railway track."

"You can't," Ahmed shouted back. "There's no road. You'll have to try the riverbank."

"No," shouted Arnaud. "If we do that we'll lose the truck."

"Wait, I'll try it," shouted Bruno. "Give me a rope and those waders."

One of the volunteers on Arnaud's truck handed him a long loop of the sturdy yellow rope the firemen used, and another gave Bruno a set of step-in waterproof waders that came halfway up his chest. Bruno climbed into them, feeling slightly ridiculous. After some juggling he fastened the straps and took off his helmet to help the fireman loop the rope over his head and tie it around his chest beneath his armpits. It was only then that Bruno recognized Tim Birch.

"Thanks. It's good to see you as a volunteer," he said. The Englishman slapped him on the back and wished him luck.

Bruno handed the loose end of the rope to Birch and watched

him tie it to the bumper of the winch truck. Then Bruno slowly walked down toward the riverbank and waded into the water to see how deep it would be. It rose steadily, to his knees and then to his thighs and then above his waist. It was hard to keep his balance, and he could still not feel the tarmac of the riverbank road beneath his feet. He hauled himself back to safety with the help of the rope.

"We can't come this way," he said firmly, stepping out of the waders. "We'll have to come the long way around, over the grade crossing. I'll go first so Arnaud can see if he can make it."

"If not, what then?" asked Ahmed.

"Then he comes along the railway line as far as he can and then down the bank toward you," Bruno said, taking off the rope. "And if that doesn't work, we'll have to try it from the far side of the river. We'll be with you as soon as we can."

Bruno got back into his van, turned, waited to check that Arnaud was following and then headed back up the rue du Port and took a right toward the grade crossing that was about a hundred meters from the railway station. Normally the road went left toward a new housing development which had already been evacuated, but Bruno turned right onto rough pasture, following the raised bank that carried the railway line. It was bouncy, but passable, and the winch truck was able to get through a grove of trees and head toward the river without trouble. Bruno could see Ahmed's truck on the riverbank about forty meters ahead, and when he reached it, the ground was already muddy and becoming sodden.

Bruno climbed out of his van and went back to ask Arnaud the length of the winch cable. Sixty meters, he was told. He looked up at the bridge with its nearest span blocked by the fallen tree.

"How did you get your cable into the tree?" Bruno asked Ahmed.

"Two of us climbed up the bank onto the railway line, then

Jeannot lowered me on a rope, and I fixed the grappling hook onto the tree, and he pulled me back up."

"In that case, I think you and Jeannot are the right guys to do it again with another grappling hook on the second winch line," said Bruno. "It had better be quick because the river is rising all the time."

"Merde," said Ahmed, and called for Jeannot, a volunteer whose usual work was installing swimming pools.

Arnaud began unspooling cable from the winch and attaching the hook, then he and his team and Bruno helped push Ahmed and Jeannot up the steep bank onto the railway track. They followed the two men to the point above the first arch, where Ahmed tied a rope around his chest. Then, with great care, he made a second loop around his crotch to make a rough harness and had himself lowered to fix the hook onto a chain around the tree trunk. There was very little of the winch line to spare. Finally, he waved the signal that they could haul him back up.

They all climbed back down the slope of the berm. Under Ahmed's direction they took logs from the back of the truck, placed them in front of the trucks' wheels and held the logs in place with long spikes hammered into the ground. Bruno saw how this would stop the truck tires from sliding on the mud. They began winding in the winches until each line was taut.

"Everybody, stand well back in case those cables break and come lashing back," yelled Ahmed. "Now, drivers, double-check that your gears are in reverse and your handbrakes fully engage. Then give me full power in three. One, two—and three."

The truck engines roared in unison, and the two winch lines went taut, seeming to vibrate almost like guitar strings at the strain, and the truck engines protested. Bruno thought perhaps the tree was too big even for both winch teams. But then the branches of the tree seemed to move, and the trunk of the tree itself began to shift. Then into view rose the white and severed roots that had been wrenched from the ground somewhere upstream by the river's mighty force. They surged from the water and then fell back as the crown of the tree, the great boughs and branches, began inching back under the power of the doubled winches.

And now the flooding river itself began to help, making it easier to haul the tree back because the water on the bank road was now deep enough to help float the tree onto the muddy land and out of the river's grip.

"This isn't over," shouted Ahmed. "I want chain saws taking off those roots right now and loading them into the back of the trucks."

Four men dressed in firemen's overalls and slicks, already sodden from the rain, fired up their chain saws and began to attack the roots, some of them thicker than a man's thigh. Bruno wanted to help but knew his shoulder wasn't up to it.

"I'll want those trucks reversing as one," Ahmed shouted. "Keep the winches locked but all the power now has to go to the wheels of the trucks to tow this tree well out of the river's reach."

It took about twenty minutes, but the massive trunk was finally hauled to the far side of the grade crossing and held securely in place by those same long spikes hammered into the ground.

Once the trunk was secured, Bruno turned to Ahmed. "Do you still need me here, or should I go back and report to Albert?"

"Go on back," Ahmed said. "I'll send Arnaud's truck back as soon as we've hauled the other limbs from this trunk out of danger. My team will stay here. Please be sure that the rail-safety guys check the bridge before sending any trains. And thanks, Bruno."

Bruno was about to go when a thought struck him, and he asked, "How long have you been up and awake?"

"Since about six this morning."

"And your team, how about them?"

"Most of them put in their usual day's work and then came to the fire station, why?"

"I had time for a good sleep before coming out here, so why not let me stay on watch, and you and your guys get some sleep in the trucks," Bruno said. "I'll wake you if we have more trouble with trees getting stuck. You know it makes sense, Ahmed, because you have to be at your best tomorrow when we have to deal with the Dordogne back-flooding."

Ahmed looked dubious and asked, "What if some police business comes up to call you away?"

"I'll call you and stay on here until I'm replaced."

"You'll fall asleep."

"No, I won't, I slept until just before eleven and had breakfast, I'm fine."

"Tell you what. Take one of my volunteers, he's not much use but willing. Sit up with him, watch that bridge and call me if it takes another tree hit. Just make sure the two of you stay talking."

Bruno nodded agreement, and Ahmed turned to the volunteers sitting in the back of the truck.

"Hey," he called. "Yeah, you, the new guy, come over here a minute."

Chapter 32

To Bruno's surprise, his new partner was Borghese in borrowed rain gear and a fireman's helmet. Bruno remembered hearing that Borghese had volunteered. He shook the Italian's hand and said, "Thank you for joining us. It looks like you've been making yourself very useful."

"Just a willing pair of hands," said Borghese, and then Ahmed held up a hand to silence him.

"You two are going to wait on the bridge until the surge comes, and you tell us how high it is. Then you sit in Bruno's van as near as is safe to the dam and keep each other awake while watching to see if we get any more trees slamming into the bridge and getting stuck. If that happens, Bruno, hit your Klaxon or your police siren or whatever and turn on your lights, and we'll get up here as fast as we can. Me and my guys have been on all day, so we'll all try to get some sleep. Okay?"

"Okay," said Borghese. "We start now?"

"Not quite," said Ahmed. "Any minute now we're expecting the peak of the flood, so I'll wait with you to see how it looks. We expect about a meter, but it could be more, depending on the inflows."

"A meter means what, exactly?" Bruno asked. "That would reach us here, right?"

Ahmed nodded. "A flood of one meter means we pull back as far as the old parking area of the railway station. Anything more and we pull back as far as the old Hôtel de la Gare. Two meters and we'll move uphill to the far side of the main road to Les Eyzies. Two meters also means we'll probably have to evacuate the *mairie* in St. Denis and probably the fire station. Anything more than that and we'll have to evacuate the old folks' home."

Bruno pursed his lips, thinking of the logistics involved, moving more than two hundred elderly people of reduced mobility and many with special needs. Most would have to be cared for nearby, since moving all of them to Périgueux would mean at least fifty ambulances, which they didn't have. And with a flood heading for Bergerac as well, the capacity of the *département* to take care of everybody would be strained far beyond its capability.

Ahmed's phone jangled. "*Oui,* Chef?" he replied, evidently seeing from the screen that it was Albert, the fire chief, calling.

"The bridge at Campagne, right," Ahmed said. "What was it?"

A silence. Ahmed closed his phone and said, *"Merde, merde et encore merde."*

"How high?" Bruno asked.

"Too damn high. One meter sixty-five at the Campagne Bridge," Ahmed said. "That means the foie gras canning center is screwed.

"All pull back to the station parking lot," he called out. "Bruno, you and the Italian come with us, but then return on foot along the railway track to keep watch on the bridge. If it gets blocked, call me."

"But you'll never get back here through the deeper water," said Bruno.

"I know, so from the parking lot we'll go back to town over

the bridge and come up the road on the other bank, where the high ground comes close to the river."

"I don't think the ground comes close enough for your sixty-meter cable to reach all of the bridge," Bruno objected. "It might just about reach the two closest spans."

"Well, we'll just have to do the best we can, probably try and link it to a second cable."

"Don't you want to watch as the surge reaches us?" Bruno asked. "It's not something you see every day."

"No, I need to be with the crew and the trucks so we can get to where we're most needed the fastest. Albert and I will need your best estimate of the surge height when it reaches this bridge. Try to mark the bricks where the level is now and then count how many rows of bricks get covered, at ten centimeters per brick. Call me with that as soon as you get it, okay?"

Despite the firemen's waterproof overalls, the men were cold, wet and miserable sitting on top of the railroad tracks on the bridge, using Bruno's flashlight to scan the oncoming water for big trees. Smaller ones, bushes and branches were commonplace, but they were swept through the arches on the rushing flood. The sound of the river and the steady patter of rain on the protective slicks hardly encouraged conversation, although Bruno knew that talking would help keep them alert. He told Borghese that his staying on and volunteering to help was really appreciated.

"Happy to help," said Borghese. "I might be coming back to see Abby, since I really enjoyed our time together. I could see why she'd been attracted to prehistory, and she was the perfect guide."

"Is that because she flattered you by asking about the Borghese pope and your illustrious family?" Bruno teased him.

"No, no," Borghese protested. "American women are different, I find. They're more direct, it's refreshing. And I never met a female archaeologist before. I've been interested in it since I was a boy, and I'd always wanted to visit this region. Abby also offered to give me a special tour of the museum at Les Eyzies. It was going to be tomorrow."

Bruno turned as he heard someone stumbling their way over the railroad track toward them. He called out a greeting and heard a vague reply, and then Birch was squatting in front of him, holding out a flask.

"We're all sitting in the trucks, dry and warm," Birch said. "So I thought you two might appreciate a little warming sip of scotch to keep the cold out."

"Thanks a lot," said Bruno, passing it to Borghese, saying, "Guests first."

Bruno remembered what his Scottish friend Dougal had told him about taking a tiny sip, letting it evaporate in the mouth and then taking a deep breath through the mouth to feel the warmth going down the throat and into the chest. He was savoring the sensation when the sound of the river increased to a roar, and he saw the surge coming toward them.

It was as though some giant were pushing a heap of foam and debris at them with a huge broom. It didn't look like water at all. Bruno looked at the side of the bridge where he'd made a mental mark, just above the surface of the water, a line of bricks exactly twenty rows below the top of the arch. Now, as the debris rushed into the bridge, his flashlight revealed that there were only six rows of bricks still visible. That meant fourteen rows of bricks freshly covered, or a hundred and forty centimeters, so the retirement home should be safe. He called Ahmed to pass on the good news, and Ahmed asked if any more trees had come down the river with the flood.

"No," Bruno replied. "A lot of debris but nothing blocking the bridge."

"Okay. Get back to the main bridge in town, but park up the Grande rue so you're higher in case we get more flooding," Ahmed said. "Albert is worried that we lost a couple of trees by the swimming pool, and if they hit the bridge we could be in trouble. At least for the moment we've still got streetlights and power."

Telling Borghese and Tim they were all wanted back in town, Bruno led the way along the railway line to the parking area by the station. They climbed into his police van, Tim Birch having to squat in the rear, and drove back to the Grande rue. The thought struck Bruno that after that healthy slug of scotch, he might fail a breath test, not that he expected any gendarmes to be out on drunk patrol tonight.

The three of them left the police van and walked to the main square, wet underfoot from the rain but not, mercifully, from the river. Even now, at the peak of the flood, it was still about five or six centimeters below the highest point of the arches of the bridge—close to half a meter below the level of the town square. That meant there would be no evacuation of the *mairie.* But just downstream of the bridge, water was lapping over the dining terrace of the hotel, into some of the private gardens beyond, and had flooded the old mill and the waterfall that had powered it.

The river was backing up the stream known as Ladouch, which flowed through the Domaine de la Barde. Bruno couldn't see that far, but he assumed that the town library, the Vietnamese restaurant, the post office, the Hôtel Le Cygne and even the fire station were either flooded or at great risk of being so. He should go down and check on the *maternelle,* the nursery school.

On the center of the bridge they found Albert, standing like a statue and staring over the rushing water, a phone to his ear. Four grappling hooks were lined up on the parapet before him, each with a metal cable attached. By the medical center to Albert's right, the cables led to two winch trucks. Two more hawsers led to Albert's left, to the short gap in the houses along the rue de la République where two more trucks waited. But this gap was more than sixty meters from the bridge, so the cables had been doubled.

Albert was speaking, inaudible to Bruno over the sound of

the rushing water. But he nodded as if satisfied and turned to see Bruno.

"The winch team by the town swimming pool got the first tree and hauled it ashore," he said, almost shouting into Bruno's ear. "The other one just landed itself at the launching stage for the kayaks, and it's now being hauled farther inland."

"So we got lucky," Bruno shouted back. "Let's hope it lasts."

Farther back upstream, only the roof of the bandstand could be seen, and the whole stretch of riverbank where small concerts were held was now underwater. On the opposite bank the stone steps that rose from the river had disappeared, and water was lapping at the parking lot in front of the medical center and the Crédit Agricole. It could have been much worse, Bruno thought, before reminding himself that this might not be over. The Dordogne flood was yet to come.

"So, we've been spared the worst, at least for the moment," came a familiar voice, and the mayor had suddenly appeared.

Albert ignored him, staring fixedly upstream. The mayor walked up to him and put a hand on Albert's shoulder. "Well done, old friend. Time for some sleep, I think."

"Not just yet, I want to see if my fire station is flooded," replied the old fire chief.

Chapter 33

Bruno followed the mayor and Albert as they walked off the bridge, and when they reached the *mairie* the mayor asked, "What can we do now that might help tomorrow if the Limeuil outflow gets blocked?"

"We've had half the hydraulic experts in France thinking about that all day," Albert replied. "It all seems to come down to the ability of the lowland valleys upstream to absorb a lot more water than we ever thought possible, which is what saved us here with the Vézère. Maybe it's because the farmers have been pumping out the underground aquifers or perhaps it's just that the limestone around here is porous, or even that the valleys are made up of millennia of sediment soils washed down by the rivers and can absorb more water than we ever estimated."

As Bruno overheard them talk, from somewhere far back in his mind came a memory, of lying in Pamela's bed one winter's morning. She was reciting poems she had learned in her youth. She had assured him it would help him learn English, but they each knew it was more for the pleasure of watching each other as she recited for him a poem that had moved her. And it came to him now:

In Xanadu did Kubla Khan,
A stately pleasure-dome decree:
Where Alph, the sacred river, ran
Through caverns measureless to man
  Down to a sunless sea.

Maybe that was where the waters were going, to those caverns measureless to man.

"Bruno." His name was being called, loudly, startling him.

"*Oui,* Monsieur le Maire," he replied, groping his way back to the cold, wet present. The mayor, Albert, Birch, Lorenzo and a group of firemen were all staring at him.

"Sorry, I was thinking of what Albert said, of the river soaking into spaces deep underground . . ."

"I'm sure we all hope that Albert is right, but we're going to look at some of the damage, if you want to join us, Bruno," said the mayor.

Feeling a little foolish, Bruno fell into step as they strolled down past the Royal Hotel toward the fire station, stopping at the break in the wall which in drier days revealed an entry road to the quayside.

Now it was all flooded, including the road that stretched inland past the retirement home to the building that housed the town's finance department, both structures still mercifully dry. But the water was about a foot higher than the bottom of the six big fire station doors. The fire engines themselves had long been dispersed to higher ground. The Ladouch stream, usually fifteen meters above the river, which it reached over two man-made waterfalls, was now level with the flooding river. The old mill, the sunken gardens and the lower floors of the building whose upper floors housed the town's library and art gallery had all disappeared beneath the waters.

But St. Denis was not cut off and the streetlamps were still working and there was light shining from the windows of the *mairie.* The road east to Les Eyzies was still open, and the main road north to Périgueux might be blocked in front of the fire station, but it could still be reached by taking the old rue de Paris through the middle of town. The road south to Le Buisson and Bergerac was blocked again, as so often in winter for a few hours, but the roads across the town bridge to Audrix and St. Cyprien, to Souillac and Belvès, were still open. So if the bridges held, they could get to Bergerac that way. The roads west to Limeuil and to Ste. Alvère and the back road to St. Avit were now closed by the flood.

"The water level on the fire station doors hasn't shifted in the time we've been here," said Albert. "But the Vézère isn't finished with us yet. We'll get another surge when they start releasing water from the highest dam, the one that holds back Lac de Viam."

"So our Vézère may not have passed its peak," said the mayor. "But what do we now expect from the Dordogne?"

"I wish I knew for sure," Albert replied. "We'll find out tomorrow, but right now I need some sleep. The latest estimate for the Dordogne flood to peak is from seven to eight in the morning. Thanks to all for your work tonight, and I look forward to seeing you all again then. Since the way to my office is flooded, I'll catch a couple of hours of sleep in the *mairie.*"

He and the mayor stomped off, side by side, most of the firemen following. A few volunteers lingered, especially one unusually tall one whom Bruno did not recognize until her hood was pushed back, and he saw it was Marta. She came up and pecked him on each cheek, and he introduced her to Birch and Lorenzo.

"That Ladouch stream is the one that flows through the Domaine de la Barde," Birch said. "I think I'll go and take a look and see if the main building has been flooded. And the grave."

"I'd like to see how the grave is doing," said Lorenzo. Marta and Bruno agreed, so they returned to the main roundabout and walked along the rue de Paris past the old gendarmerie to the *domaine*. The lower part of the garden had several pools but was not entirely flooded, and the *domaine* itself, the forge and the buildings intended to become *gîtes* were all dry, to Birch's great relief. Bruno's flashlight showed that the bridge was only thinly covered with water now that the rain had stopped. Although the ground squelched beneath their feet, they were able to reach the grave where the higher ground was dry.

"We'd better go back over the bridge," said Bruno. "The road past the retirement home is flooded all the way to the fire station."

"Would anyone like some coffee, something to eat?" asked Marta. "I've got the key to the restaurant, and I'm starving. I can make sandwiches for us all. And don't worry about Ivan, nothing wakes him until he's ready to get up."

Birch and Lorenzo eagerly agreed. Bruno glanced at his watch, surprised to see that it was already past five in the morning. He said he'd look around to see who was still on watch and who might want to join them. He'd be back for coffee, he said as Marta opened the restaurant door, turned on the lights and led the way inside.

Bruno found Arnaud back at his old post at the far end of the bridge, Ahmed with him. Bruno told them he'd take over if they wanted coffee and some food at Ivan's. The latest word, Ahmed replied, was that the Dordogne flood had passed St. Cyprien and at current speed would reach Limeuil before seven. He'd wake Albert and the mayor at six-thirty. The current estimate was that the flood height would be close to four meters, on a river three or four times wider than the Vézère.

"It was six meters at Souillac, so it's losing a lot to the meadows, just like the Vézère did," Ahmed explained. "If it loses another meter before it reaches Limeuil, we may be okay, and there are nearly ten kilometers of meadowland between St. Cyprien and

Le Buisson and another couple between Le Buisson and Limeuil, including one of those oxbow *cingles* Albert was talking about."

"How's our own flood on the Vézère?" Bruno asked.

"Dropping a bit, see for yourself." Ahmed pointed his flashlight at the peak of the nearest arch, where the surface of the water was now perhaps a hand's-width lower.

They went off to Ivan's and met Tim Birch coming their way, holding two cups of black coffee. He handed one each to Bruno and Ahmed and then poured a slug from his whisky flask into each one.

"I thought you'd appreciate this," he said, and pulled two packages wrapped in paper from his pocket. "Marta sends her love and a toasted cheese-and-onion sandwich for each of you, still warm."

"You're leading me into bad habits," said Bruno, grinning. "But a drop of scotch goes down very well on a night like this."

Ahmed went off to wake Albert and the mayor, and Bruno and Tim headed back to the warmth of Ivan's.

"I know I should be tired and sad for all the damage, but frankly I'm feeling great, really optimistic now that the *domaine* has come through all this untouched," Birch said as they walked. "It feels almost like a sign that it's all going to work out, that we'll get this glorious property and make it work."

"And Lorenzo is going to be your first guest," Bruno said. "Not bad, having a real prince as the first name in your guest book. And if he's staying there when your TV cameras start filming, you and your *domaine* will be famous."

"I'm not sure about that," Birch said. "He's entitled to his privacy, like everybody else. But I think this new history that's been uncovered with the grave will certainly help, and that song that Rod and Amélie gave us. We'll have to see if they can repeat it for the TV cameras."

"I heard that you were a chef in some chalet in the Alps," Bruno said. "Does that mean you have a French cooking qualification?"

"Yes, I had to get a *brevet,* but since I already had a British version it wasn't a big problem," Birch replied. "I knew that I wouldn't be able to run a cooking school without one."

"You could run one for foreigners, but not for French people," said Bruno. "It's the same for Abby, wanting to be a guide."

"Yes, I remember the fuss made about British ski instructors having to get a French qualification, even a guy who'd been a skier in the Winter Olympics."

They chatted on, enjoying each other's company, until Arnaud joined them, saying that the flood, still close to two meters, had now passed Le Buisson and was expected at Limeuil any moment. Albert and the mayor were in the *mairie,* awake and checking that all the teams were ready.

"We've got one of our men watching the bridge at Limeuil to tell us when the flood hits and what it does to our river," Arnaud went on. "Any minute now, I reckon."

"I'd better go back and tell Marta and Lorenzo," said Birch.

"Tell them to join me where we were earlier, opposite the fire station," said Bruno. "I want to see if the flood has gone down."

It had, but very much less than he'd hoped. The water still lapped at the doors of the fire station, and he thought that neither the nursery school nor the post office was likely to reopen on Monday.

"Merde!" came a shout. It was Arnaud's voice, and as Bruno turned to reply he heard his name called. It was Birch, hurrying down the street toward him with two figures following him, one of them very tall. That must be Marta and probably Lorenzo.

"They say it's nearly three meters, the flood at Limeuil," Birch said. Bruno had no idea whether that would be enough to block the flow of the Vézère and deepen the flood in St. Denis. But it would certainly put his town under more pressure. Was it his imagination or was the water already higher at the fire station? It was hard to be sure. Then he felt real dismay as the streetlamps suddenly went out.

At that moment he heard the sound of a car engine revving powerfully and turned to see headlights coming fast, too fast, down the route du Single, the road that came from Limeuil and Ste. Alvère. It had been carved into the cliff face above the river some two hundred years ago and was still an impressive feat of engineering, but that road had been closed because of the flooding. The car must have used the chemin des Noisetiers, one of the farm roads on higher ground.

Still going too fast, the car hit a speed bump and the headlamps pointed at the sky as the car almost took off before landing hard. It plunged at once into the flood, sending great plumes of water soaring on each side of the vehicle. It seemed to skate toward Bruno and then began to sink, and even when underwater, the headlights remained lit, like the eyes of some deep-sea creature of which Bruno was the prey.

Bruno backed away but saw that the car was slowing as it advanced into the deepening water. Then it skewed to one side as some of the backwash from its initial plunge hit its side. The engine was still roaring, although he thought the exhaust must be underwater. The car continued its slide as Bruno shouted to his friends to stay back, but then it bounced off the low stone wall that protected the Vietnamese restaurant. Its engine died with the collision; the headlights went dark and the hatchback flew open. It slid along the front of the town library and the railings, now invisible, that protected the sunken garden.

Evidently floating but still with some momentum, the car skewed again to face the river at the point where the side road led down to the quayside. Then it stopped, caught on some railing. Bruno plunged into the water to try to help any passengers get out before the car slid into the still surging river.

The driver was slumped over the wheel and the man in the front passenger seat was leaning back between the seats to try to release the belt on a child's seat. But he seemed to be getting in the way of the woman, presumably the mother, who was sitting beside the child on the back seat. Bruno could hear them screaming at each other.

Now the man was trying to open the front passenger door, but it was held shut by the force of the water. Bruno could hear another voice in a timbre that sounded like that of a child. He wrestled with the door handle as the window rolled down and water surged into the vehicle, balancing the force of the water holding the door shut. He reached in, trying to undo the seat belt of the woman in the rear seat. He seemed to succeed and, with a strength he didn't know he had but which sent jolts of pain through his damaged shoulder, he began hauling her out. Then Birch was there helping him, and they dragged the woman through the water and up to dry land.

They almost collided with Marta, who was reaching through the open hatchback over a stack of suitcases, lifting a shrieking child from the rear seat while Lorenzo held on to her to stop the water from sweeping Marta away. As he and Birch helped the woman, and Marta and Lorenzo together brought the child to safety, the white car began to slide again. With the two men still in the front seats, it rolled over as it was swept into the rushing water and was carried off toward the even more powerful river downstream at Limeuil. A wail from the child in Marta's arms told him that one life at least had been saved.

It was while he was trying to give mouth-to-mouth resuscitation to the woman that Bruno recalled the couple with the child in the white hatchback that had been parked at the *gîte* near the old Resistance camp. The dark night and heavy rain were challenging his senses, but could this be Gary Barone's sister? There'd been two men in the car, and if he was right then one of them was presumably Barone, the other possibly the husband of his sister and the father of the child. Bruno continued pumping her chest and breathing into her mouth until Fabiola arrived to push him to one side and take over. He feared it was too late even as Fabiola labored desperately to bring back a spark of life and gestured at him to keep pumping the rib cage. He had to do it with just one arm. The other was too painful when he tried to use it.

After what seemed an endless time, the woman gave a jerk, almost sat up and spewed out a flood of water over Fabiola, some of the jet strong enough to hit Bruno as well. And then she coughed and began sucking in great gulps of breath.

Even as the woman spluttered and coughed back to life, and Marta knelt beside Bruno to put the child's head against the mother's cheek, Bruno knew that this was already a double tragedy. There had been two doomed men in the front seats of that car. One was the father of the child. The other was Abby's ex-husband, Barone, the man who should have been in a police cell in Périgueux, about to be shipped to Paris to be extradited back to America. He would have been safer if he'd stayed in jail.

Bruno's eyes shifted to the river, and he was surprised to see the white roof of the car had barely moved downstream. He'd expected it to be out of sight on the way to Limeuil by now. That meant the Vézère River was no longer flowing, but when he looked at the level of the water against the fire station, it did not seem appreciably deeper. It wasn't backing up, somehow finding enough space to flood the meadows downstream.

"Three meters at Limeuil," came a shout. Bruno recognized Arnaud's voice. "The Vézère is still flowing."

And as Bruno watched, the roof of the white car moved a little farther downstream, and then a fraction faster as a crosscurrent shifted it to the right bank, where the flow seemed stronger. These coherent thoughts were soon replaced by an awareness of a pain that was increasing beyond endurance, and he was falling and seeing only darkness.

Epilogue

It was like the dream again, like the time he had been in hospital. He was being kissed by a woman whose hair was brushing his cheeks, and he heard a soft purr that told him that she was enjoying it as much as he was. The lips moved away, and suddenly he sensed small bodies up on the bed on each side of him and loud kisses on his cheeks of a very different kind, and then he heard two childish voices calling for Balzac as his hound snuffled around the foot of the bed.

Bruno tried to open his eyes and struggled in vain to raise himself, but his vision was blurred, his limbs were so feeble he couldn't even raise his head, and his shoulder throbbed in agony with each breath he took.

"Lie still, doctor's orders," came Florence's voice from far away. "You're drugged up to your eyeballs and strapped to your bed to keep you immobile."

He wanted to say that her twins kissed very well, but her kisses were even better, but his mouth didn't seem to work. He had no idea of the time, or even which day it was and whether it was daylight outside or night. The hand on his good arm was being held, and from below he could hear the laughter of Dora and

Daniel as they romped with a playful Balzac. At least, it sounded like romping, and he hoped it was.

When he woke up again, a thin morning light came from the place where the curtains had not quite met. It might have been evening, he'd have to wait and see, but after a moment he recognized the imperious cry of his cockerel, Blanco, named for France's greatest rugby player. He was not sure what day nor even what time of day it was.

He heard a woman's voice, speaking quietly. It sounded like she was talking on a telephone. "I think he should be in the hospital," the voice said. "Will you come and look at him? I'm really worried."

His head was being gently raised and a cup held to his lips, and as he sipped the water Bruno realized how thirsty he was, and the image came to him of all that mass of freezing water that had been flooding around him and how little there had been to drink. That thought began to trigger another, but before it could take shape, his head felt stuffed with cotton wool and he drifted gently down into sleep again.

Later, awake again, he was aware of movement, the sound of conversation against the background—no, he told himself, against the background of something mechanical. He swayed a little, aware of a turn. He was being driven, strapped to something, and his hand was being held and a thumb was softly stroking his wrist. He tried to say a greeting, felt the words stumble and warp in the thickness of his mouth, and then a second hand was on his cheek, stroking in time to calming words.

His sleep felt disturbed and fractious as he was dimly aware of being moved, lifted and lowered, on wheels, in an elevator, in daylight, and smells of antiseptic, sudden coldness as a cream was applied to his chest. Then he was being slid into a dark tube, soft voices speaking a technical patois he didn't understand. Then intense pain as his arm was moved and he was slid back again into the dark tube.

When he awoke again he knew from the smells that he was in a hospital, and that he was sitting up in a bed. There was a tube going into his right arm, and his left arm and shoulder were strapped into a raised position on a small cradle. He felt not so much a pain, more a steady ache, and his head felt clear for the first time since the flood. He was in a pleasant room with one other bed, for the moment empty, and wondered what he would do about food and peeing now that both his arms were occupied. Through the window he could see only sky, which made him think he might be in Sarlat, where the hospital was perched on a hill above the old town. Beneath the window were two chairs and a table, on which were several imposing bunches of flowers.

He drifted off to sleep again, woke when a nurse who could barely be out of school injected him with something. He slept until a male doctor of about his own age came in to ask why he'd been working when he was supposed to be on convalescent leave after being shot. Bruno said something about the flood being an emergency.

A cheerful nurse came in to give him a bedpan and then feed him breakfast of stewed fruit, coffee and a croissant. She said the surgeon would be along soon, "on his rounds." Bruno knew from experience that this meant he would enter with a small retinue of medical students, say some hearty words to the patient and speak to his coterie in technical terms that might as well have been a foreign language.

Instead, Fabiola came in with a male doctor who seemed to defer to her. She introduced him as Monsieur Barak, the best surgeon in the region, and gave Bruno a brisk kiss on the cheek. She looked at his chart, assured him that the surgeon had done a magnificent job to save his shoulder, but that Bruno would never play rugby again. This was just as well, she added, given the head injuries that she had seen from the game.

He thanked her and the surgeon. "How long will I stay here?" he asked.

"You can go home later today." Like so many men in Fabiola's forceful presence, the surgeon seemed content to say nothing and give the occasional nod to support her words.

"It's all arranged. Florence and the twins are moving into your house to look after you, and Félix's mother will be there on week-days to make you lunch. You have a physical therapist coming every morning to get you exercising your shoulder."

"What happened to the American woman and child in the car?"

"They are fine, or at least healthy, and back home in America," she said. "Despite your best efforts, her brother and husband disappeared in the flood. Bits of what may have been their car have emerged, along with livestock, tractors, boats and jetties, all looking as though they were ripped up by giants. Nobody else in town was hurt except for you. Half the town has been bugging me about when they can come to visit you. Now that you're going home, however, you'll have to sort out the visiting hours yourself. Half of the Pilates group is talking about what dishes they should prepare for you, and the other half wants to invite you to Christ-mas Eve supper. Gilles can't wait to cook you his chicken satay again, and Pamela is having us all for Christmas Day."

She gave him a warm smile. "You have been warned, my dear Bruno. Enjoy it while you can, because early in the New Year your friends and neighbors will start grumbling again about speeding cameras and parking fines and it will all get back to normal."

"What day is it?" he asked.

"Friday, five days after the Sunday morning when you almost ripped your shoulder off hauling that American woman out of the car. You were taken home and very sensibly Florence persuaded me to come look at you. We thought you wouldn't be nearly so good a cook one-handed, so we put you into an ambulance."

"Thank you. Are we in Sarlat?"

"No, in Périgueux. And you'll be back here next week to see Monsieur Barak again. We'll put you in a taxi because you'll have to keep your arm in that cradle, probably through Christmas and into January. Now that I think of it, Bruno, it looks quite fetching—as though you're permanently ready to take to the dance floor and give a girl a waltz. Now, do you have any pain?"

"A dull ache, nothing like as bad as it was."

"Good, we've started cutting the painkillers. I brought your underwear, tracksuit trousers, and Madame Brosseil found a very ancient tracksuit top from the rejects pile at Action Catholique and cut the left arm off so you can poke your arm and the dressing through it. Otherwise we'd have had to wrap you in a cloak."

"Do I get a taxi home?" he asked.

"No, Florence has a free afternoon, so she'll be here at two to collect you, and you have an appointment with the physical therapist at four."

He lay back against the pillows with a small sigh of relief. He would be home soon and everything was under control.

Author's Note

This is a work of fiction, and (almost) all characters are figments of the author's imagination, however much their kindness, decency and cooking skills may owe to my friends and neighbors in the lovely valley of the River Vézère in the Périgord Noir, the jewel of southwestern France.

The history, however, is as accurate as I can make it. The tale of the Franco-British agent Roger Landes and the assassination of the French Resistance chief Grandclément, who had been turned by a clever Gestapo official, Friedrich Dohse, is entirely true. Grandclément indeed planned to build an alternate and conservative *maquis,* with German and Gestapo support, in order to fight what he thought would be the inevitable civil war against the Communists. The story of the Italian submarine flotilla based in Bordeaux is true, as is the account of the miniature-submarine teams and their frogmen and their courageous feat in putting two British battleships out of action at a crucial point in the North African campaign of the Second World War.

Abby's hopes of becoming a guide dedicated to the American connections to the Périgord are entirely reasonable, and I had great pleasure in researching the links. They are all true: from the

Cactus Hill excavations, which indicate human settlement of the eastern shore of North America some eighteen to twenty thousand years ago; Thomas Jefferson's reverence for the writings of Archbishop Fénelon; the paratroopers of the Percy Pink mission of American paratroops dropped near Cadouin in August 1944; the Marquis of Biron's role in the American War of Independence nearly two centuries earlier.

While writing this book in the summer of 2023, I was invited to a splendid dinner and weekend book festival that celebrated a great American and her connections to this region. I have written before of the legendary American jazz singer and dancer Josephine Baker, the international superstar who became an honorary Frenchwoman and a member of the Resistance. Baker tried at her Château des Milandes on the banks of the River Dordogne to raise her adopted rainbow family of a dozen children of different faiths and colors.

She went broke in the process, lost the château in 1968 and was rescued from homelessness by the film actress Grace Kelly. She had become the Princess of Monaco in the years since they had first met in 1951, at the Stork Club, where Kelly and Baker between them broke the color barrier and became firm friends in the process. In 2021, Baker's remains were deposited in the Panthéon, the great church atop Montagne Ste. Geneviève in Paris that is now the resting place of the heroes of France.

In that same summer, we learned that for the first time the surface temperatures of the coastal waters around Britain, Ireland and France had suddenly soared by as much as 5 degrees centigrade, which meant more water evaporating into the prevailing winds from the Atlantic, heavy rains and water building up in the dams of the Massif Central. At the same time, temperatures in France broke all records, reaching 43 degrees centigrade, 108 Fahrenheit, in our garden. This was climate change with a vengeance. Meanwhile, my friends in the vineyards were battling monstrous outbreaks of mildew from the sultry weather that was destroying up to 80 percent of their grapes.

So if anyone wants to know the strange alchemy of coincidence that leads a writer to a new novel, here is a classic example. The wartime history of the Resistance, the Italian submariners in Bordeaux, the flight of hundreds of thousands of Germans from southern and western France in August 1944, the unusual weather and the history of flooding all came together with my getting to know some new friends. Tim Birch and his family have been doing a great job in restoring a lovely old building near my home called Domaine de la Barde, to turn it into a set of *gîtes,* bed-and-breakfast rooms and a cooking school. So with thanks to Tim and Krys (whose names are used with permission) and the whole Birch family, and my salaams to their work, this novel came together.

It could not have done so without my wife and coauthor of *Bruno's Cookbook,* Julia Watson, and our daughters, Kate and Fanny, who are always my first readers. My literary agent, Caroline Wood, is an unfailing support and provider of sound advice. My peerless British editor, Jane Wood, of Quercus Books, along with my tireless U.S. editor, Jonathan Segal, of Knopf, turn my clumsy manuscripts into novels, and I am aware how much I owe to their efforts. Translators and editors in many other countries work in ways I can only admire, but my friends at Diogenes Verlag, the Swiss-German publishing house, have become special because over the last seventeen years they have organized more than seven hundred readings and pubic events for me in the German-speaking world. Philipp and Daniel Keel, Anna von Planta, Ruth Geiger, Marion Hertle and my German translator, Michael Windgassen, have thus become honorary citizens of St. Denis, that lovely place that exists mostly in my head.

Martin Walker, the Périgord, 2023

After studying at Oxford and Harvard Universities, Martin Walker served as a foreign correspondent for *The Guardian* in Africa, the Soviet Union, the United States and Europe and was also the editor of United Press International. In 1987, he was awarded Britain's Reporter of the Year prize for his work in the Soviet Union. He was a senior scholar of the Woodrow Wilson Center and senior director of the Global Business Policy Council, both in Washington, D.C. He now shares his time between the United States, Britain and the Périgord, where he writes, chairs the jury of the Prix Ragueneau for cooking and is proud to be a grand consul of the wines of Bergerac. He enjoys writing a monthly column on wine for the local English-language paper *The Bugle,* and with winemaking friends produces an agreeable and unpretentious red wine, Cuvée Bruno. He has been awarded the Gold Medal by the French Republic for his services to tourism, and, in 2021, he was awarded the Prix Charbonnier by the Federation of Alliances Françaises for his services to the French language and culture.

A NOTE ON THE TYPE

This book was set in Adobe Garamond. Designed for the Adobe Corporation by Robert Slimbach, the fonts are based on types first cut by Claude Garamond (ca. 1480–1561). Garamond was a pupil of Geoffroy Tory and is believed to have followed the Venetian models, although he introduced a number of important differences, and it is to him that we owe the letters we now know as "old style." He gave to his letters a certain elegance and feeling of movement that won their creator an immediate reputation and the patronage of Francis I of France.

Typeset by Scribe,
Philadelphia, Pennsylvania

Printed and bound by Berryville Graphics,
Berryville, Virginia